STRIKER

AN INIQUUS ROMANTIC SUSPENSE MYSTERY
THRILLER

STRIKE FORCE
BOOK 5

FIONA QUINN

Strike Force

THE WORLD OF INIQUUS

Ubicumque, Quoties. Quidquid

Iniquus - /i'ni/kwus/ our strength is unequalled, our tactics unfair – we stretch the law to its breaking point. We do whatever is necessary to bring the enemy down.

THE LYNX SERIES

STRIKE FORCE

CERBERUS TACTICAL K9 TEAM BRAVO

Warrior's Instinct

Rescue Instinct

Hero's Instinct

For an up-to-date list, please visit FionaQuinnBooks.com

If you prefer to read the Iniquus World in chronological order you will find a full list at the end of this book.

STRIKER

AN INIQUUS ROMANTIC SUSPENSE MYSTERY
THRILLER

By

Fiona Quinn

AI Statement — Fiona Quinn relies on her imagination and experiences to write her stories. She pays for professional services by humans who use their education and unique creativity to help her bring quality works to this platform, including editors, artists, and audio narrators.

Fiona Quinn uses AI as part of her word processing software (spellcheck, for example) and does NOT use AI to create her stories.

THE PLAYERS

Strike Force

  Striker Rheas — Commander Strike Force
  Deep
  Jack
  Blaze
  Randy
  Gator

Striker's Family – Miami, Florida

  Dad
  Mimi — stepmother
  Mercedes — stepsister (deceased)
  Lynda — stepsister
  Cammy — niece

The Players Continued

Iniquus

Lexi (Lynx) Sobado — Iniquus Puzzler, Striker
Rheas' fiancée.
General Grant
Colonel
Mr. Spencer

Wombats

Auralia Rochambeau — Gator's sister
Remi Taleb
Nicole Street

The Map

1

Auralia Rochambeau

Dressed in her night shirt, with leggings that she'd hastily tugged on underneath, Auralia stood next to Remi in the middle of the hotel room. The women draped scarves over their heads, tying them in place to cover their mouths and noses, a small protection against the cloud of dust that powdered the air.

As Remi poured champagne into their plastic cups, the women's candle-lit silhouettes danced on the walls, distorted by the cracks and bubbles in the peeling green paint.

Outside, bombs screamed out their displeasure as they tumbled from overhead planes. In Auralia's mind, she conjured up images of sentient missiles shrilling their high-pitched terror as they plunged toward the ground.

Each one ended with the impact, the detonation, and the roaring collapse of some structure.

There was nowhere else for the two women to shelter.

No safer space outside the walls of their hotel.

Their life expectancy at this point was luck of the draw.

Might as well drink the champagne.

Each explosion sent more debris into the atmosphere. Chunks fell quickly back to Earth. The fine chalky particulates thickened the atmosphere like one thickens a gumbo with roux.

An unctuous potage of air.

Unsavory. Unwholesome. Unwelcomed.

Auralia Rochambeau watched her friend and mentor, war correspondent Remi Taleb, closely for actions and reactions. Remi had been in these kinds of situations for most of her career. And Auralia was still getting used to the idea that she was in front of the camera, explaining what was happening to the news audience. Auralia had dreamed of seeing the world —all of it, even the horror-filled parts—since she was a little girl, watching the news with her mom while they washed the dishes side by side. Auralia had practiced her skills in the mirror, lifting her pink bristled hairbrush and annunciating, "Well, Jake, that's a good question. The situation on the ground is bleak."

Surreal.

It was easy enough for Auralia to suppose she had the mettle to stand up to a situation like this when she accepted an assignment.

Living through it, though, tested the theory.

Whenever Auralia felt her body giving in to the terror, she'd conjure the image of her brother Gator, a retired Marine Raider who now jumped into hot spots all over the world as a security operator.

Gator was unshakable.

The last time she'd seen Gator, Auralia had noticed a new tattoo, a tiny skull inked in the webbing between Gator's thumb and forefinger.

"What's that about, Gator?" she'd asked when she discovered it on their last visit.

"A *memento mori*. I'm gonna die. We all are. This reminds me to do what I can while I've got a breath."

"Why now?" Auralia had whispered as she painted her thumb over the tattoo. After all, his stint in the war with the American military was over.

"D-Day's still in the fight."

Ah, well, that made sense. Gator had met his wife, D-Day, on assignment. Together, they'd battled to stay alive. Now, they battled apart. D-Day was a Night Stalker who flew special ops groups into the fray in the dead of night, mere feet off the ground, at breakneck speeds. One twitch of her arm muscles, and she could be nose down in a fireball in a split second.

Gator, too, still took off on missions that required the finesse of a special operator.

If there was a couple that faced death on a daily basis, it was her brother and sister-in-law.

They were calm and accepting of their potential demise. "We came here and did what we could while we could," they'd said when Auralia asked for pointers on how to face her fears.

As global hot-spot reporters, Remi and Auralia spent a good portion of their time hunkering under falling buildings to report the news to the world. They didn't have the same level of hazard as Gator and D-Day's jobs.

But there was a risk.

Tonight, a bigger risk than usual.

Auralia wanted to be brave in the face of danger like her brother and Remi, but her own brain screamed that she wasn't ready to die, wasn't done with life. She needed more time to accomplish something to help humanity.

Maybe that was the difference.

D-Day, Gator, and Remi had been doing this for so long that their accomplishments were undeniable. They'd made their mark.

BOOM!

Auralia squatted with her feet spread wide like a surfer on the wave, riding out the tremble of the building. She covered the top of her cup with her hand. The champagne sloshed against her palm. Auralia chuckled at how ludicrous it was that she'd volunteered to be here.

Remi checked her watch, then leaned over to open her laptop. She placed a pre-arranged video call to the Wombats - Women's Mentorship in Battle, Achievement, and Trials. Just a handful of women who knew each other from the danger zones. Different skills. Different career trajectories. All of them people that Auralia aspired to become.

One by one, images populated the screen.

Remi leaned in so her face showed up front and center. "I've opened a bottle of champagne, ladies."

They each raised their own glasses, whatever was handy —depending on where they were in the world—from champagne flutes to ceramic mugs to Remi and Auralia's plastic, collapsible hiking cups.

A bomb whistled its way down.

"Do you hear that?" Remi asked.

BOOM!

The room shook, throwing Auralia off balance. She hovered there, arms outstretched, gasping for air through the dusty cloud, struggling to let go of her hold on life so fear wouldn't incapacitate her.

Remi calmly stretched out to catch the laptop as it skidded off the table.

"Whew, close!" Hailey said from the top right corner of the screen.

"Too close. But let's get to it, shall we?" Remi asked. "I have called you all here tonight because I thought this might be the appropriate time, place, and circumstance to welcome a new Wombat into our wisdom."

A wisdom, Auralia knew, was a group of wombats out in nature.

And the wisdom of Wombats in front of her was an elite group of women who had bonded as they did their jobs in the most desperate of circumstances—reporters, humanitarian aid workers, medical aid workers, engineers, CIA agents, linguists. In that group, the expertise had depth and breadth. They used their resources to help each other accomplish their professional goals. And more importantly, to stay alive.

Remi lifted her champagne with one hand as she turned the video camera toward Auralia with the other.

The women started cheering and calling out welcomes to her.

Auralia's eyes stretched wide at the honor that they were extending.

Remi's words weren't a surprise to any of them. Obviously, the women had discussed and agreed upon her invitation. They had opened the door for her and extended their hands to her; now, she needed to live up to their example.

"We have some rules," Remi explained. "First, whoever is under imminent threat is the only one to share a hardship. If the threatened sister needs to break down and emote, excellent. If others needed to, they excuse themselves to do that privately."

"Fear is infectious," Hailey said.

"Panic, too," Nicole added.

Remi took a sip of champagne. "The next rule: once the situation is understood, once all resources for aid are exhausted, it is time to collapse into the warmth of our sister-hood. To create an often-false sense of safety. A bit of rest. A webbing of support. Like tonight, there's nothing more we can do to stay safe. So here we gather."

"And if worse comes to worst—no sugar coating here," Julie added, "well, we won't die alone. Think of it as hospice surrounded by family but without the I.V. meds to bliss you out."

The women laughed.

"Remi," Hailey said, "let's save the rules for when you're not coughing up bomb dust. Let's get the distraction going."

And so, they did.

While Auralia couldn't completely block out what was happening outside, hanging out with people who understood the circumstances did take the edge off—and time passed, which was the only remedy to the situation.

"Hey, do you hear that?" Nicole pointed upward.

Everyone stopped talking and listened to silence.

"How long?" Auralia whispered.

"Since we started our last round of camp songs." Nicole grinned.

The all-clear siren shrilled.

Remi filled Auralia's plastic cup, then hers with her Wombat-welcome champagne. "One last 'Hurrah!' Ladies. And then let's all get some beauty sleep."

The Wombats whistled and welcomed, then with the customary "see you later," rather than the fate-tempting "good-bye," each square on the video grid went dark until only Remi, Auralia, and Nicole were on the line.

Auralia took a gulp of champagne that went up her nose and made her sputter.

"Hey, Auralia, can you stay and speak with me for a minute?" Nicole asked.

"Absolutely." She dragged the back of her hand under her nose.

Nicole Street functioned as a sociologist for an NGO, studying patterns in women's reproductive health in both post-war zones and present-day conflict areas. She had seeded her share of journalistic stories by passing on insights and observations to Remi and Auralia, depending on who was reporting in which region.

It was a win-win.

Remi and Auralia knew which stones to turn over. Nicole got the public's eyes turned toward women's issues, helping to shape public awareness and understanding with the hopes that the outrage of the circumstances might turn to public pressures where policymakers might otherwise overlook these issues.

Her work in Kabul came to a screeching halt when the Afghan government decided that non-governmental organizations couldn't employ women. The NGOs, in turn, said they couldn't operate without their women. Auralia wondered where Nicole might be heading next and if she had a new story up her sleeve.

2

Auralia Rochambeau

Monday

Patiently, Auralia waited as Nicole searched the bottom of her cup. In their communications, carefully picking words wasn't unusual. Auralia understood that Nicole often walked a fine line on what she could ethically share with reporters.

When her gaze came up, Nicole said, "I was going to go through Hailey on this since she's a Wombat with an Iniquus connection. But she's another degree of separation from getting information passed, and this is really very sensitive. Now that you're a Wombat, it seems tighter to tell you and see what you think."

"Wow, okay. Listening." Auralia shifted into a seat in front of the screen.

Nicole lifted her voice. "Nowhere for you to go to make this a private conversation, Remi, but could—"

"I'll put in my earbuds and crank the music," Remi said as she flopped onto the bed, pulling out her phone and earphones. No bad feelings or curiosity. Such was the level of trust and support within the wisdom of Wombats.

"Auralia, with this conversation, I'm putting you in the middle of something, in a way." She paused overly long, so Auralia nodded her head by way of encouragement.

"We Wombats support each other, but there is never a responsibility," she started again, then shook her head. "You have no obligations here. I'm trying to fulfill a family debt. If you can help me, that would be great; if not, I'll find another way. Okay? No worries."

"Okay, well…" Auralia pulled her brow together. "Let me hear, and we'll figure out the best steps together. How about that?"

"Your brother, Gator, still works on Strike Force at Iniquus?"

"Yes."

"There's a woman there who works with him. Her name is Lynx Sobado."

"Yes." Auralia canted her head. "I know Lynx. But how in the world would you know that name?"

"I don't know her. I know *of* her. So the back story is, about a decade ago, my cousin Kaylie—Kaylie Street—was working in Africa on reclaiming desert and making the land farmable. Kaylie was kidnapped and not ransomed. They explained that it was most likely that she had been killed."

"I'm so sorry."

"Yes." Nicole swallowed hard. "Whew, this is…a big decision to tell you this."

Auralia locked her teeth, not sure she wanted to know what happened to Kaylie.

"Okay, step by step. These things are still okay to tell."

Auralia pulled a long breath through her nose and promptly sneezed out the dust.

"It turns out that Kaylie was sold to Isis as a slave. She was alive. Held in Syria. Lynx not only helped discover where Kaylie was, but she personally went there to save my cousin's life, fighting off the man trying to drag his knife across Kaylie's throat." Nicole wrapped both hands around her own throat as if self-protecting. She took in an audible sniff of air. "That was about two years ago. When I discovered what Kaylie went through, I changed my focus with the UN's global women's health research to specify women in crisis areas." Nicole's face turned red, her eyes watery, as she looked down at her lap, and a breath juddered past her lips.

There was the boom and shake as a building collapsed nearby.

The air filled again with particulates.

Auralia coughed into her elbow. "Keep going. There's nothing else to do here but pace and shake. It's good to focus on something else."

"I know a secret about Lynx." Nicole paused and looked up, rolling her lips in and out with indecision. "Well, surely Gator knows this, and surely Lynx knows this, so I'm just bringing you into the fold."

Auralia couldn't imagine what this could possibly be about.

"Lynx is married," Nicole said in a sudden burst.

"Was married, yes," Auralia corrected. "Her husband died in an IED explosion while on a mission with the Rangers." Auralia stopped to smile. "She is engaged, though. To Striker, Gator's commander. But they—" Auralia felt some strange sensation move through her body, then whispered, "keep putting off the wedding."

"Lynx's husband, Angel, is alive. Lynx discovered that when she was saving my cousin. Kaylie only told *me* and only because I needed help getting dangerous information to the right people, and she… That doesn't matter. Angel Sobado is alive."

"Wow," Auralia whispered. The only way that made sense was that Angel was doing something extra-legal. Nicole had said "right people," so that must make what Angel was doing something for the greater good. Auralia could only think that he was black ops—that he'd staged his death to lose his identity and protect his family and friends.

If Lynx knew he was alive and kept it secret, just kept carrying on as usual, then she had to agree that what Angel was doing was for the greater good. Otherwise, she'd go to the courts, the newspapers, and the Pentagon and create chaos. She had the contacts to bring a hailstorm down on the situation.

Nicole gave Auralia's mind a chance to churn. To figure all of that out. When Auralia looked up to catch her friend's gaze, Nicole nodded. "Okay, you get the situation. Now, why I'm telling you: I overheard a phone conversation by a CIA agent when I was…that doesn't matter. The agent said they were wedged between a rock and a hard place when it comes to Lynx. They need Lynx's special expertise in ongoing geo-political issues. She's, according to that agent, an insanely important asset. He also said they've failed to live up to their obligation of helping her get a secret divorce from Angel. They had promised to help make that happen."

"So, Lynx can't get on with life because she discovered he was alive—"

"And if Lynx hadn't gone to save my cousin, she

wouldn't know. She'd just have moved forward, unaware. Saving my cousin meant...well, it put Lynx in this bad place."

"Okay."

"That dangerous information I mentioned? As a sociologist going in and collecting data, I see and hear a lot of things. I've become a CIA asset. I'm not supposed to tell anyone. But this whole conversation is top secret. Yay for Remi's encrypted channels, right?" She laughed nervously. "I am supposed to meet with...well, I guess I have to tell you the agent's name, so if you decide to pass the information on, Lynx will know it's trustworthy. The CIA guy's name is Grey, John Grey. Grey will meet with The Angel—that's what they call Angel now. I guess it references the fact that he's supposed to be dead."

"Maybe." Auralia's ribs were a tight cage around her lungs.

"I have the name of the hotel where the two of them will be next week in Jordan. Like I said, I'm meeting them to discuss something. I thought that particular information might be interesting to Lynx. She can choose what she wants to do with it. That's it. I was hoping you could get that out to her."

Screams rose from down the street, the high-pitched lament of someone finding a loved one dead. Once Auralia had heard that cry, she found it unmistakable no matter where she was in the world. It always sounded the same, a call to the universe.

Auralia's skin pebbled with goose bumps. "I can. I will. I'll do that. Yes, thank you."

BOOM! Another building collapsed.

"That is," Auralia grimaced, "if I'm still alive in the morning."

3

Striker Rheas

    Tuesday

THE SHIFTING NYC CROWD PRESSED IN FROM ALL SIDES AS
Striker took up the left rear of the protection formation.

His teammate, Jack, was to his right and a step ahead of
him as they moved forward.

Blaze and Gator walked shoulder to shoulder in front of
the group up ahead. In this way, the four operators created a
security box around their protectees—father, mother, child,
and nanny—as they took their leisurely stroll up Madison
Avenue at eight in the morning, smack dab in the middle of a
work week.

Despite the early hour, the humidity levels in the July air
pressed the scents of the city down to street level, where they
heated against the black surface, cooking the odors to a

ripeness that would be difficult for someone not used to these kinds of smells.

To every man on the Strike Force team, the odor was hardly noticeable. They'd all served as special operators in swamps, open sewage fields, slaughterhouses, and communities where sanitation was an unaffordable luxury.

That military life wasn't entirely in Striker's rearview mirror. For the past five years, he'd commanded his own tactical team for Iniquus, a private security firm whose letterhead bore their Latin motto that translated to "Whenever. Wherever. Whatever."

Their assignments led them into war zones, high seas, natural disasters, and personal ones—saving kidnapped loved ones or repatriating American remains from countries where few would willingly go.

Comparatively speaking, this city was fresh as a daisy, and this protection assignment was cake.

Suddenly, the child dropped into a crouch in front of him, dragging at his caretaker's hand.

"Hold," Striker called out, extending a stiff arm as a blockade, keeping the hurly-burly from tripping over his protectees. He flicked his gaze down to assess the flash of red and shiny being lifted by the boy.

Blaze pivoted to close the third side of their security framework by extending his arms wide.

The masses swirled around them as if a stream had encountered a boulder in its path. Those on the right side of the walk blended and shuffled in with the left. Few had any curiosity about the disturbance of the flow. They just pulled their limbs in tighter and kept their gazes forward.

The caregiver tightly gripped the child's hand as he examined the red ribbon he'd found. Their contract family simply called her "Nanny."

It seemed that Mr. and Mrs. Westgate had difficulty with proper names.

Striker's team was all lumped under the general name of "security." Their client addressed the team members as a collective rather than individuals making up the on-duty team of four close protection operators on scene and a remote operator, Deep, who supported them from back at Iniquus Headquarters in D.C.

Addressing all of them by the name "Security" had already led to some communication confusion that the team was working through internally.

This pattern seemed to go beyond the couple's employees.

The Westgates referred to their child as "Son" and directed others to call him "Sonny."

Sonny was non-verbal and on the autism spectrum.

The parents had warned the team that Sonny liked to take off when he became agitated or confused.

Concerned about bringing a child who "eloped" into such a congested city, Strike Force had offered a monkey-shaped backpack that could buckle across Sonny's chest. Holding the long monkey tail, Sonny would have a range for his four-year-old curiosity, a safe circumference for exploration, and an added layer of safety.

Sonny rejected it. The sensation of rubbing wasn't tolerable for him.

The second and less effective piece of equipment was to secure a tracking device to him in some way. They tried a soft wristband. Sensation, again, was their nemesis. Finally, Striker fastened the device to the back of the child's tennis shoe with an epoxy adhesive. Each operator had the tracking app queued up on their phone.

Looking down, Striker focused on the very interesting way that Nanny gripped Sonny's hand. Making a loop with her pinky and thumb, the child wrapped his tiny fingers around the circle like a handle, then Nanny used her middle three digits to make a claw of sorts, trapping Sonny's wrist between her middle and index fingers.

That grip looked like a good one to know. In the field, the team never clasped hands. The operators clasped wrists; it was a much more secure hold. Striker would share what he saw with his team when they had a moment alone.

Mr. and Mrs. Westgate chatted as they patiently waited for Nanny to resolve the stop.

Striker cast his gaze around, looking for anyone who focused on their group with curiosity or malintent.

Sonny stared at the piece of satin he pinched between his fingers, then moved to put it into his open mouth.

Nanny's reflexes were no joke.

In Striker's peripheral vision, he watched her snatch the ribbon away as she thrust a cracker into his hand so quickly and efficiently that the boy probably didn't even notice the exchange.

Sonny stood, contentedly crunching his cracker while Nanny shoved the ribbon into her pocket. "We're going to the park, Sonny, where you can play. Won't that be nice?" She had to change sides so that she could capture his free hand in her clasp, moving Sonny behind Jack.

"Security," Mr. Westgate pulled a linen handkerchief from the inner pocket of his suit jacket and pressed it under his nose, "it smells of urine."

"Yes, sir," Striker responded. There was zero Striker could do about the smell of dog piss in the gutters. Madison and 47th were about as upscale as one could get in the city, but their dogs needed to pee just like a dog from any other neighborhood did.

And as if on cue, a dog trotted across the street on the end of a leash.

Sonny shrieked and lunged toward the collie, but Nanny's grip held firm. She leaned back to counterbalance the tug. Once again, Striker extended his arm to stop the crowd from barreling over them.

Striker remembered his niece Cammy would desperately try to get to any furry animal that scrambled into her line of sight when she was Sonny's age. Striker took those mental pictures of Cammy, with the same ebony-colored hair as Sonny, and put them in a box to take out and look at later. When Striker was on the job, the job had his full focus.

The dog disappeared. Sonny calmed. They started forward.

As the time spun toward the typical eight-thirty start time at work, folks were picking up their speed.

The scene was growing dynamic with pushing and jostling. The leisurely pace set by the Westgates was becoming problematic. But even getting the family off the street—dipping into a coffee shop for a few minutes—would move them from one press to another.

Dressed in their Iniquus uniforms of military-styled boots, dark gray tactical pants, and black compression shirts, their professional attire and surely the sheer size of the men on his team meant that no one was challenging the way their group took up space on the sidewalk. Folks eased by with little curiosity.

Their group was getting closer to their first destination. They'd be out of this swarm in a matter of minutes.

The Westgates had decided to get some exercise by walking Nanny and Sonny the five blocks from their hotel to Bryant Park, where Sonny could play, then rest with books in the public library that was right there. Meanwhile, the "adults" (the noun that Mr. and Mrs. Westgate used to refer to themselves) would be four blocks back in the direction they'd come, in the Diamond District, so that Mrs. Westgate could choose a present for her upcoming birthday.

The team planned to split until the gift was found: two operators with the parents and two with Sonny and Nanny.

At that point, a limousine would collect the parents, along with Blaze and Gator, and then drive over to pick up the rest of the group at the library.

"Security."

Striker slid his attention away from Sonny when Mr. Westgate's nasal whine cut through the street noise of idling engines and impatient horns.

"We won't be walking anymore during this trip. This is just too much. Please arrange for the limo service to provide our transportation. In fact, we need someone to meet us at the park, a taxi even. This is untenable."

Striker pressed his sternal comms to access Deep, who could make those arrangements. "Striker here. I need a—" From the corner of his eye, Striker caught movement in the road.

A car suddenly made a left turn toward the sidewalk without slowing.

It was a split-second shift that mobilized the whole team.

Blaze and Gator spun on a dime, each grabbing one of the parents—all but lifting them from the ground—and pressing them toward the building, using their bodies as shields as the New Yorkers scrambled out of their way.

Striker had Nanny, who gripped at Sonny as Jack scooped the boy—screaming—up into his arms and jumped forward to clear the danger.

Not quick enough.

The corner of the car plowed into Jack.

As Jack fell to the ground, he spun to hold Sonny up away from his tumbling weight. That move protected the boy from being crushed but also wrenched him from Nanny's grip.

In the split second that had passed, the pedestrians' reflexes didn't keep up with the danger. They fell over Jack and hit the car as the vehicle plowed into a cement garbage container.

Striker managed his adrenaline as he evaluated the scene.

Those on top of the pedestrian pile stood and shook off their shock.

Those coming up the walk yelled out information, "He's passed out. Call an ambulance," as they tried to access the doors to help the driver.

Not an attack on their protectees; the guy was experiencing a medical event.

Striker and Nanny pulled people off the pileup over Jack and the car. Nanny was diving low. "Sonny!" she screamed. "He's gone."

Blood flowed from Jack's open head wound, where the underside of the bumper slashed his scalp. He jumped to his feet, eyes on a swivel.

"Protocol E," Striker called out as he pressed the comms unit taped to his chest so Deep would get the NYPD en route.

E was for elopement; it was the plan they had in place if Sonny were to bolt. It didn't differ significantly from what they'd do for any child that went missing.

As Striker pulled up the app to track Sonny, each of the other operators grabbed the arm of one of their protectees. They each paced out and began the call in a cadence that carried out past the city commotion: "Four-year-old, non-verbal, autistic boy, running. Short, black hair. Forty inches tall. Thirty-five pounds. If you see him call out."

If a bad guy were in the area and had gotten hold of Sonny, they wouldn't want the kind of attention the operators' calling would produce. Striker watched the pedestrians' eyes searching about them as they tried to help.

When a child went missing, it was almost always the best action plan to get as loud as possible as quickly as possible.

As Striker jogged forward following the progressing red dot on his phone app, his men fanned out, moving in the same general direction, hoping to create a safety net.

If Sonny were taken, most people wouldn't consider pulling off the child's shoes when the tracker wasn't readily visible.

Striker shouldered through the crowd as he forced his way up the sidewalk. The boy was moving fast. And that made Striker think that an adult had him in their arms and was making a dash for it. If Sonny was just on a tear, Striker needed to beat him to Park Avenue, where traffic wouldn't see a small boy.

As Striker passed Vanderbilt, the red dot on his app stopped moving.

The moment of relief quickly gave way to frustration as Striker found the child's shoes in the gutter.

Striker pressed his comms with his head on a swivel. "No joy. The shoes are off his feet."

With that information, the men turned, each taking a cardinal direction, dragging a protectee along.

Striker pressed down the jolt of adrenaline when he saw the entrance for Grand Central up ahead.

The announcement the men called now added, "The child is not wearing shoes. He may have on socks or be barefooted."

Striker checked hands to see if anyone was leading Sonny away. What he found was, understandably, other parents tightening their grip on their own children's hands. A mom pulled back her stroller's sun shield to ensure her baby slept safely tethered within.

He also watched with gratitude as pedestrians moved their eyes away from their cell phones, tipping their heads this way and that as they scanned about them for the endangered child, concern tightening their faces.

"Here! Here!" Came a deep base near the end of the block. An arm extended up and waved like a flag.

A linebacker of a guy in jeans and a football T-shirt had Sonny in his arms. The boy gripped the man's beard with both hands.

Striker moved into the roadway so he could sprint. He pressed his comms. "I have eyes on. Jack, bring Nanny up."

The man tipped his head and, with a cheerful voice, started singing to the tune of "Row, Row, Row Your Boat." "Look here, what did I find? A boy who needs his mom! Straight black hair and neither shoe. He'd like to go on home."

Striker raised his hand in the air, not wanting to startle the child, who was wholly engrossed in the man's long beard.

Striker's move caught the man's eye, and he nodded.

It was good that both men were head and shoulders above the crowd.

As he approached, Striker noticed the practiced and gentle way the boy was held. The sway of the hips was calming. A gold ring on his left hand. No red flags.

Striker approached from behind Sonny's head.

And interestingly, and very astutely, the man asked, "Do you have proof that you and this child belong together? How do I know he hasn't run away from you purposefully?"

A police officer moved toward them, his K9 held on a

tight lead. Sonny jerked his head around toward the dog and twisted his body into a dive to get to the K9.

The man juggled the slender limbs as the boy scrambled from his arms to get down. Lifting his beard, he tickled the boy's arm. Sonny went back to focusing on the man's beard.

Striker held his phone out for the officer with Sonny's picture and Iniquus credentials. His eyes never left Sonny.

There was a firm gentleness to the man's hold—utter calm. Striker caught the man's eye.

"My daughter's on the spectrum," he said. "This is very familiar to me. But best safe, right?" He nodded toward the officer handing back Striker's phone and credentials. "Shall I try to hand him to you?"

Striker wanted the boy in his own arms but had seen over the last few days how someone incorrectly touching him sent Sonny into fight or flight, and Striker didn't want to traumatize an otherwise contented Sonny. The police here, Striker, made the gut call to let this stranger continue to help. With a watchful eye unblinkingly on him, Striker said, "If you wouldn't mind, his nanny is just behind us."

"That would probably be good," he agreed.

Jack arrived, blood dripping from his hairline down his face and neck.

A sobbing Nanny was snorting hard to calm herself, then with a quivering lip, smiled as she reached out her hands. "Hi Sonny, I missed you." She reached into her pocket and pulled out her crackers. "Do you need a snack?"

When Sonny was back in her arms, the thank yous being extended all around, the Westgate's arrived.

"You're bleeding," Mrs. Westgate told Jack.

"Yes, ma'am." Jack pulled his first aid kit from his thigh pocket.

"Stitches," Blaze said as he reached out a hand to hail a

cab. "Are you concussive? Do you need someone to go with you?"

"Not necessary," Jack said as he stepped off the curb toward the taxi that had pulled to a stop.

Striker bladed his hand toward the doors on their left. "Why don't we head into the hotel lobby for a moment and make a plan for moving forward while Jack gets medical attention."

And frankly, Striker needed a minute to reseat his heart. He couldn't imagine what it was like for a family to always be on razor's edge, worried their child would disappear.

Nothing sent terror through his blood like a child in danger.

Now, how was Striker going to make sure this didn't happen again?

4

Saadiq

Tuesday

SAADIQ SHUFFLED HIS SANDALS OFF HIS FEET BEFORE stepping into the wooden crate. Squatting, he folded his legs under him as he curled into a ball on his side. Pressing his weight into his elbow, he slid one of his shoes under his hip bone to protect himself. The other he wedged behind his back. And lastly, he used his outer cloak to make a pillow for his head as he nested inside the small space. He gripped a stack of family pictures in his hand—family who had already died. Pictures that endangered no one.

The stranger's bearded face swam above him, blocking the glow of a setting sun. "Ready?"

No! "Yes, ready." Saadiq took one last glance at the nectarine sky, one last breath of unobstructed air.

The stranger lowered the top. The slats on the crate were

wide enough to allow airflow and narrow enough to stop curious eyes from easily seeing what traveled inside. Around him, the driver stacked other crates with onions and garlic, burlap bags of rice, and baskets of apples.

The driver rounded the cab and climbed in. The engine growled awake, and off they lurched, just a vendor heading out to make a delivery.

Saadiq was prepared for the misery, for the cramps and stiffness that would leave him crippled for hours once those who moved him from one secret location to another were able to get him safely out of his box.

This mode of transport had been the same over the past month as they moved him from safe house to safe house.

He hadn't had much choice.

This felt like he was living some strange parallel existence with history. Saadiq had read about slavery in America. Back before the emancipation of those suffering souls from their bondage, there was a thing called the "Underground Railroad." Not a railroad at all. Not even a train. But people, who believed slavery was immoral, helped the enslaved escape to Canada, where they could live freely.

History intrigued Saadiq, the history of the United States in particular.

American culture had fascinated him from the time he was a boy. In school, he studied English as hard as he had studied science. Saadiq dreamed of attending medical school in America and returning to his people to provide healthcare.

And he succeeded with the first part of the plan.

Saadiq spent thirteen glorious years becoming a pediatric surgeon in the United States. It had been everything he'd hoped for and more.

As he was finishing up his residency in Baltimore, he had big dreams for his future. That was back before four airplanes changed his life and exploded his plans and thousands of others' lives.

As the political winds shifted, Saadiq felt compelled to return home to Baghdad to be with his family.

Hoping to help America, he had offered his medical expertise, which they turned down. The military said they needed his language skills most, so he served the U.S. as an interpreter. Hoping...

Yes, back then, Saadiq was filled with hope and purpose. He saw the potential for good things for his people that weren't available under the regime that ruled with a mighty fist. Under America, maybe things would be better—just the right to shave one's beard, to sing a song, to allow girls an education.

He believed Iraq could have a brighter future with the Americans opening new possibilities for a happier existence. He *believed* his sister could use her brilliant mind to improve lives rather than letting it rot on the daily task of making bread and sweeping dust.

He had been so optimistic about the possibilities that, from the first American boots on Iraqi soil to the time well past the drawdown that turned the U.S.'s presence from a river to a rivulet, Saadiq was doing his part.

His hope bloomed, then the rose dried on the stem.

Saadiq had dealt first with American special forces. They needed someone intelligent enough and competent enough, loyal enough but mostly strong enough to work alongside them. Saadiq was a natural athlete. Small and wiry, his muscles were steel bands. He didn't have any tactical skills like the team's men. But he could run alongside them with ease and carry his share of the load.

At least, he could in his younger days, but he was now decades into this effort. His body was older now, rusty, and worn.

Then it was time for a majority of the coalition soldiers to leave. The time when the suffering of those that had aligned with the Americans would multiply. When life itself became fragile.

Little by little, as the military efforts wound down and the missions were fewer and farther apart, the CIA came knocking on his door. After all, Saadiq had traveled all over the country and held a security clearance that allowed him to know all kinds of things from the American side as well as having a deep cultural understanding and network of contacts on the Iraqi side.

In the last decade, the CIA provided the salary that kept Saadiq's family thriving.

Saadiq was supposed to have—had been promised by the military—a visa back to the States. For someone like him, being left here as a terrorist target was a death sentence. And that was only if he was his most optimistic. In reality, it was probably years of torture and pain before he succumbed to injuries or malnutrition. He'd rather shoot himself in the head.

But there were others to consider—his widowed mother and sister, his wife, and his daughter. Four women without a man here? That was not feasible.

Love and loyalty to his family trapped Saadiq.

And the CIA knew it.

He did what they'd asked of him. And now, his name was at the top of a terror cell's wanted list.

And he was on the run.

One point of hope, just before the last mission he'd done for the CIA, Saadiq felt the walls closing in around him. Just before that last mission began—as if by miracle—Saadiq stumbled across Striker Rheas, who was working on a close protection mission in Baghdad. "Striker, man, I have a big ask. I'm terrified to leave our family's documents here in Iraq. If the terrorists take them and burn them, there is little hope of my ever leaving my country again." Striker had taken the documents back home with him. They were safe on the other side of the world.

EACH TIME SAADIQ CLIMBED INTO A VEGETABLE CRATE, THE underground helpers moved him in a roundabout route toward the border where he could sneak over the desert and face prison but not torture. But he knew that if he could get over the border, Striker would fly over to deliver the documents and would throw the weight of Iniquus into the diplomatic fray.

After all, Striker and his team were only alive because of Saadiq.

And Saadiq believed in Striker's ethos; he was an honorable man.

For right now, Saadiq would survive the hours in a crate, bouncing painfully over the potholed road toward his goals: Get out. Find his family. Get the papers from Striker. Start anew. *Inshallah*—God willing.

He kissed the photos gripped in his hands, praying for fortitude.

5

Lexi

WASHINGTON, D.C.
   Tuesday

LYNX SAT IN HER OFFICE, STARING AT THE CORK WALL WHERE she'd push-pinned pictures, words, and news clippings. She looked like a conspiracy theorist, a female schizophrenic incarnation of John Forbes Nash of *A Beautiful Mind* fame. Though, his fame was really from being a Nobel Prize-winning mathematician. And she, most certainly, was not.

She was confused by the components that Command had handed her to sort.

The puzzle pieces weren't falling together.

And since that was her title, Iniquus Puzzler—the placer of pieces, the former of coherent pictures—it might be nice if she could figure this out.

When her phone buzzed on the table beside her, Lynx leaned over to see Deep's name. Standing, she signaled to her

Dobermans, Beetle and Bella, to stay where they were, basking in a ray of sunlight that stretched out over the industrial grey carpeting.

Strike Force War Room was a short walk down the hall. She pressed through the heavy wooden door to find Deep scowling at his computer monitor.

"What's going on?" She pushed the door shut behind her.

"We just had an incident in New York."

"Incident?" Lynx scrambled over to join Deep behind his desk. "Is everyone okay?"

"Yes and no," Deep said as Lynx plopped into the captain's chair beside him. "Jack might need some stitches."

Deep was queuing up the video on her screen while he continued to monitor three chest cameras on the active Strike Force members. Deep pointed at the box at the top of a feed that wasn't running a camera. It had Jack's name, GPS positioning, and vitals. Through sensors embedded in the team's compression shirts, an AI system monitored the active operators' physical conditions—temperature, oxygenation, hydration, and heart activity. In this way, the system could warn the operator support team before something like a minor hydration issue turned into heatstroke while the field operators focused on other things.

Jack's vitals seemed fine.

"The sirens on all four of these were screaming ten minutes ago. Heart rates were through the roof."

"Adrenaline?"

"That's about right." Deep tapped a button and pointed to the monitor in front of her. "This is Striker's feed. I have it queued to the point just before the incident."

Lynx focused on the screen as their group ambled down the otherwise bustling city street. Pedestrians swerved around the team in their haste. She watched the child, Sonny, lunging toward the street when he saw a dog, but the caregiver handled that professionally. Typically, children walked on the inside, away from the curb, but—given that the sidewalk was protected by parked cars and on the other side of the nanny, there was a crush of people—this configuration made sense.

Until it didn't.

As the group passed a stretch of space that posted "No Parking" signs to protect a loading zone, a car suddenly turned toward the sidewalk. It was if someone jerked the wheel to aim directly at the contractor's family.

"Holy moly!" Lynx clapped her hands over her mouth and nose as she took in the chaos.

Deep tapped the button to move the video to slow motion. Lynx's trained gaze absorbed the information.

The driver slumped over the wheel.

Each team member grabbed a protectee.

Jack was hit. From the angle of Striker's camera, Lynx couldn't tell whether he was under the tires. "Jack!"

"Bleeding head. He said he didn't feel concussive. He took a taxi to a clinic."

"Clinic?"

"There was a three-hour wait time at the emergency department. During our planning session, we identified two clinics that could provide fastest care. We contracted with both, so if we ran into a problem, the facility would prioritize our mission group. The problem, though," he flicked a hand at the screen, "ran into us."

"They have the equipment to check Jack's head for signs of concussion?"

"Both clinics have full capacity. I sent him to closest proximity." Deep tapped the side of his head to indicate he had someone in his ear. He pressed the comms button. "Documented. Keep me apprised. Out." Deep turned toward Lynx. "Jack's taxi just pulled up. We'll hear back soon enough."

"You have a call into his wife to let her know?"

"He's lucid and ambulatory. That one's on him."

"Right. Okay." Lynx tapped the video to get it to play. She put her finger on the screen. "Sonny fought himself free of that pile. The adults don't see it. And he's out of camera range."

"He took off. Depending on the kindness of strangers, they got him back. It was two minutes and thirty-seven seconds from crash to recovery."

"I bet it felt like hours. So, the team's adrenaline going ballistic was about a babe in danger. *Whew*. I can't even imagine what that felt like. How are they doing?"

"I haven't talked to them. They're still out with the family. They finished the walk to the park. I think that since the boy has an issue with running away, his mom and dad are a little more used to the situation. That has to be it. Mom is still heading off with the dad to pick out her birthday gift along with Gator and Blaze. Striker is going to stay with Nanny and Sonny at the park. Nanny isn't covered by protective services, and the parents counted that as two adults watching the one child and felt it was sufficient."

"I'm not going to comment," Lynx said. "But you called me in. How can I help?"

"In the planning stage, we got support from our psychological team. Strike Force tried all the interventions they suggested. For this reason or that, they all failed. I'm looking for a new idea, something to keep the kid safe until tomorrow night when the family is back at the airport."

"Do you have that list?" Lynx asked. "That way, I know what the team tried and rejected."

"Yup." Deep pulled up a file on his computer and dropped

it into the ribbon on Lynx's monitor. "You'll find notes about why each intervention was unworkable in the file."

"Okay." Lynx leaned forward as she opened it. "Anything else besides today's incident video and this file to help me figure this out?"

"Yes." Deep sent a URL to her ribbon. "This is a social media site where the nanny posts short videos of Sonny's day. It's only accessible by the parents and the nanny. Nanny gave Striker the URL and password, and he passed it on to me."

Lynx looked at her watch. It was not quite zero nine hundred hours. "Okay, let me see what I can come up with."

6

Lexi

    Tuesday

The notes in the file said that when Strike Force conferred with the Iniquus behavioral psychologist about best practices in keeping Sonny safe, everyone agreed this was a high-risk place for the family to travel with Sonny's issues. Not just the elopement but his being averse to commotion and sounds.

Well, if they had to be in New York City with its series of triggers from square one, at least the family hired Iniquus to safeguard them from dangers.

The list of security interventions—it said right at the top, highlighted in red—only worked when they worked with the child. If Sonny's nervous system couldn't handle the intrusion, they were to find a different means.

A different means... Her brows drew together.

Nothing that touched or constricted him... Lynx realized how little she knew about neuro-divergence. She had read that compression was helpful to children on the autism spectrum. But this contradicted that notion. "Don't lump," was Lynx's immediate takeaway.

Lynx tapped the button that told the computer to scroll through the private social media page, playing each video at the highest speed. The moment-to-moment particulars weren't important; Lynx was looking for a repetition of themes.

Deep leaned in. "What have you got, Lynx?"

"There are an awful lot of pictures of Sonny with dogs. In many of these little videos, he grabs at what looks like stranger-dog's leads and walks along with the owner." She slowed one of the videos to show Deep the surprised look on the dog owner's face and the search for a responsible adult. There was Nanny jogging up, calling out her explanation.

Sonny was a cute kid. And the joy on his face as he walked along would melt anyone's heart. But Lynx could see this becoming problematic as Sonny got older.

Deep leaned over and did some wizardry on the keyboard. Now, there was a series of videos in a grid. "The computer searched *dogs*. You can look specifically at that now if you want. Press the back button if you want to scroll again."

"No, this is good." She picked one randomly.

There was Sonny, having a meltdown because Nanny was trying to get him to release the lead so the owner could go home. He was even ignoring the offer of a cracker that seemed to stave off a good ninety percent of the cusp-of-a-meltdown videos Lynx had watched.

Lynx tapped a different square. Another video came up; this time, it was of Sonny asleep on the couch, still holding a dog's lead. Some doggo was curled contentedly on the floor.

Nanny snuck in and unclasped the leash from the dog's collar, clipping it to a stuffed dog.

With her fingers curled into the dog's collar, Nanny tiptoed the dog out of the room. In the kitchen, she handed the dog over to what Lynx assumed was the owner, who tied a piece of kitchen twine to the collar, accepted a hundred-dollar bill and a handshake, and went out through the back door.

The body language between the two of them read as strangers caught up in an unexpected turn of events.

Lynx's across-the-street neighbor Justin's rescue husky, Sitka, found joy in running. And she was a Houdini when it came to getting the door open. Every day of the first week that Sitka was at his house, she'd disappeared on her daily exploration. Every day, Justin waited for the inevitable "I guess it's dark, and I should probably stop playing with you and get you home" phone calls following a Sitka-escape. He'd arrive with a "thank you, I appreciate the call" case of beer, piled a tired Sitka into his truck, and headed back home. Justin quickly realized that making an investment in a top-notch tracking collar was the way to go.

And that crisp green bill had that "thanks, sorry I put you out" feel to it. Lynx wondered if there was a drawer that held crisp hundred-dollar bills for just such an event. And if that were the case, why not just get a dog for the kid?

Lynx lifted her cell phone to quick dial over to Cerberus Tactical. Headquartered on the east side of the Iniquus Campus, that part of the Iniquus compound was where the K9 teams trained and prepped for mission work. While some of those dogs worked solely in search and rescue, all the doggos had trained in technical feats like parachuting into a crisis zone when they responded to mass disasters. About half the K9s had tactically trained as force multipliers when an operator team went out on a security mission.

And while Strike Force wasn't exactly doing a military-style operation up in New York City, Lynx thought a chat with K9 handler Ash Gideon was in order.

Before Lynx could press the quick dial, the first note of Striker's ringtone sounded, and she swiped to open the call. "Striker, hey, you're on speaker. I'm in the war room with Deep.

"Good."

"I heard you had a rough start to your day." She leaned to the side to get a look at Striker's camera feed. He was at the park. With ribbon streamers fluttering from their hands, Nanny and Sonny twirled around, watching colors dance with their movements. The ambient tinkling of a children's song about rainbows jingled happily in the background of the phone call.

Lynx peeked at Striker's vitals. All were back to normal —crisis contained.

"Scared the life out of me," Striker said. "And to make it worse, just before it happened, Cammy flashed into my mind. I was hoping you could maybe give her a call."

"Just in case you were suddenly tuning into your sixth sense? A little woo-woo happening for you?"

"Ha. No, that's your specialty. I leave all the woo-woo to you, but—"

"Yeah, I'll ring your dad and casually ask." Her gaze landed on the picture of Sonny, and yes, she could see why Striker's mind went to his niece. The two children looked enough alike that they could be siblings. Though Cammy turned seven last January. She had been just a year younger than Sonny when she was snatched away from her mom in broad daylight.

Strike Force tore up Washington, D.C., trying to find her. Save her.

That Cammy was a surface thought when Sonny took off running must have sent Striker's nervous system into a spiral. But he was textbook in his action/reaction from the camera feed she'd been analyzing.

After more than a decade of training, his body and mind served the situation well.

"I can't have that happen again." Striker's voice was granite. "I *won't* have that happen again. And to that end, Chica, I was hoping—"

"That I could figure something out? Deep already called me in and brought me up to speed. I'm going through the videos. But you guys did a stellar job. The family is safe because of your reflexes. That accident was crazy town."

Deep leaned in to get his voice closer to the speaker. "I got a readout from the 911 calls of the accident. The guy that jumped the curb had a heart attack and was trying to park in the loading zone to get out of the street."

"When I slow-mo the tape," Lynx added, "at the point where you turned your head, you can see the driver grip his right hand into his chest as he leans left, jerking the wheel harder. Jack saved Sonny's life. Looking at the angle of that car, Sonny would have been under that front tire had Jack not acted."

"Anything on Jack?" Striker asked.

"He's at the clinic," Deep said. "They rushed him right back to the examining room. He's getting his wound cleaned out. He doesn't think he needs stitches, just road rash and lots of blood. Once he's got his bandage on, they'll scan him for brain trauma and keep him if he's concussive."

"Okay. Keep me abreast. That might put us one man down, and I'll need someone to get up here."

"Copy," Deep said.

"Lynx, Nanny told me about a private social media page."

"Deep already handed that to me," Lynx said. "I'm on it."

She could hear the smile in Striker's voice. "Thank you. Love you, Chica."

"Not me?" Deep contrived a wounded tone.

"Love is a nuanced word, isn't it?" And without waiting for a response, Striker ended the call.

Lynx tapped Cerberus Team Bravo's headquarters' number.

"Growing up on Long Island, I can tell you for sure," Deep shifted back to face his monitors, "if someone saw something happening to a kid, they'd pile on. I'm not just talkin' men here. A silver-haired granny would haul back and whack the guy with her purse. They'd step in. But that call-out technique, that's the way they got people's heads up and scanning. It worked as planned."

Lynx chewed at her lip as she listened to the phone ringing. "I loved that the father that found Sonny wanted proof that Striker and Sonny belonged together. That was actually kinda ballsy, don't you think? Especially given the way Striker dressed for intimidation. Some fiercely protective papa bear energy going on there."

"New York. A hundred percent."

Lynx raised a finger and nodded at Deep to let him know someone was on the line.

"Cerberus Bravo, Juan Ortega speaking."

"Lynx here. Hey, I need to have a conversation with Ash. Is he available?"

"He's in the pool doing an evolution with the team."

"This is about a mission in progress and high priority. We may need to send Ash in immediately."

She heard a muffled. "Ash, Strike Force War Room stat. I'll get Hoover cleaned up."

Followed by a resonant "Yes, sir."

"Where's the mission?" Juan asked.

"New York City."

"Ash is out of the water," Juan said. "He needs to drag on some dry clothes. Then, he's on his way. Ten minutes."

"Thanks. Out." Lynx chewed on her lip as she set the phone down.

"Ash? Is this to take the place of Jack?" Deep asked.

"I hope we hear good news about Jack's head soon. But more importantly, I hope they take the time needed to get his assessment correct. I'm not a fan of head trauma. But as to Ash, I had a thought that may or may not work. I wanted to chat with him about Hoover's capabilities. Hoover might just be the key to Strike Force's mission success."

While she spoke, Deep was scrolling through a file, multi-tasking. "I don't know exactly what you're thinking about, but Hoover's a no-go. The client is allergic to dogs. It's on his medical form."

"Who is 'his' in that sentence? The dad? Sonny looks fine in all these videos."

"Father."

"Okay. Well, that sucks. How allergic? Like he gets the sniffles, or does he go into anaphylactic shock?"

"Checking."

As Deep scanned the file, Lynx watched another dog video. The dog walker looked around for the Nanny, who was jogging up. She quickly explained Sonny's situation as she rushed forward. The stranger waved her off. "Chauncy is laid back, and I'm glad for the help taking him for his exercise." The guy smiled, and along they walked.

Deep tapped his screen. "Allergies: dogs, cats, chestnuts,

avocado, and banana. Mild symptoms include—congestion and itchy eyes for fur and oral reactions to the food intolerances."

"I'm not worried about mild. I'm worried about Sonny running into traffic."

"Too bad you don't get to set the hierarchy. Based on my interface with the family, there's a solid structure in place. Dad is king."

"Got it. How about this angle? Can we keep them separate enough to protect the dad from sniffles in order to protect his son's life? Or maybe offer him an antihistamine?"

"All right, Lynx, you made your point." Deep pulled up the filed activities schedule. "But Dad is the signer of contracts and, therefore, the wielder of power." He scrolled down the timeline. "After this morning? Let's see. Family walks to the park. His wife gets her gift. She goes to see a fashion show while he has meetings." Deep read the schedule. "Nope, that walk was their only family time. Sonny and Nanny have their own suite next door to the parents. Tell me what you're thinking. I have a good suspicion that having the dog there would give Dad permission to limit interaction. It could work."

"If Hoover has the capability that I think he does."

"I'll let you surprise me. But just in case, let me book a room for Ash and Hoover at the hotel."

Deep's words faded into a blur as dread slid down Lynx's spine. For a moment, her lungs forgot how to inhale. She couldn't for the life of her fathom what could have caused her body to react with that level of survival reflex.

As Lynx tried to self-talk her way through the sensations, her phone buzzed.

She looked down at the screen and read: **Auralia Rochambeau**.

7

Lexi

Tuesday

As Deep maneuvered himself through the booking page at the client's hotel, Lynx stood and gave him a pat on the shoulder. "I'll be right back."

She bustled out to the hall and didn't swipe the call open until the War Room door clicked shut. "Hey, Auralia. How are you?" Lynx scampered down to her Puzzle Room, where she shut the door and headed over to plop between her doggos, looking for support.

As Auralia would say, something about this phone call just felt like bad juju.

"Lexi?"

"Hey, girl! What's up?"

Auralia exhaled loudly. "Look, I promised I'd pass on some information. I'm doing that, living up to the promise."

"Okay…"

"Are you alone right now?"

"I am." Lynx's system sizzled and snapped. "Are you safe? What part of the world are you covering right now?"

"I, uhm…yesterday was bad. Lots of explosions, but I got what I needed, and I'm in Amsterdam now. Listen." The line was silent for a long moment. "I was handed an address, date, and time where two people will be meeting in Jordan."

Lynx frowned. "Jordan the country?"

The receiver was silent with another long pause. A stress-relieving exhale.

"Yeah." Auralia's voice stretched thin. "Two men are meeting with a woman. The men's names are John Grey and—"

Lynx knew. She *knew*. Yes, *she knew*.

The next name Auralia would push past recalcitrant lips would be her husband's.

"Angel Sobado," Auralia whispered, then cleared her throat. Quietly, she read out the information about where the men would be staying on the date in just a few days. "Did you get all that?"

"I wrote it down," Lynx said, hoping against hope that Auralia wouldn't demand an explanation. She tried to preempt that with, "Whoever gave you this information surely, they warned you about the importance of secrecy."

According to the US government, Angel was dead and buried. He didn't exist in a mortal form. He wasn't in any computer bank, erased like they did the Delta Force operators and other governmental black ops. Not even disavowed. Just non-existent.

"Of course." Auralia was back to whispering. It didn't sound like she was trying to hide her words from others in the area. It sounded like the panic attack Lynx was experiencing actually belonged to Auralia. "Absolutely. Mum's the word."

"Auralia, you're okay. Everything's okay. I appreciate this information," she soothed. "Did the person who gave you this tell you *why* they were giving this to you? Did they specifically ask you to pass it on to me? Do you trust them?"

"This person is indebted to you. They shared the story with me about why. I knew a bit about it already. Not secret stuff, just a general timeline, and location. It lines up with what I know about Gator's coming and goings. I think that's the most that this person would want me to say."

"That's fine. As long as you trust the source."

"Yes. This is—I hope for the best. No matter what happens, you deserve to be happy. I'm shaking. I don't know why." She laughed without mirth. Nerves. "I think I should probably hang up."

"Thank you," Lynx was able to slide in just before the call ended.

Lynx sat there, stunned. Her mind scrolled through a mental list of all the people who might have helped Auralia get this information, and Lynx couldn't figure out a single one that would have used Auralia as a vehicle. It wasn't Color Code at the CIA, that was for sure. And that group was the only group out of Langley that—as far as Lynx knew—was aware that Angel still breathed, that his heart still beat.

Auralia was right to be frightened. Now, she knew about a black operator's whereabouts. That was dangerous information to hold. The existence of the black ops community was one of the most tightly guarded governmental secrets there was. And surely, Auralia was a smart enough woman that she'd figured that out.

It meant that people out there knew about Angel and were willing to share with others. That felt risky for him and his missions. Lynx wanted nothing to do with endangering him. Or him in general. That part of her life was over. Mourned and done.

This put her in a bad place. When she was working with the CIA to save Angel's life, Langley had promised her a secret divorce. That had *not* come through. It wasn't like she prioritized her freedom over others' lives. She'd handed the issue over to the intelligence agency. Surely, they could put the matter before a judge and get it sealed until a time when it didn't matter anymore.

Lynx refused to be the one to pursue her divorce for oh-so-many reasons. Mainly, she didn't know what she didn't know. She didn't know what could be deadly. In fact, she didn't know if her own life and that of her team might be in danger just because they knew that Angel was out there alive and functioning.

She'd been silent. They all had. And Striker had handled it all in his trademark stoic manner. He didn't care about the courthouse paperwork or the preacher's benediction. In his heart, he had already made the commitment.

Who knew? Who knew enough to get the information to Auralia—a journalist!—and trust her with it?

From Auralia's tone of voice, she understood the ramifications of her message.

Her mind scanning, Lynx was sure that those at Iniquus who knew—her team, Command, and the Montana group that had helped her find and save Angel—all kept a tight lid on that information.

But someone was talking. Reaching out. Including others into the fold.

Dangerous. Just flat-out dangerous. And now that she knew about the situation, she'd have to take steps to warn Angel.

Action was needed. But what action would that be?

Lynx looked down at her paper with the three logistical pieces written in blue ink with a shaky hand.

Next steps weren't decisions that she should make in a vacuum. She'd talk to Command and Striker. Have a strategy session. That would have to wait until Striker got back the day after tomorrow.

Lynx swiped her phone open and tapped the memorized phone number to Command onto the pad.

"Hi, Leanne," she said to General Elliot's secretary. "Listen, I need to talk to the general after Strike Force gets back. Can you find me a time slot?"

"Sure, let me coordinate that. Can you give me a sense of what this is about?" Specifics were usually classified, and Leanne knew better than to ask.

"Just let him know this is a matter of national security."

LYNX GAVE HERSELF A SHAKE. BEFORE SHE FORGOT, SHE SENT a quick text to Striker's dad: **Hey there, checking in. All's good?**

A moment later, a text came back: **Mimi's making tacos!**

No crisis in Miami. Lynx kissed her dogs on the head and asked them to stay put. She used the slow walk back to the war room to compose herself. With the ding of the elevator, she turned with her hand resting on the doorknob.

Ash strode crisply up the hall dressed in his Iniquus uniform. His short-cropped black hair was damp, and there was concern in his eyes as he paused by Lynx's side.

"That was fast. Thanks so much." She pressed the door open.

"Are you okay?" he quietly asked as he reached over her

head to grasp the door, holding it wide for her. Following her in, Lynx watched as Ash flicked his gaze toward the corner of the room where Deep sat behind his monitor, tapping at the keyboard.

Lynx knew that Ash, an ex-SEAL who had served under Striker back in the day, had learned over his deployments how to sniff the air for nervous energy. That, and he handled dogs, where body posture was its own form of communication. Of course, he would read the anxiety in Lynx's stance.

"We have a challenge that we're working to resolve." With a shift of her shoulders and the flash of a friendly smile, Lynx forced on her fluffy-bunny persona. Edging toward a chair at the conference table, she skated her hand down the back of her full pink skirt to tuck it under her as she sat. Where everyone at Iniquus wore black and grey, military-cut clothing, she alone, in her girly colors and feminine silhouettes, was supposed to stand out as a soft spot. A siren that wooed people into feeling comfortable enough to let down their defenses.

And Lynx, in turn, used the clothing and her ability to slide into her girl-next-door persona as her own defensive camouflage. Nothing to see here; everything is fine, thank you.

"I think you and Hoover might just be our solution to a mission debacle." Lynx gestured toward the comfortable leather chair across from her. "Won't you take a seat? Or first —you're just getting out of your water training—maybe you'd like something from the snack cart. Coffee, tea, water? Would you like to grab something to eat?"

Ash pulled out the closest chair. "I'm good, thanks," he said, taking a seat. "What've you got?"

"Strike Force has a four-man team on a close protection mission in New York City. It concludes tomorrow night."

Ash nodded. "That's what my commander said."

"Our protectees include a father and mother and their non-verbal son on the autism spectrum. This morning there was an event, and he took off running."

When Ash lifted his brows, Lynx added. "A driver's medical crisis caused a car to jump the curb and was plowing over the sidewalk toward our protectees." She held up both hands. "The team got everyone safely away from the vehicle. Jack sustained a head injury. We're not sure yet how severe. He's getting checked as we speak." After tucking her hands onto her lap, Lynx leaned in. "But in the chaos that followed, the child, Sonny, slipped away from the scene and took off running through the crowd. I can show you the camera feed, but the bottom line is Sonny was out of pocket on the city streets for almost three minutes."

Ash let out a low whistle. "How little are we talking here?"

"Four-years-old. Sonny likes to wander off on the best of days. On days when his senses light up, he panics and runs."

Ash slowly nodded as if he were picturing the scene.

"And Sonny is hyper-sensitive to anything rubbing his skin. Sonny doesn't like to wear clothes, so as soon as he was out of his family's sight, he took off his shoes where Striker had attached the trackers."

"Not good. But..." he looked between Deep and Lynx, "how can I help?"

"Sonny loves dogs with long fur. And I think that's going to be our best means of protecting his safety. In thinking about the Iniquus K9s—their dispositions, their training, and their fur type."

Ash smiled. "Long?"

"Exactly. The first doggo I thought about was Team Alpha's search and rescue dog, Valor. Her nickname, Little

Mama, says it all. When a child is endangered, she won't leave their side. And, of course, Valor wears a collar with a two-way communications device."

"But—"

"She's trained to search, working away from her handler. We need a K9 who knows how to work close protection. I think Valor would sense Sonny's needs and adapt to them."

Ash leaned in. "Even so, a twenty-four-hour window is a short time to take a dog from one kind of work to another. And I've been with Valor in a city. She's better on a mountain where she has space to think and react."

Deep lifted his voice. "Checking rosters, Valor and Trip-wire are in Colorado right now."

Lynx turned his way. "Oh, well, that answers that. She's not available." Lynx turned back to Ash. "Which is fine because I was thinking about Hoover and the mission we were on with the CIA. Hoover went in playing the role of a stability assistance K9."

"Not a service dog," Ash qualified.

"Just generally assisting, yes. He did a fantastic job acting. But then again, he was trained for that job. He took over for Noah's stability dog, Hairyman, when Hairyman was injured. Did you train Hoover for that task, or was it Reaper and Noah?"

"I worked with Hoover to test a theory. Noah refined the training as he used Hoover for those three weeks while Hairyman was healing."

"Great. Good. I can ask you about how that went down. So, from my own dogs," Lynx reached up and tucked her hair behind her ear, "I know that a dog task is a series of compo-nent parts put together. There was a lot going into the idea of Noah—who's what, about a hundred and eighty pounds?—

taking hold of the stability harness and propelling himself from a seated position up onto his feet."

Ash shook his head. "I'm trying to put Noah's problems with vertigo together with a four-year-old with elopement issues."

"Stick with me." Lynx smiled. "When you broke down the task of standing there solidly while Noah got up, was there a command for that one step?"

"Cement," Ash said.

Lynx tipped her head. "When you say 'Hoover, cement,' how does Hoover define that command exactly."

"Don't move no matter how much pulling or weight."

"And once Noah was up, did the command 'Cement' just stop? Or does Hoover require a release command?"

"The word is 'heel,' or the non-verbal is to step off with the left foot."

"I was afraid of that." Lynx swiped her hand over her mouth. "What if you said 'cement,' but the person holding the handle stepped off with their left foot."

"Okay, I think I get where you're going with this. If I'm commanding Hoover, Hoover will only follow my authority. For example, if I gave the signal for sit/stay and someone else —even someone from our team—then tried to get Hoover to break that sit/stay with a verbal or hand command, Hoover would ignore them. I'd put Hoover into his stability harness in the New York scenario. He reacts to the uniform he's wearing. It helps him define the job he's tasked with doing. If this child loved dogs and was willing to hold onto Hoover's harness, I don't think Sonny would have to put his hand on the stability harness. He could hold something else, Hoover's fur, his collar, a lead—then I could command Hoover to walk or cement as needed. My concern would be that the child would let go. Do you think that's possible?"

"Absolutely." Lynx's brows tugged together. "But Hoover's trained in scent work, right? Can he track specific human scent?"

"Yes and no. He's a tracker. But that task gets a little more complicated in the city with so many people and so much movement. That's not something we work on regularly. Hoover is more the kind of dog that can sniff the driver's seat of an escape vehicle and chase down the fleeing bad guy. A city search is a different skill set."

"Rub the kid in meat sauce?" She shrugged and patiently waited as Ash looked down at the table and processed.

When he finally looked up, he said, "I mean…" He spread his hands wide. "This kid really loves dogs?"

"*Loves* them," Lynx said emphatically. She stood and beckoned. "Come over here and look at this footage that I've bookmarked and see what you think from Hoover's training and temperament." As they both moved behind the wall of monitors, she added, "I was tasked with finding a solution, and frankly, this is the only one that I think is viable."

"What else are you considering?" Ash asked.

"Strapping him to helium balloons and flying him around."

"Oh."

"Yup. I'm really hoping that Hoover the Wonder Dog can do the trick."

8

Saadiq

IRAQ

Wednesday

WITH THE MORNING LIGHT CAME THE HEAT. AS THE EARTH twisted toward the sun, the intensity of the rays would broil the land. Saadiq was so grateful that the truck had traveled at night when the limited vegetation in the desert meant the nights were cool when fires would be welcomed, even if just in his imagination. Being stuffed into that crate during the height of the sun would have moved beyond torturous to being unsurvivable.

Saadiq was even more grateful that the delivery truck had *finally* pulled up at their destination. Throughout the long journey, the driver stopped every four hours to get him up and walking just enough to get circulation back in his limbs. Then back into the crate, he'd go. Each time it took Saadiq longer to talk himself into the box. Saadiq had no idea where he'd pin his location on a map. None. Now, in the moments before the men hefted up his crate and moved it to a safe room, Saadiq listened to the domestic clatter of the compound. He tried hard to catch the accents or to snatch a piece of feathery information that fluttered out of a mouth and into the air.

He waited impatiently as the men unloaded the truck. Each crate scraped along the wooden bed. The men grunted as they shifted the weight of their staples onto their shoulders for the transfer to a storage room. They would do the same with Saadiq, balancing his slight weight between two men who clasped the side handles.

His was the last crate off the truck.

There was a jangle of keys and the familiar words of well wishes and gratitude to the delivery guy. Then came the slow sway as his protectors moved carefully forward. The sun's angle was just right to stab Saadiq in the eyes. But he didn't chance moving his head. The only relief Saadiq allowed himself was to squeeze his eyelids tight.

The light dimmed. The room was cool and echoing. The door clicked shut, and the interior bolt slid into place.

A man gently tapped the crate's lid as if he were knocking on a guestroom door, then pried the top up. "We're turning you now."

At that point, that maneuver was the only way that Saadiq could get himself out of the crate. They'd lay the box on its side, and he would inch his shoulders and hips until he lay on the dusty ground like a beetle on its back.

Sometimes, the host would leave him like that to recover as best he could.

Sometimes, they would grab his feet and arms and drag him open like the Chesapeake Bay oysters Saadiq would dig up and wrench open back in his halcyon med school days.

If his protectors took the time to pry him open, they

usually followed by rubbing circulation back into his numb limbs. As his body came back awake, the pins and needles were excruciating, yes, but it was a kindness, nonetheless. "May Allah know of your compassion and return it a thousand-fold. Your generosity is a blessing." Saadiq's words were dry crackers that crumbled and fell from his mouth.

On this trip, he had only allowed himself sips of water that he'd used to keep his tongue moist. He had learned the hard way how painful a full bladder could feel on rutted roadways.

"All right?" both helpers asked over and over, one man on his left rubbing, the other on his right. "How do you endure?"

"I focus on what's in my mind." Saadiq pressed the words past gritted teeth. "Today, it was the great poet Rumi who filled my thoughts. 'Those who don't feel this Love pulling them like a river, those who don't drink dawn like a cup of spring water or take in the sunset like supper, those who don't want to change, let them sleep.'"

"And your thoughts?"

"I am living a nightmare," Saadiq whispered, making sure not to open his eyelids, protecting his hosts' anonymity. "I only hope to awaken to a fresh dawn."

"I wish this for you, my friend. Today, though, will be very hot. In here, you will be comfortably cool. Did you sleep at all? I don't know how you could have," the man on his left said.

They never told Saadiq their names. Not even made-up names like the Americans used on operations, names like ReadyMan, Havoc, and Viper. Names that meant power. Dangerous names.

His own name, Saadiq, had meaning too. His name meant "honest, trustworthy, and true." His mother and father had meant for his name to guide him in life. *I'm doing my best, Mama.* "Sleep? No," Saadiq answered his caregiver.

"I have food and mint tea on the crate behind you." The man's voice was thick with compassion.

Saadiq's stomach begged to taste the offerings as he drew the scent of aromatic spices into his nostrils—the fresh flatbread, garlic, cinnamon, and lamb. "Two buckets. One has warm water and soap. One is for your waste needs. You will find everything with the lantern that I will leave with you. Right now, this is, unfortunately, a dangerous location. There is inter-tribal anger. *They* will move you again tonight. Take what rest you can."

"Moved again?" Every cell in Saadiq's body screamed that he wasn't ready to be back in a crate. It was a torturous way to seek freedom. "Where will they take me?" Was his body language and voice nonchalant enough to pry loose some information?

"I know no more." Saadiq read the worry in his tone. "Except that I ask that you are very quiet and alert no one that you are here. You will be locked in for now. For your safety, I alone carry the keys." Saadiq heard the rustle and shift as the man got to his feet.

"Thank you."

"If you can move now, we will leave you."

Stifling a groan, Saadiq twitched this way and that. "Enough, my friend. Enough that I can cope on my own." He pressed into his hands until he sat. "Many thanks." He touched his heart to emphasize his words while he could not with the strength of his voice. "May your family be blessed." He quietly stared at the lantern light as the men left, not taking in their faces. It was better that Saadiq could not identify them.

The key turned in the lock.

Saadiq dragged himself to the crate with the tray and took a moment to appreciate the bounty before him. Childhood memories of his mother and aunties working on such a meal filled his mind.

After intoning a du'a—the personal prayer he spoke before each meal —Saadiq ate slowly, savoring the food.

Tearing a piece of flatbread to scoop up the meat and juices, Saadiq thought about the strange turns that his life had taken since most of the American soldiers had left Iraq. He was grateful at this juncture that he was a reading man and that he had always enjoyed history books.

While Saadiq had learned survival techniques working side by side with the special operators and the CIA, he'd learned things that kept him alive now by reading books about World War II.

In Europe, the Resistance made heroes out of everyday people. Shopkeepers fed those hidden from the Gestapo. Grandmothers sat on park benches and turned information into a knitted code. The scarves they made were then offered to the right people to wear as they moved from one place to the other. Teenaged girls would seduce the Nazis into the woods, where they would shoot them dead.

From those books, Saadiq was aware of methods to escape and hide. He taught these to his friends in the same circumstances as him. They developed code words that could be easily worked into their conversations. Words that would warn of dangers or capture.

Torture worked.

Once detained, the sadists would wrench information from the prisoners' mouths.

It wasn't an *if;* it was a *when.*

If a friend was compromised and forced to call people in his circle, the code words were worked into their conversations. A word might mean abandon everything and flee. Other words might mean, "Go to my place and destroy everything" —a last-ditch effort to keep others from being compromised, arrested, and dragged into their own interrogation rooms.

Friends would put loved ones on the phone when possible during these "gotcha!" phone calls. It could well be the last time that they ever heard, "I love you. Peace be with you," from the prisoner.

And as soon as they hung up, the person who had received the encoded call would rip the SIM card from his phone and destroy it. That man would never return to his home. Instead, he would flee to his safe location, gather his backup gear, and head off on his planned escape route along the underground railroad of his own construction.

Saadiq had been composing such strategies for over twenty years, always with the hope that they would be unnecessary. And in his mind, it never looked like this—locked in a food pantry, squatting in front of an onion crate, eating a silent meal.

No. All of his plans had been momentary plans. A week. A few days. Nothing, *nothing* like doing this for over a month —trucks, boxes, storage rooms, passed from hand to hand.

Reaching for the tea glass that scalded his fingertips, Saadiq relished the fresh, sticky-sweet, minted steam that he slowly inhaled.

After a sip of tea, he placed it down gingerly.

Pushing himself into a crouched walk with his hands pressed into his low back, he made his way to the far corner of the room, where he pulled off his clothing. Holding breath, he shook as much of the road dirt from the fibers as possible, then pulled the pieces back on to try and finish his meal without a swirl of dust assailing his nostrils.

As he chewed on a tender piece of mutton, he mulled his

assumption that as the Americans retreated that so would he —back to Maryland and his friends there. Back when the Americans left Iraq and all but a couple thousand troops went home, he had a visa and was ready to go. When he had tried to make the logistical arrangements for the move, Saadiq discovered his get-out-of-jail-free card—the visa to America —was issued in his name alone. Saadiq had flailed. He could not—*would not*—abandon his family to save himself.

Grasping at anyone who might help, he continued his interpreter's work for the U.S. military and the CIA—mostly the CIA.

Things had been okay—certainly not ideal, not his druthers—but it had been fine. Dangerous, but fine. Until they weren't.

Saadiq got the anticipated warning call. His name showed up on a list of men hunted by a terrorist cell. His family's survival was fragile.

He reached out to the CIA.

With that thought, Saadiq dragged an arm over his mouth as he choked on that last bit, a chunk of meat lodging in his throat, as he coughed into his elbow to clear it. What would happen if he choked while locked alone in here? He'd die. And then, it would be over for him, but his family would still need to find a way to survive.

Once he knew he was on the terrorist's list, Saadiq's first thought had been about his family. His first call had gone out to a longtime friend and colleague, John Grey. Grey worked along the Syrian-Iraqi border and was willing to hide Saadiq's family outside of Baghdad, keeping them away from the areas with heavy terrorist activity, like along the border between Iraq and Jordan.

Yes, there were men with a solid ethos whom Saadiq could trust.

The CIA Color Code said they would put his family into hiding near the capital while Saadiq continued to work for America. He would have to stay away from them, and Saadiq agreed with that assessment. He kissed his family goodbye, waved as they climbed into the vehicles, and prayed that they would be safe if they had some distance from him.

That's when another group within the CIA approached, offering Saadiq an opportunity to work one final mission in return for visas for his family to go with him to the USA.

Saadiq had, as the American idiom goes, "rolled the dice" that they would follow through with their end of the bargain. But he had worked with these off-book, black ops men; he knew who they were. He hadn't trusted them to fulfill their word, but that didn't mean he didn't go along with their plan out of desperation. Saadiq would have nothing to do with them if it weren't life or death.

Yes, to get those precious visas, he did that one last soul-damning thing for one of the CIA Numbers Group called Double Zero.

As in, double-zero shits to be given about anything.

As an interpreter, Saadiq had always hated it when he showed up for a mission and saw the DZ symbol on a patch on someone's pack.

Double Zero builds their ethos from some crazy fever dream of domination. Not *world* domination. Well maybe. Yeah, the Numbers were the psychopaths.

Double Zero—DZ—were the hell-bound. They didn't seem to care who they took along with them.

They were the devils who wanted him to sign on the line.

And for those he loved, he had.

The "what ifs" haunted him every day since the end of that mission when he alone was left standing there with full culpability of aiding an illegal mission, standing there with his name scrawled on the terrorist's most wanted list, unsure if DZ could or would produce the dangled carrot of survival.

"Don't put all of your eggs in one basket" was one of the first American idioms that Saadiq had memorized as a boy.

A good portion of his eggs went into the Iniquus basket via Striker Rheas. In Saadiq's mind, the protection of their documents was vital.

Iniquus was the white hat, the military beret, the cowboy ten-gallon, the baseball cap—the America that he had believed in.

Double Zero, though, wore black hats over stygian souls.

Having finished his meal, Saadiq drank the minty syrup of his now-cooled tea. He stood like a creaky old man. He felt twice his age. One foot in the grave.

Staggering the few steps over to the warm-water bucket, he dragged off his clothes, looking forward to washing the road dust off his skin.

He'd be back in the crate again tonight.

Saadiq pushed those thoughts away. It made his heart pound, made him lightheaded.

How much more could he endure?

Here in the food storage chamber, Saadiq arranged the sleeping pallet behind bags of rice and raisins in the window-less room. Stretching long, he arranged his aching limbs in the most restful way he could manage.

The pad of his finger hovered on the solar lantern's off button. The rubbery give under his finger had the feel of a blister. He hesitated to press it, wanting to keep the darkness away a moment longer.

This darkness was unlike that in Baghdad, with its streets and high rises. There, even when the electricity failed, there was still the hum of a generator to run a light, a stove, and a fan. The windowpanes would flash awake from the headlights as a car moved down the road.

His finger pulsed on the button.

When he finally gathered the courage to extinguish the light, the room plunged into nothingness. Fear skittered across his scalp. It was the terror he'd felt during his interpreter days that always foreshadowed a deadly night.

As Saadiq drew a blanket over his prone form, he heard men's shouts and women's wails. Gunfire clapped an enthusiastic applause.

The door to the food storage room bashed open with such velocity that it banged against the wall and bounced back to meet a man's fist.

With faces obscured by shemaghs, dusty sandals descended on him.

Hands grabbed and trapped Saadiq's arms, forcing him to his feet.

As his bones turned rubbery, a black hood dragged over his head.

9

Saadiq

Thursday

THE ROOM HE HAD LANDED IN WAS COMFORTABLE ENOUGH for a holding cell. If that was what this was. It was hard to categorize it.

Saadiq was having a tough time figuring out what the hell had happened to him.

It could be that he was a captive.

It was equally possible that the only thing that had happened was that Saadiq was moved the way his last host had cautioned him that he would be. Though, Saadiq hadn't anticipated the change until that evening.

Perhaps the last safe house had explained how crippled Saadiq had been when they pulled him from the crate, and his helpers determined that it was too soon to fold him into such a confined space again. Perhaps they used the hood to keep

83

Saadiq from seeing faces or being able to describe his route to the next safe house.

Over and over, the scene from the food storage room tumbled in his mind.

Ruminating. Ruminating.

What else did he have to do with his time than fold what few facts he had over and over, this way and that, trying to create something that had a vague resemblance to a representation of reality he could grasp?

The origami of a distraught mind.

The man who locked the door and said that only he had a key had been kind. It was in his touch and his voice. Saadiq had trusted him.

As a pediatric surgeon, Saadiq knew the doctors who were there for the job and those who were there because their souls told them to be. He didn't care much about money or prestige. He had been there for the children. He'd been there to stop their pain, to extend their lives, to give them functionality so they could just be kids.

The men who took him from the crate had been like that —people destined to be kind and make things better where they could not be fixed.

He had laid down.

There was that warning spike of adrenaline with the frozen fingers that scratched at his scalp.

The bang of the door. That was the part that was confusing Saadiq. But then, there had been shouting and gunshots. It could be that the bang was part of a rescue. The man had said there was unrest between the neighbors.

Saadiq had been out on enough missions to easily recognize the sound of a breaching ram—certainly, not a key.

The bag over his head.

His hands had been bound with zip ties.

He'd been brought here. The zip ties cut. The door shut and locked.

It was true that he'd been confined in one way or another at each leg of his journey over the last month. And it was also true that Saadiq had been locked in most places he'd been hidden.

In his mind, it was to keep people out, not keep him in. Perhaps, to also make sure he didn't wander around the compound, making people look at the stranger who suddenly appeared amongst them.

He was so confused. Should he be grateful or terrified?

A room with a bathroom. A sleeping pad. A stuffed bookcase. A ladder-back chair was pushed neatly under a desk. There was a tray with a traditional meal, the kind a family would eat. Not at all the sort of food you'd give a prisoner to break his will.

The lock was in place. The door was so thick and solidly placed in the opening that Saadiq couldn't rattle it.

Pushing the chair under the window that was high enough up the wall that it lit the room easily, the height and angle also kept the heat of the day from turning the glazed floor tiles into lava. There was nothing to see here—the stretch of a roof. The bleats of livestock and an occasional call from a child rode the wind into his room and perched there in the corner, looking at him.

Was he brought here like this to confuse the people shouting and shooting? To make *them* think he was a prisoner rather than an ally? Were the zip ties part of a subterfuge?

Prisoner or guest?

His system didn't know how to respond.

Should he rest, eat, and read?

Should he pace and pray?

In the end, Saadiq decided to bathe.

It was the first time he'd been able to properly wash his hair in over two weeks. Once his bodily filth washed down the drain, Saadiq filled the tub with the lukewarm water heated by the sun and gravity-fed through a pipe stuck through the roof. For no discernable reason, Saadiq shook the pipe to see if it could be dislodged. It was a small enough pipe that Saadiq could wrap his hand around it. What was he thinking? That he could suddenly shapeshift into a snake and slither his way out of here?

Anxiety whirred through his system, looking for a perch. It landed on his family and that last mission with Double Zero. "We need this one thing from you," they'd said. "And then we can get all five of you to safety. You and your family —we can get everyone out."

Saadiq had reached for that life belt and shook hands on the agreement. "But first," he'd said, having watched the CIA get what they wanted and not, in turn, lived up to their end of the bargain, "I need proof that my family is secure outside of Iraq." That had been the plan.

Until his family refused.

Leaving would have been safer—and been a lot easier on him in so many ways. Though, he understood their fears. They were women from a culture that didn't raise females to be independent. They couldn't fathom being alone in a strange country where they couldn't speak the language and knew no one. The thought terrified them.

With him? Yes, of course, they'd go.

Without him? No. They would not budge.

"But things will go badly for you. It's possible that you will be beaten, starved, imprisoned." Nothing he could say would change their minds. So, he contacted his friend Grey. "Will you hide my family?"

And he did.

At least, Saadiq *thought* that he did.

Saadiq had no idea where his family was, what kind of life they lived, or even if they were still alive.

He was no clearer about their situation than he was of his own.

Was he a prisoner now?

He had, after all, aided and abetted what some believed to be the enemy, U.S. spies. With his fluency levels and high-security clearance, Saadiq had been there when dangerous things were discussed. And he had a *very* good memory. There was much that could be extracted from him in a torture session, especially if they inflicted pain on his mother or wife, on his child.

Saadiq had already decided that he'd tell them anything and everything to protect his family. There was no reason to be tortured when it would all be told in the end. No one could resist forever.

All the names. All the policies. All the missions. All of it.

Ruminating. Ruminating.

Stripped of anything other than the clothes on his back, what did he have to trade other than what was in his head?

What weapons of self-protection could he brandish other than the memories from his work over the last two decades?

Lying back in the water, it was a luxury to soak his muscles. But the fear that he would be caught and punished for using the water quickly drove Saadiq out of the tub.

He pulled on the fresh pair of traditional trousers and a *dishdasha*, the loose cotton robe worn overtop, then went to lie on his bed.

Adjusting the pillow under his head, he stared at the ceiling. *They never asked my name.* Saadiq worked to calm himself. *I never saw them photograph me.* This thought calmed his nerves, and he began to relax in the heat of the day. Exhausted from being awake for so many days, his eyelids grew heavy.

Suddenly, Saadiq felt himself jump to his feet. Crouched with his arms spread wide, he watched the door to his room swing wide.

There, without readable emotion, stood the old man who had brought him food earlier, gesturing him out of the room.

Others ranged behind him with rifles clasped in their hands.

Terror blazed through Saadiq's system.

"What?" He twitched his head from one man to another. "What do you want from me?"

No one grabbed at him.

No one smiled.

It was so disorienting not to have a verbal or body language clue. This was like being in a sensory deprivation chamber. There was nothing for him to latch on to. He floated in his confusion.

They walked through a long corridor. Doors shut all along. No other people, though Saadiq could hear children calling to each other in the distance and bleats from the herd.

The old man opened the door to a dark room. A silhouette of black against charcoal gray asked in a gruff voice, "Do you have any friends whom you trust to come to your aid?"

No preamble. No welcome or hello or blessing.

Saadiq immediately said the name at the forefront of his mind since the black hood went over his head, "Striker at Iniquus." He then rattled off the Iniquus number that Saadiq had memorized after Striker took possession of his family's documents.

"Striker?" The silhouette paused. "Is this man a Navy SEAL?"

"He was, yes." Saadiq nodded enthusiastically, but no one

could see that. Was it good that this man knew Striker? Or had Striker's job harmed this man in some way? "He's retired from the military and works for a security group named Iniquus."

"I'm familiar with the security organization," the gruff voice warmed. "Let's give Striker a call and see if he can't be of some help righting this problem."

Problem. There is a problem.

Was Saadiq himself the problem?

Was his safety a problem?

Saadiq didn't understand the word *problem* in this context.

There was rustling in the corner.

Before they initiated the phone call, the shadow told Saadiq what he could and could not say. Saadiq would only give enough information to identify himself, and then, he'd return to his room.

But to be honest, other than his identity, Saadiq didn't have any more information to give about his present situation.

There was the slightest illumination from the light on the man's phone. Saadiq was able to make out another man's figure who brought him the phone to speak and then snatched it back away.

He was turned and pressed.

Not pushed, just encouraged to leave.

The door shut, and their footsteps retraced.

And now, back in his room, with this enigma of…*everything*.

10

Striker

WASHINGTON, D.C.
   Thursday

JACK TURNED ONTO THE MAIN ENTRANCE AT THE FRONT OF
the Iniquus Campus, glad the five-hour drive from N.Y.C. to
D.C. was all but over. "Anyone call Lynx with our ETA?" he
asked as he pulled to a stop at the Iniquus front entry.

The team shook their heads to the contrary.

As Didit and her K9 stepped out of the guard house,
Blaze leaned forward. "I got a twenty that says Lynx is
waiting in the Cerberus parking lot when we pull up."

Didit looked into the front window and caught Ash's
gaze. After he gave her the all's well signal, she waved them
forward without having her K9 sniff their passenger van for
explosives.

The electric gate slid wide to let them pass.

Iniquus had her friends. She also had her enemies. They stayed vigilant.

"Lynx in the parking lot," Ash reached over the seat to rub Hoover's muzzle, "when no one told her we were coming in? I'll take that wager."

When the team laughed, Ash turned to Striker with a look of confusion.

"Just don't mention we were bettin' on her," Gator said. "She hates that somethin' fierce."

As they rounded down that side road, Striker could see that Lexi was indeed standing right in the middle of the parking lot, not paying attention to the approaching van. She was still. Her arms hung from her shoulders as if weighted. Her feet spread a little wider than normal as if trying to keep her balance as the Earth shook beneath her.

Striker's body reacted, shifting into high protective gear. He knew it was coming. Over the years that he'd loved Lynx, he'd learned to spot the early signs of something dark and dangerous heading their way. When she did this, it was always a tsunami.

How high would the dangers rise this time? How devastating would the crash be?

A tsunami wasn't the largest wave of an ever-increasing series of waves; it resulted from water pulling away from the shore, gathering the force in strength and power.

That draw had started before he left for New York City.

"You're humming it again," he'd whispered into her ear as she cuddled up on his lap.

"What's that?" She tipped her head up to accept his kiss.

"*Three Blind Mice.*"

"Mmm, yeah. It's the nursery rhyme that Little Guy likes the best. Kate's been super tired with her pregnancy, so I was watching him earlier while she took a nap." Reaper and Kate lived on the adjacent side of Lynx's duplex. That explanation would have been perfectly reasonable for anyone else.

Just not when it came to Lynx.

"So that's it?" he'd asked, keeping his tone neutral. "You were keeping Zack happy?"

"I think so." She pushed herself up a bit to look him in the eye. "Why?"

He'd smiled because he loved her with every damned cell in his body. "That was nice of you, helping Kate," he said. And while he smiled so she would know he loved her, that conveyed only half of what he was thinking. Hiding behind his expression was the feeling that something dangerous was gathering force.

Compartmentalization was a tactic, especially when it came to Lynx and her sixth sense.

Striker had learned, over time, that it was best to let her percolate something up—a thought or a psychic "knowing." Asking too many questions at the beginning could make the dark and dangerous burrow deeper into her psyche. Like early cancer detection, the sooner the team got the information, the better the outcome.

Lynx had uncanny, otherworldly abilities—just one tool in her remarkable toolbox.

Her skills in the ether had saved his sister, Lynda, and his niece Cammy's lives. They had protected the team. The truth was that without Lynx's abilities, Strike Force would all be dead.

But that sixth sense information didn't come for free. They were often brutal hell rides for Lynx as she went behind the veil to fight where the team couldn't follow.

Now, Striker had a scientific mind. In high school, he'd set his goal of becoming a NASA engineer. After starting dual enrollment at age fourteen, attending most of his classes at the community college, he went to school year-round, trying to gain as many credits as possible. In his mind, Striker was shaving off time with his undergraduate work, excited to go after that Ph.D. in rocket science.

A Navy recruiter approached him when Striker captained his school's water polo team at the state championship in his senior year.

"Son, if you want to send rockets to the stars, you've got to get leadership under your belt. The SEALs will give you real-world experience applying that engineering you like so much."

Calculations. Formulas. Science. Cold hard facts.

Crazy that he'd end up loving a woman that upended his understanding of how the world worked and what was possible.

Lexi Sobado, AKA Lynx, was the biggest challenge of his lifetime—a paradigm buster.

Striker was in awe of her bravery. And he feared for her, especially when a children's story or nursery rhyme tumbled from her lips. Striker knew that they were her etheric danger language. Or, as she put it, "the way my subconscious informs me."

In his experience, that information was never benign.

And it often had to do with things she had never seen or heard before. She just snatched things from the air.

A miracle and a poison.

"Don't look at me like that." She tucked back into his arms.

Striker held her a little tighter. "I just get a little paranoid whenever you start chatting about Grimms' Fairy Tales or Mother Goose." He dropped a kiss onto her nose. "Not a *knowing* then?"

"I'll always tell you if I pick up anything on my psychic

channels. But you know…the mice…" Her words wavered off unsteadily.

"Tell me, Chica." He kept his voice light and even. Lexi had the bad habit of keeping her cards to herself while she worked out puzzles in her head. A habit of necessity. Who in their right mind would go around telling people about their psychic experiences, especially in Iniquus's line of work?

"Just dreaming a lot about something underground. Voles, maybe?"

"What are they doing?" He used the same voice quality that their mentor Spyder used when he was hypnotizing someone.

"Running around in tunnels underground."

Striker opened his mind to a picture or a thought, but all he got was, "Huh."

"Yeah, weird. Right?"

"A lot, Chica?" Striker combed his fingers through her hair, hoping to soothe her, hoping she might offer more clues to the big and bad that he sensed—the ocean of water pulling from the shore.

"What?" she'd murmured.

"Have you been having the dream about rodents in tunnels a lot?"

"Last few nights."

"But that's not why you're singing *Three Blind Mice* to me?"

She'd chuckled. "You're cuddling me in your arms. You're rocking me in a soothing way. I did this with Zack, *Three Blind Mice*."

Since then, Striker had caught her humming throughout the day. "*Three Blind Mice*" put Striker's system into combat readiness. He had worked very hard not to let that distract him while he was on the close protection job in New York.

Typically, he was well-practiced and very good at compart-mentalization, but the idea that her team would be hours away if the farmer's wife came after Lynx with the metaphorical butcher's knife? Yeah, that was tough.

As Jack pulled into the parking space, Striker thought he'd be relieved to get back to her. But seeing her like that? He was in warrior mode.

Ash pulled out his wallet. "I owe you a twenty," he told Blaze, dragging the bill out.

Gator leaned forward. "You see what I'm seeing?"

"Yep," the team said as they focused on Lynx.

"Shit is about to hit the damned fan," Jack said as he unclipped his safety belt.

Ash looked over at Lynx, who stood smiling from the middle of the parking lot. "What am I missing? What's going on?"

11

Striker

AS LYNX HEADED THEIR WAY, THE TEAM CLIMBED OUT OF THE van, happy to stretch their legs.

Their boots were on the ground for all of ten seconds when everyone's phone sounded at once with a summons to get to Iniquus Command pronto.

Even Ash and Lynx were pulling out their cellphones, tapping out: WILCO, and turning to Striker for orders.

Striker pointed a finger at Ash. "Run Hoover inside and hand him over to one of your teammates. We'll take the van back to Headquarters."

Silently, the men stood while Hoover unloaded, and the two jogged toward Cerberus Training Center.

Striker squinted past the broiling glare of the mid-day July sun. "Do you know what this is about?" he asked Lynx.

"No," she whispered.

"Tunnels? *Three Blind Mice*?" he pressed.

"I don't know." She bit at her lips. Her face had gone pale, and she looked like she was going to pass out—all typical signs of the looming big and bad. Striker wanted to reach for her, to drag her into his arms. Every instinct in him screamed *protect her*! But touching Lynx when she was like this fried her wiring. Still, he moved behind her enough that he could catch her if she took a dive.

"Heebie-jeebies?" Gator asked. "Knowings?"

Blaze jabbed his hands onto his hips as his gaze scanned the area. "Anything at all buzzing your psychic antennae?"

"Sweat. Fear. Kinship." She turned to Gator. "You?"

"I got nothin'." Gator had trained his own sixth senses over the years, but he was a rookie compared to Lynx.

Jack lifted a hand to indicate Ash jogging toward them. "Let's mount up and go see what Command wants."

Lynx climbed past Jack through the passenger door. The white bandage neatly covered the stitches along his hairline. In the sunlight, the purple and green bruising running down the length of his face was much more pronounced—just another day in the life of an operator.

"I watched that video of the accident. You look better than you should." She swiped her hand down the back of her skirt to smooth it under her as she sat. "Did something more happen in New York? Do you think that's what this is about?" Her phone pinged, then pinged again. Lynx swiped, and she said, "That's Deep. Command requested Randy, and he joined the meeting, too. They'll wait for us at the elevator outside of the Command Suite." She caught Striker's gaze. "That's all of us. Interesting that they called in Ash. But if it included Randy, since he was on loan to Tidal Force, it means this meeting has nothing to do with New York."

Ash jogged over. Holding the door frame as he swiveled his hips onto a seat, he asked, "Is this usual for you?" He dragged the door shut. "I've never been called into Iniquus Command before. I only talked to them during my interviews. It's always the Cerberus Commanders who go, and my team gets read in."

"It's unusual," Striker said.

The silent drive across campus was quick. They exited the vehicle and took the elevator to the Command wing of Iniquus. The team fell in step, their shoulders back, their chins tucked. Lynx moved at a slower pace. When Striker sent a glance back to check on her, she was sliding a hand along the highly polished, walnut chair railing. She was off balance—and the team each took that information in their peripheral view. But they knew better than to offer an arm or hand for stability. At times like these, Lynx couldn't stand to be touched.

By the time Leanne opened the massive carved door to the Command Suite for the team with an "Oh good, Command is waiting for you in the conference room," they were mentally prepared for a hard conversation.

Leanne pulled the second door wide and gestured them in. There was a ping on her computer, and she scurried behind her desk.

General Elliot stood by the window. Colonel Grant and Mr. Spencer sat across the table from the operators as the team filed in and stood at attention. White shirts rolled to the elbow, and ties loosened at the neck, balding heads, deep lines around their steely gazes. These were the men who had envisioned Iniquus, then made it a thriving reality.

"Find seats, gentlemen," Spencer said, "and Lynx, of course."

"Sir."

Striker waited for Lynx to find her spot. She moved to a side chair away from the conference table. His team waited for Striker to sit. Then, they filled the chairs.

Leanne ran in, flapping papers above her head. "Signed and ready to go, sir." She handed them off to General Elliot, her face unusually tense.

General Elliot looked the pages over, nodding. "They clearly understand the seriousness of the situation." He looked over at his fellow commanders. "Good, they decided not to drag ass over this." He looked at his watch. "Seven minutes. That's the fastest signature we've ever received."

The look on the colonel's face was battle ready. "Gentlemen, we've signed a Pentagon contract for an Iraqi mission." He tipped an ear toward the papers the general handed back to Leanne. "As you heard, Iniquus instigated the contract just minutes ago." He pointed at the wall behind them, and Leanne scrambled over to push the painted canvas aside.

"Sir." They swiveled in their black leather captain's chairs to face the newly exposed screen as Leanne dimmed the lights.

The photograph was of Saadiq, an interpreter that Striker's team had worked with on most missions in Iraq. Saadiq was one of the few terps that had the physical stamina to keep up with the requirements of a special forces team.

"Ash," Colonel Grant said, "You're here because you served with the same SEAL team as many of the Strike Force operators. You know this man?"

Ash shifted to the edge of his chair. "You've got that right, Colonel. He saved my life more times than I can count."

"And that's why we want you here." Colonel Grant stood. "This operation is personal. It's about one of our own." He pressed his fingertips onto the table's surface. "Background for all of you who weren't on Striker's SEAL team: Saadiq al-Habib was an American interpreter from 2002 until present. Since the main withdrawal from Iraq, Saadiq has worked as an interpreter for the military in their narrowed scope, for State, and for the CIA in the field. About a month ago, Striker made contact with Saadiq in Baghdad. At that time, Saadiq had asked Striker to safeguard his family's documents. Iniquus now stores those documents in our vault." He lifted his chin and adjusted his shoulders. "The nature of that contact, the idea that he wanted his family's documentation out of the country, concerned me. I didn't know that Saadiq was married and had a child, and that was why he didn't leave Iraq. My understanding was that he was there to continue his job with our government." Colonel Grant clenched his jaw and dragged in a noisy breath.

Everyone understood the sentiment conveyed. The U.S. made promises to the men who had worked as their interpreters in both Iraq and Afghanistan. And in many cases—way too many—American red tape and bureaucracy got in the way of the United States living up to their word. All the men in that room owed their lives and the success of their missions to their interpreters, and they had all tried to keep track of and push for their immigration to America, usually to no avail.

"After Striker returned with Saadiq's papers, I put out some feelers to reassure myself. I," Colonel Grant said, "like all of you, owe much to Saadiq's intelligence and bravery. But, too, I know what types of things Saadiq knows from working with special forces—data, names, even protocols, and techniques—that we don't want in terrorists' hands. A man like Saadiq…" He dropped his chin and shook his head. "You all get it." He lifted his gaze to Saadiq's picture on the screen. "Through my inquiries, I discovered two things. One,

Saadiq approached the CIA's Color Code and asked them to protect his family as he went out on a mission. They agreed. The family is under the CIA's protection in western Iraq, close to the border."

"Why would that working group take on family protection?" Striker leaned back in his seat, crossing his arms over his chest.

"Protecting assets is one of the functions Color Code has taken on in the region. Their toe hold is an elliptical working area from the Mediterranean that includes parts of Israel, Lebanon, Jordan, Syria, and Iraq," Spencer said. "The fear is that if terrorists captured a family at the same time that terrorists seize a high-value target, they could use the family to pry sensitive information from our allies." Mr. Spencer came from the industry side of war. He financed the start of Iniquus and focused on the financial side of the business.

"You said family as if they are in a separate location from Saadiq?" Lynx asked.

"Exactly. Saadiq was heading into the field on a CIA mission with a different working group when Saadiq reached out to his contacts in Color."

"The mission was with which working group?" Lynx asked.

"Numbers," the general said. "That mission is classified. But after I pulled a chit, I found out it was Double Zero."

Cold washed through Striker. Double Zero had a specific purpose—and it was dark.

He could feel Lynx's gaze on him. She would have seen and read his reaction. And she'd have questions, but honestly, he didn't want what Double Zero did in her head; he didn't even want it in his own.

Striker spun toward Colonel Grant. "Saadiq is after more visas?"

"My thoughts. Given the timing of his marriage and the birth of his child, we can surmise he didn't leave Iraq because he didn't have visas for his family."

"And that's just the kind of thing Double Zero could dangle," the colonel finished.

Striker leaned forward, resting his forearms on his thighs, his gaze intent. "What do you need from us?"

12

Striker

"I spoke with Black at Color Code a week ago," Colonel Grant said. "He indicated that Langley hadn't heard from Saadiq since the Number's mission. It's been over a month since Saadiq stopped answering his cell phone, and the cell phone isn't pinging on the map at Langley anymore."

"Can we ask Numbers about his status?" Lynx asked.

"There's no way to get information from that team," the colonel said. "The missions are classified and compartmental-ized. Like Delta Force for the Pentagon, Numbers for CIA work at the behest of the President. Both organizations exist and also don't exist. That's the level of secrecy." He cleared his throat. "And at this point, unnecessary. Bringing this time-line up to present moment, a man called the Iniquus hotline a short time ago. Since we have a digital recording of Saadiq's voice, our AI system was able to compare the two audio frequencies, and they were a match. Apparently, Saadiq was in hiding when he was scooped up in regional unrest. Saadiq convinced his captors to allow him to call Iniquus to affect a trade."

The team was tightly focused.

"Per our policy," Colonel Grant said, "once our communications staff determined the nature of the call, they transferred the line to a hostage negotiator. In this case, the call went to Honey Honig."

"Good. Best of the best." Lynx nodded. "What did he come up with?"

"Let's take a listen, shall we?" The colonel turned to Lynx. "How's your Arabic?"

"They spoke it in my Kitchen Grandmother Jadda's home. But she spoke Arabic as a second language, so you can't look to me to pick out nuance."

As a SEAL team leader, Striker had worked to keep his team's brains and bodies in good condition, and one of the ways that he did this was to require local language classes every day that they were out on an active mission. It had the added benefit of helping to stave off boredom and the substance abuse—especially alcohol abuse—that he saw with other teams.

And he had done the same as a Commander here at Iniquus. Striker and his team kept up with their language skills by watching the news and reading newspapers every week. They would pick meals and speak amongst themselves in a rotation of shared languages. Most of them spoke French for their work in Africa; Arabic got them by in most of Iraq— a smattering of other regional languages from Afghanistan.

And Lexi participated; her Arabic was very good.

Leanne walked along the line of operators, handing out

pages with the conversation in Arabic and translated to English and giving the last one to Lynx.

The colonel pressed a button, and the team followed the readout as they listened to the recording in Arabic.

HONIG: "SAADIQ? THIS IS HONEY. I WORK WITH STRIKER. I'm here to help."

Saadiq: "Thank you. I have a message from my," he paused as if searching for the right term and ended with, "hosts."

Honig: "Ready to receive."

MUFFLED CHATTER IN THE BACKGROUND THAT SOUNDED LIKE a reprimand and a warning.

HONIG: "WHERE ARE YOU?"

Saadiq: "I will leave that for the moment."

Honig: "How are you? Do you need medical assistance?"

Saadiq: "I am physically well, thank you. My needs are met, though I haven't been here very long. I knew my days were *numbered* with my last job a month ago. I have *zero* ideas where I have been since my last translation job. *Double zero* ideas."

Honig: "I see. I'm sorry that Striker isn't here to speak with you. But I'm happy to help. What is it that you need from Iniquus?"

Saadiq: "My host says that he is friendly with Striker as well. That they worked together many years ago when Striker's SEAL team was in Iraq. It's very fortunate that we have this great friend in common."

Honig: "I agree. Can you tell me this man's name so I can pass it along to Striker?"

Saadiq: "I needed you to verify that I am truly speaking to you. My host is signaling that I should hand the phone to them. I send my brotherly love and my gratitude to the friendships I've enjoyed with the men of Iniquus."

The recording stopped.

STRIKER RECOGNIZED SAADIQ'S VOICE IMMEDIATELY. A CHESS player, Striker was aware that Saadiq was trying to game the call and insert information that might clarify the situation for Iniquus. Surely, Saadiq had no idea that the colonel had been working the phones on his behalf since Striker encountered him in Baghdad and that Command had some idea of what had happened. Still, as Lynx would say, that conversation was an affirmation. And affirmations were usually welcomed.

"He was on the phone long enough," Jack said, "did the computers get an estimated location?"

"We believe we know where he is." The general tapped a button, and Saadiq's picture changed to a topographical map showing the terrain of western Iraq. A blue circle had a wide enough circumference that it was useless in pinpointing where the call initiated.

Not atypical. When using a satellite phone, pinpointing a caller was much more difficult. There were no cell towers to triangulate.

The general tapped the button again, and the image changed to an aerial of a family compound.

Ash stabbed his finger at it in recognition.

"Yes," Striker said. "We know the place, and we know the players. That's Mahmoon el-Sahl's compound."

"How friendly are they with you?" Spencer asked.

Striker pressed the pads of his fingers together. "We share a mutual respect. They do what they need to survive. Their loyalties are generally fluid, with the objective of living to see another day. I'm not aware of any specific animosity toward America. But a lot can happen in a decade."

Spencer flipped to a new image: this time, three compounds were identified on a satellite map.

"After Saadiq got off the line, Honey spoke with Saadiq's captors. They were very forthcoming about the situation," the colonel said. "You have the readout. This is the situation—stick with me here. It's a bit like a shell game. As part of an ongoing rift between local families that mostly centered around herds and grazing, Naseem el-Pars captured Mahmoon el Sahl's eldest son and was holding him for ransom. Mahmoon doesn't have the kind of money that Naseem demanded of him. Mahmoon found out that Naseem el-Pars's son was going to confront another neighbor here." The colonel lifted a laser pointer and circled a compound to the south of the other two on the map. "It so happened that this is the compound where Saadiq was hiding as friends moved him toward the Jordanian border. This compound is only relevant to this discussion in that Mahmoon's people didn't find Naseem's son, so they took Saadiq instead."

"Naseem's son wasn't captured. He's still a free man?" Striker asked.

"He never showed up, and his well-being was neither confirmed nor negated," the colonel clarified. "Which leaves us with Mahmoon el Sahl holding Saadiq, hoping to get enough money to buy his son back from Naseem el-Pars."

Striker opened his hands. "Give them the money. We've dealt with Mahmoon. While this is exactly the kind of thing we've seen happen in the past, he's a man of his word."

"Not so simple," Colonel Grant said. "Trust has fallen off

between these families, and they want an esteemed common denominator—specifically, Striker and his men—to affect the exchange. The plan as of right now is straightforward." He leaned over to tap the button to change to a map that included the southern American base. "You will fly in. Here, you will be supplied with vehicles." He tapped the highway. "You will drive west to Naseem el-Pars family compound, where you will blend in as you attend a wedding with the other guests. There you will pay the ransom for Mahmoon el Sahl's son. You will then drive to Mahmoon el Sahl's compound and exchange his son for Saadiq. Once you have Saadiq in pocket, you'll head back this way to the base, unless he's injured. If needed, we can get a medical evac. The Pentagon prefers we keep this low-key. Use your best discretion." He sniffed hard and drilled Striker with his gaze. "It's best for everyone if we can keep this as small a footprint as possible."

Striker gave a curt nod. "Sir."

"Tomorrow morning, zero five hundred, rally here." He pointed down at the conference table. "Logistics was able to get your team onto a military supply transport heading over to the base. Tomorrow you will be provided with appropriate clothing for the wedding, but you'll want your own gear for the rest of the mission."

Spencer rapped his knuckles on the table. "All of this has transpired in the last hour. Our support teams are spinning this up as fast as they can. This is where we are right now. We'll have a better target package to hand you by morning." The colonel referred to the intelligence summaries that included information about a location, applicable groups, and individuals. This information helped give the operators with boots on the ground a better picture of the environment they'd be working in.

"Gentlemen," Colonel Grant said, "as you embark on this

mission, you will ensure that you follow all laws and customs. And you *will* come back safely. We aren't adding to Uncle Sam's issues by having a team of retired SEALs on terrorist Darknet videos. Understood?"

Striker gave a curt nod. "Sir."

"Yes, sir," the team responded.

"Deep will be coordinating from your war room." He turned to Deep. "Nutsbe is backup and can spell you during the operation."

"Yes, sir."

"Since you're looking at about twenty hours in the air," the colonel said. "I'm going to suggest that Deep gets going with our logistics team. The rest of you have been in the field. Go home. Get cleaned up, water your plants, pack a bag, and get some good shut-eye because it's going to be a long haul once you get in the air."

"Yes, sir." The men stood and snapped to attention.

"Questions?"

"Sir." Ash turned his head to catch the colonel's gaze, "Is my tactical K9 Hoover going in with me?"

"Cerberus," the colonel squinted at Ash, "remind me about Hoover's training."

"Hoover's a German shepherd, sir. Tactically trained and deployed to hot spots. He's a nose and a bite. He can scent munitions and track individual scents."

"Right. Yes, he goes. And to that end, it's good that you're landing on an American air base. We'll figure out how to get you all home once you have Saadiq in hand. Thank you, gentlemen. Dismissed."

Striker noticed that they hadn't mentioned a role for Lynx. Not even in support of Deep. That was unusual.

As the team shuffled toward the door to leave, General Elliot said, "Lynx and Striker stay put."

Striker glanced at Lynx to see if she knew what Command needed.

Lynx laced her fingers in a tight grip. Her face flamed red as she turned toward the general.

She knew what this was about, all right, and she was *not* happy.

13

Striker

The team filed out the door while Leanne pushed the painting over the display screen, then moved to adjust the precision placement she preferred for the chairs around the table.

"Thank you, Leanne. We need the room." When Spencer dismissed her, she turned and bustled out, shutting the door behind her. Lexi rose from her chair to the side of the room and moved across to sit closer to the general. And this was telling because they had a grandfather-granddaughter-like relationship. While her relationship with Spencer and the colonel was much more professionally distant.

She was in that cloak of fragility that she sometimes wore. The one that threw him off balance. Striker would admit that there was something about this side of Lexi that appealed to his male ego—brought out his most caveman-like instincts—puffed out his damned chest. Lexi, in the persona of a fairytale princess in need of a prince, was the stuff of his niece's bedtime stories.

And absurd.

Yeah, that fantasy princess role wasn't a good fit.

Highly gifted, in her twenty-five years, she'd lived more —and through more crazy trials—than most people would in their entire lifetimes.

Striker thought that the image of a medieval queen was a better metaphor. Regal, learned, accomplished.

But like a medieval queen, Lynx could don her armor and ride into the fray with cunning and courage. And equally, she could swish her skirts as she meandered amongst the trees in a sun-dappled wood, feminine and vulnerable, knowing her knights were standing ready in her defense.

It was this strange combination of fragility and immense power that challenged Striker over the five years since he'd met Lexi. At that time, the team had moved Lexi to an Iniquus safehouse. Since the second he laid eyes on her lying vulnerably in that hospital bed, he knew in the marrow of his bones she was his to love and to protect. It was hard to believe they'd been a couple for almost four years. During that time, he was always impressed by how strong she was, physically and intellectually.

Yet, when she showed up like this—like glass that could shatter if it weren't handled correctly—there was something to those fantasy images. He wanted to drag his sword from its scabbard and fight the dragon coming against her.

Rarely in their relationship had that happened.

Once, he'd thwarted her from racing into a confrontation with a madman on PCP. But typically, he arrived after she'd slayed that dragon on her own—often in a fight to the death where she barely escaped with a breath in her body.

He'd scraped her off the sidewalk, bleeding out from a stalker. He'd defibrillated her back to life after she'd escaped a prison and stolen a plane to fly to safety and crashed.

He'd watched while she'd pitted her wits against powerful, egomaniacal men twice her size and age, where she always walked away the victor.

He'd stood by as she used her sixth sense skills, working in the ether to save his sister Lynda not once but twice in acts of selflessness that left him in awe and in visceral pain from her audacity and courage.

And equally, she was mule-like and headstrong, too.

She was a goddess divine.

Yes, a powerful, amazing woman.

This side of Lexi, as she sat vulnerably beside the general, was every bit as much of her personality as the side she suddenly switched on—the nerd girl with a vast store of factoids—when Spencer leaned in and asked, "Did you find a solution to that puzzle we handed you?"

It was a toggle switch of a question that flipped on her analytic brain.

"I tried. My gut says that the client grabbed the wrong guy. But the reasons I think it's the wrong person are murky." She shrugged. "Okay, a lot murky."

"Tell me about that." Spencer leaned back in his chair, resting his laced fingers comfortably on his chest. "Murky, is that because you can't prove he did it?"

"The pieces don't fit together. It seemed off, and I couldn't put my finger on the why. I still can't. But when Striker," she tipped her head his way, "had an incident in New York that needed some attention, I had a few ideas bubble up. On Striker's mission, I was looking for a way to keep the client's child, Sonny, safe. To learn about him, I watched their family videos. Two things occurred to me." She pressed her lips together.

If they saw someone else doing that, Lexi would explain to Striker that this was a body language tell, indicating that she didn't want to share her ideas.

"Listening," Spencer said.

"First, my understanding is that this guy, who is American, was raised as the only child of a mom working two jobs without a lot of support—so no cousins in the house acting as siblings."

Spencer nodded.

"I don't know if this is true to all cultures, but in America, if one has siblings, it's often true that you habitually announce where you're going. As in, 'I'm going to take a bath.' 'I'm going to bed,' 'I'm going outside to play.' Ask any only child in America, and they'll tell you they think it's weird when people narrate where they're going. Only children typically never say, 'I'm going to the restroom.' They just go."

Striker had never noticed that before. But yeah, he had a blended family since he was five after his mom took off with a new guy. He grew up with an older stepsister Mercedes, now deceased, and a younger stepsister, Lynda. Though the term "stepsisters" was correct, Striker never considered them anything other than his tight nuclear family. And to Lexi's point, Striker constantly announced things like 'I'm taking the trash out.' And thinking back, he didn't remember Lexi doing that unless it would affect his timeline somehow.

Interesting.

"Reading the witness's account of what the perpetrator said, it seems the killer narrated everything to his female accomplice—everywhere he was going and what he'd be doing there. If that's accurate, I'd say your killer grew up in a litter. I'd lay good money on it."

"Noted." Spencer steepled his fingers and pressed the point under his chin. "I can understand why you'd say murky. Anything else?"

"Same thought thread. The other reason I don't think this guy pulled a body across the bow of his kayak, paddled out into open waters, and slid him into the deep is the 'why' of your suspect being an only child."

"The why? How does that impact this case? His father died of suicide before Boyd Carr was even born."

"Right. So, there is a series of studies done to try to explain generational family trauma. Let's take a mouse study." She turned to Striker, a check-in.

He gave her a nod of encouragement, and she turned back to the commanders.

"I came across this study while helping Panther Force on their Paris mission to save Arya Khouri. During that mission, the researcher...sorry, too much information. You don't need to know about that mission except that I learned about this mice experiment."

"That applies to humans?" Spencer asked. Obviously, this case was his baby.

"In theory. There haven't been human studies. You know, ethics... But this is what they did in a nutshell—think Pavlov's dog only with torture. So, they had a group of male mice that were standing on a bed that could be electrified to the point of causing excruciating pain. As the scientists flipped the switch on, they released the scent of cherry blossoms."

"To what end?" General Elliot asked.

"Pavlov linked the sound of the bell to food for the dogs. Here, the mice now linked the smell of cherry blossoms to torturous pain. Whenever the mice were exposed to the scent, even in the absence of a shock, the mice had the physical response of a life-or-death event. And they measured this in the mice to ensure that was true."

"Okay." Spencer's brows pulled together.

"Later, when they weren't in an aroused state—" Lynx looked down at her lap with bemused confusion. "Let me reword that—when not experiencing the scent of cherry blossoms, the mice were having a normal day with their vitals all in the normal range, the scientists gathered their semen and impregnated some lady mice. It's important that you know that this was merely a sperm donation. The male mice and female mice were never in the same physical room."

"Again, to what end?" Spencer pushed. "You started with generational familial trauma."

"Right. The researchers discovered that the scent of cherry blossoms produced a fight-or-flight response in the baby mice. Again, the baby mice had no personal reason to react to cherry blossoms. And that cherry-blossom-scent fear persisted for several generations. They, of course, had mommy mice in the same lab who were impregnated with sperm from non-traumatized daddy mice as a control. The control offspring didn't react to cherry blossom with any discernable vitals' reaction."

"Interesting, but…" Spencer shook his head.

"This is one study. And again, it can't be replicated in humans for ethical reasons. But what if it's true? What if life-or-death fear goes into the DNA, the revulsion and pain? Why would our DNA want to do that as a survival technique? Because daddy-caveman might not live long enough to see the kiddo grow up. He might not be able to verbally pass on the information that 'it's best to avoid the saber tooth tigers.'"

"Sound advice," Spencer said with a wry smile. "Now

apply this to Boyd Carr."

"Boyd Carr's father was released after being held hostage by terrorists in Afghanistan. Those terrorists tried to get him to tell his military secrets; according to his file, they waterboarded him. While being waterboarded, he died on three occasions to be brought back with artificial breathing and a defibrillator." Lexi frowned deeply with her eyes squeezed shut. After a moment, she mastered the emotions. "Returning home with PTSD and clinical depression, he shot himself. That background was withheld from his wife. Mrs. Carr didn't know the details of what her husband had experienced. She is like the mother mice in the experiment I was describing. Also, we know that she discovered she was pregnant with Boyd after Major Carr's funeral. Because those details lined up with the mice experiment, I found it interesting that in this case, Boyd Carr is accused of going out into the water to dump the body."

Spencer shook his head. "I'm going to need more here."

"Looking back at Mrs. Carr's social media, she recounted in her early posts that from when he was born, Boyd screamed his way through tub time. He was better about showers, which he started as soon as he could sit because putting the child in water, no matter the temperature, was so traumatic. She couldn't take him to the pool because the idea of drowning terrified Boyd."

"Mrs. Carr is deceased, is she not?" Spencer asked.

"She died when Boyd was eighteen. That's when he joined the military. Airforce. Little to no water."

"And you're saying Boyd couldn't have put the body in the lake because he has a lifelong water phobia?" Spencer asked.

"I don't think Boyd could physically handle taking a body anywhere near the lake. But you could test my theory."

Spencer canted his head. "How's that?"

"Get his vitals sitting in a room without telling him your plan. Then put him on a floaty, float him out into a pool, get his vitals again, and draw some blood for adrenaline and cortisol. See if he's panicking. The person who witnessed a man putting something on the front of his kayak said that individual seemed calm—just a guy going out for a paddle." She licked her lips. "Anyway, that's my theory. I think our client needs to keep looking."

"Back it up a minute, Lynx. That experiment would mean that trauma is passed through DNA, right?" the colonel asked. "Fear would be nature over nurture?"

"It seems that it can be either or both. While we can learn to be terrified through nurture, it's also possible that I not only carry my own trauma in my body but my father's too." Her gaze caught and held on Striker's. "It's something to consider when thinking about having children." She turned back to the colonel.

"Lynx, I'm going to follow your advice. I'll test your hypothesis myself. Very interesting. Very interesting, indeed." Spencer checked the time on his cell phone, caught the colonel's eye, and both stood to leave.

Striker was watching Lynx that whole time. Typically, when she found some crazy way of solving a crime, her body language, and the look in her eyes, bubbled with excitement at figuring out the puzzle. Usually, when Striker sat through one of her explanations, he had a great time watching jaws drop.

But today, that explanation obviously made her feel uncomfortable.

Then it hit him that Lexi had remembered this experiment in the last few days, days during which she'd been constantly humming "*Three Blind Mice.*"

14

Striker

AS SPENCER AND COLONEL GRANT WALKED OUT, LEANNE caught the door and moved to the center of the room, waiting until the general acknowledged her. "Sir, your wife is on line one. She says she needs a yes or no."

"Sit tight," the general told Lexi as he strode to the credenza at the far side of the room to pick up the landline receiver.

Lexi leaned in. "Striker, who are those people that Saadiq was referencing, Double Zero?"

It was the question he knew she'd ask. He could paint with broad brush strokes; he didn't need to go into graphic detail. "I know very little. You might have heard talk in the halls lately about a group called Zero-One Unit?

She nodded.

"They're a clandestine counterterrorism force that the United States trained."

A frown tugged at the corners of her mouth. "Who trained them?"

"The CIA. They were looking amongst anti-Taliban and anti-al-Qaeda militias for people with the mindset and physical skills to do the job."

"So, Afghanistan?" she asked.

"Yes."

She dropped her voice. "They were special forces?"

"Black ops. Covert missions. Most of the Zero-One Unit operators didn't even tell their families what they were up to."

Her brows drew together. "What did the CIA want them to do covertly?"

"They were spears."

She braced. "Did you meet them in your work?"

"We were asked to help them with some planning. We showed them some techniques to make their missions a little safer. They did some important things for our country. Things we're incredibly grateful for."

"Like?"

"They were there when the Afghan government was collapsing. They risked their lives—and many died—getting NATO personnel and civilians out of their houses, through the hordes of desperate people in Kabul, to the airport. They're the reason so many Americans made it home."

Lexi shook her head. "That's not the whole story, CIA black-ops asset forces? Why is their name floating around Iniquus halls?"

"More than a dozen cases allege that the unit killed civilians, captured people, and tortured them. War crimes. It's started popping up in the news as these instances come to light. In that our operational forces are made up of people who had incidental contact, some are being called in to testify about what they know."

"You?"

"Not yet. And I have nothing to say of consequence. We met them at the behest of the government, and we did scenarios on paper."

"And that group was in Afghanistan. Can you make the connection to Double Zero? Are they the same but for Iraq? Did the CIA get Saadiq to commit some kind of atrocity?"

"Very little is known about Numbers other than that they are American agents who work black ops for Langley and the White House. Like the SEAL teams, Numbers have different geographical regions. I know that Double Zero is the group that developed assets, including Zero-One. And I know that the reach of Double Zero extends throughout the Middle East and parts of Africa, and that includes black sites. Their operating in Iraq is assumed."

"Oh." Lexi exhaled.

"That kind of clandestine track never interested Saadiq. I can't see him working as a Double Zero asset."

"Can't you?" Lynx uncrossed her legs and recrossed them in the other direction. Her feet now pointed toward the door. If she saw that move on a video, she'd tell him that meant that she was uncomfortable and wanted to leave the room. "It seems that for lack of family visas, Saadiq was left behind to fend for himself as best he could. I mean, it's been a huge source of concern for the American men and women who depended on interpreters in theater. Promises made. Bureaucracy. Red tape." She reached out and put her hand on Striker's. "When Saadiq gave you his family's documents and asked you to hold them outside of the country, surely, that was a red flag for you."

Striker scowled.

She edged forward in her seat. "Do you think Double Zero wanted to recruit Saadiq away from his work for the U.S. military and the State Department?"

"I think that after ten years of not having the right visas to get out and the increased efforts by the terrorists lately, the time to make a move was ripe. Double Zero had a role that needed to be filled and the right carrot to dangle. That's what it looks like anyway with my limited vantage point."

"And this was in the last month?" Lynx asked.

"Five weeks ago. And no, he didn't say anything to me that was classified. We passed each other in the street, and I was surprised to see that he was still in Iraq. We shook hands, and he invited me to dinner, which I accepted. At dinner, he put his bag down next to my chair. We talked about people we had in common back in the day. As we were leaving, I noticed he didn't reach for his bag. When we hugged good-bye, he quietly asked me if I would take his official documents to Iniquus for safekeeping, and I agreed. Looking through the papers back in my hotel, that's when I got the full picture of his family life."

"He didn't talk about them at dinner?" She sounded mystified. "Didn't show you pictures?"

"No. I thought he was still single. But then, I also thought he was in America."

Her blue eyes turned stormy. "No mention of Double Zero?"

"No. But in that quick exchange, I asked where his family was. Saadiq had just said goodbye to his family. He'd sent them somewhere to the west to keep them from becoming pawns."

"We need to make sure that when you pull Saadiq out, that Color Code figures out how to get his family out, too. Seems like a no-brainer, but this is Color Code, and I don't trust them."

15

Striker

W<small>ASHINGTON</small>, D.C.
Thursday

B<small>EFORE</small> S<small>TRIKER</small> <small>COULD RESPOND, HE LOOKED OVER HIS</small> shoulder as General Elliot set the phone down. The general dragged a chair across the room so they were sitting all together.

Focusing on Lexi, the general said, "I understand that you have a situation that needs my attention."

Lexi adjusted her hips in her seat as she shifted to the new topic. "Yes, sir. I got a call from someone I know who works overseas. They were passing a message to me, and I'm not sure what to do with this information. It's both personal in nature and has to do with United States security."

"I'm listening." The general settled back in his chair, lacing his fingers and placing his elbows on the armrests.

"The caller said a source had provided them with logistics

information about my husband, Angel. If the information is correct, I know where Angel will be this week."

The general tipped his chin. "Where's this?"

"At a resort on the Jordanian side of the Dead Sea." Lexi licked her lips. "It's concerning to me that someone—who is supposed to be dead so he can operate in black ops—now has so many people who are aware of him. That my source knows about him is *extremely* concerning."

The general gave a considered nod. "This source is trustworthy?"

"See, here's the part I don't know. I got a call from someone I trusted, but they got the information from another person. That identity was not divulged. But I asked if the caller trusted the information, and they did. I guess in some spy novel, someone could have figured out who Angel was and wanted to lure me to Jordan to hold me against my will. But that's fairly absurd. And the person who called me said this source was paying back a debt. They seemed to know what the debt was. Sorry for all the pronouns. It's confusing to talk about two people that way. But, well, Person A called me. Person B had information. I trust A. A trusts B."

The general chuckled.

"I've been going through my mental files, and I can't fathom whom we would have in common, let alone someone who owed me a debt. But there it is."

"And the point of you having this information is to give you the opportunity to go and get the divorce papers signed?" Striker asked.

Lexi's shoulders drooped as she looked Striker in the eyes. "Which, in the scope of things, is ridiculous. Sitting here and telling you this sounds so petty."

"In fact," the general pulled her attention around, "your still being married to Angel while the world thinks he's dead is not a small thing. It has ramifications for the government as well as for Iniquus. And if we drill down, it has ramifications for the American people and the rule of law. Let's talk three of those things through—the personal, the impact on Iniquus, and the law." He drummed his fingers on the table. "And I guess to the impact on broader American security. Let's start with your personal concerns."

"Well…" She sent Striker a flat-lipped smile before focusing back on General Elliot. "There's the fact that I can't marry Striker when I have seen my husband alive. Even being in a relationship with Striker, engaged to him, feels like a breach of my marriage vows. And my dad always said you are only as good as your word. If I'm untrustworthy, that has ramifications in my relationship with myself and those I care about. If I'm willing to wiggle in this area because it suits me, why wouldn't I do it in others?"

The general nodded his approval.

She gestured toward Striker. "We're both caught in this situation. When we discovered Angel was alive, we had to postpone our wedding. Friends and family don't understand what's going on and keep asking for updates. I hurt myself and Striker if I continue with this charade. The only out I can see is to go with papers in hand and ask Angel to sign them or just keep getting up every day, living this lie. I know Angel is off doing his covert stuff, so I'm blaming the CIA for not following through. And I'm afraid it's impacting or will impact my work on CIA contracts."

"Let's put that last bit off to the side for a moment," the general said. "I hear you say that the only strategic way out of this mess is to get that signature from Angel through the CIA. What other avenues do you have?"

"Strategically?" she asked. "You're right. I only see this

coming to a soft landing if the CIA would handle it like they said they would."

"*Did* they say they would?" the general asked. "Or did you hear what you wanted to hear?"

Lexi stilled, facing toward the window as she softened her focus, thinking. "No. They didn't say that. John Grey said, 'We'll do everything in our power to take care of this as quickly as possible.' I assumed that the CIA would be all-powerful in fixing this. I guess they are not, for some reason, that I'm not landing on."

"They can't force Angel to sign," Striker said.

"He doesn't want to be married to me." Her shoulders came up to her ears. "I don't know how to interpret that scene with Grey other than that he had the power to make things right."

The general scowled. "You were physically in the room with Color Code when this was said?"

"It wasn't a group of Color Code folks, just the one, Grey. By the way, I was informed that he would be at the hotel with Angel."

"So maybe they want you there?" Striker suggested.

"I would assume someone from their working group or from Langley would reach out to me. This is too wild a path for that to be true."

"Still," the general said, "this isn't the only way for you to get your divorce. It's the way you *want* to get the divorce. And you're angry because it's not going the way you'd like it to."

Lexi sat perfectly still.

"You could file with the courts yourself and declare yourself abandoned. You could go to the media; they'd eat this story up. Surely, whoever was stalling would find a way to push the pedal down."

"Yeah, I'm not doing that with an organization that has black sites run by people called Double Zero." Her head twitched from side to side. "No, sir, but thank you."

"My point is that there are options, but you don't like them."

"True. But not selfishly," Lexi insisted. "I mean, if my actions endangered anyone's life, it's going to be a no-go from my end. I'm not at risk here. I'm inconvenienced."

"There are more things to be weighed. I have concerns about legal liability—both yours and for Iniquus," the general said. "I take your point about protecting lives, but there's a whole lot of lawbreaking going on." He tapped his index finger on the table beside him. "I'll give you one example. They insist that you continue receiving Angel's death benefits though he's not dead, and you know it. That's fraud. There is, in fact, legal peril that they have knowingly put you in beyond just the constraints of your private life. And while it might be expedient, it is, in fact, still illegal. What kind of country are we living in if *easy* negates law?"

"I've thought about that, sir. I also think about if that legal liability might somehow touch on my team or even Iniquus since there is a chain of people who understand that I am fraudulently accepting that money. Though, that money goes to Angel's Abuela Rosa. Well, shoot." Lexi ran her hands up and down her thighs as she adjusted to that thought. "I told Abuela Rosa about Angel because the grief was killing her. I probably put her in legal jeopardy as well." She glanced at Striker and then back at the general. "Sir, if I could draw a straight line between them," she stopped to put "them" in quotation marks, "not allowing a sealed divorce because it meant survival of a group of people, I might be willing to go to jail and serve time to protect them. But I can't fathom why my divorce wouldn't be allowed. It makes me a liar. It makes me unethical. It makes me a criminal. And the circle radiates out from me, affecting others."

The general sat quietly, nodding as he processed Lexi's thoughts. "Let's talk about how your relationship with the CIA could impact your job at Iniquus. You said that's one of your concerns?"

"Yes, sir. In my mind, the CIA is the thing standing between me and my being free of Angel. As you've pointed out, that may not be true. Someone above them might have nixed the divorce. But Grey said to me what he said. At least two others know, Black and White." She flung a hand toward Striker. "We were at Langley when Black and White literally ran from me. Striker ended up full body slamming me into a wall so the security guard they sicced on me didn't shoot me in the head." She leaned toward the general. "Here's the thing, at work, I try very hard to separate out how I feel about the CIA and how I do my job when we are working a Langley contract. I want American intelligence agencies to be success- ful. And I'm going to admit that I feel resentful when the agents question my loyalty and ethics. That distrust is prob- lematic to me doing my job."

"This is when you go to Langley and solve puzzles for them?" the general asked. "Striker's reported that you are poorly treated in those meetings. Disdain for your age," he opened his hand, "among other things."

"I was referring to the last CIA-Strike Force mission when we were working in the Seychelles. Johnna White of Color Code signed that contract with us. I believe there were a lot of emotions-based calculations that were going on in her mind. I felt like she was safeguarding some information and that she braced for me to manipulate the situation to make her, or the CIA, look bad."

The general squinted his eyes. "I can't imagine that being true of you."

"I did nothing unethical, sir. But I did see a hundred opportunities to get the job done at their expense. I'm a human being. As my resentment festers, it might very well impact my ability to do the kind of job for the CIA that lives up to the Iniquus ethic. I feel I should say that to you out loud."

"If the divorce was complete?" General Elliot asked.

"Then we'd be back to even keel."

"I see." The general tapped his finger on the table. "Jordan. He'll be there when?"

"Strike Force will attend the wedding the day before, sir."

"It's difficult for an unmarried female to travel to the Arabian Peninsula. I could divert Margot from Panther Force before they're wheels up. Their team is about to go to Madagascar to relieve Tidal Force. Or I could send Didit from Cerberus Alpha. She has Arabic language skills."

"My Arabic vocabulary will get me through most logistical things and simple conversations. In the cities, English is widely spoken. And I have Iniquus translator earbuds available and a translation app on my phone. I'd rather not take anyone."

"Why?" Striker leaned forward, his whole body humming in protective mode.

Lexi shrugged. "I may want to use some personal techniques that I'd rather keep private. And I don't want to widen the circle of people who know about Angel because his work is important. Lives are being saved. I believe that."

"Iniquus rarely sends an operator out without backup," the general said. "I won't authorize it here."

Lexi blinked at him. "But this is a personal trip, sir."

"You've just argued that it is not solely personal; it

impacts the Iniquus business model and could well impact United States security. We can't send you with another male non-family member. That would be even worse than your going alone." The general looked over to Striker. "It occurs to me that it could work out very well that Lynx and Margot would be right there in Jordan. Once Strike Force evacuates Saadiq, Color Code will need to bring his family out of Iraq. Iniquus can receive them as they cross the border from Iraq to Jordan." The general leaned forward and tapped Lexi's knee, then leaned back in his chair, the decision made. "Yep. In this case, Margot's the best partner. Ex-CIA, she'll know the procedures and protocols for such a transfer."

"That sounds like a green light," Lexi whispered. "You think my going to confront Angel is the best course of action."

"I'm ordering you to go." The general stood. "I'm ordering you to get that signature. And if, somehow, your efforts are ineffective, Iniquus will move forward rectifying the situation in a way that will remind our intelligence and military organizations that *no one* is above the law."

16

Striker

"Hey, Chica." Striker stuck his head around the door of the Puzzle Room. "Are you done for the day? Ready to head out?"

That smile. What he wouldn't do for that smile. When she looked at him, it was like she could see every good thought he'd ever had, every good deed he'd ever done, and amplified them. When she smiled at him, he felt loved and accepted by her, and that meant the world to him. "Yup. Done." She pushed her seat back and reached out to close down her computer.

When Beetle and Bella heard the word "home," they stood, shaking themselves, making their dog tags rattle. They bowed deeply, their back legs straining as they stretched, before trotting over to Striker for a scritch while Lexi put her coffee mug on the tray for the kitchen staff to collect.

"The CIA obviously didn't hire Iniquus for this Iraqi mission. Is it interesting at all that the Pentagon did? Do you know who signed the contracts over there?" she asked, walking around her desk and out to the hall.

"JASOC."

"Wait." She tugged the door shut, then checked that it locked behind her. "JASOC didn't pull from Delta Force or any of the other special operations forces?"

They started off side by side in the direction of the elevator where Beetle and Bella were already sitting politely, waiting.

"Not when they're unsure of the circumstances behind Saadiq's situation. If it were a terrorist group, even then, it would be tricky because Saadiq is an Iraqi citizen." Striker pressed the down button. "As a ransom and rescue effort, it's better to go to contract."

"You don't think it's because they're afraid of the fallout if they went chest to chest with the CIA's counterpart? That's how you described Double Zero's work in that region, right?"

"That's too far into the weeds," Striker said. "I'm an operator. By contract, I go where I'm told and do what needs to be done." Striker reached down and rubbed the soft fabric of her full skirt. "I like this." He bent to kiss her neck. "It does good things for me."

As he stood and looked at Lexi, that wanton little smile of hers tickled her lips and was getting a rise out of him. He still had to make it all the way out the door in front of his colleagues.

She knew. That's why she adjusted the look on her face and said, "To momentarily change the subject, I'm going to remind you that you left the SEALs because that was hard on you. That you needed a little more clarity on the morality and the impact of your work." She quirked a single brow. "You collaborate with Command on the missions you go on, and you have a clear understanding of the 'why' not just the 'how' of a mission. And you agree on the ethic and efficacy."

"That was only a slice of the pie." Striker draped an arm over her shoulder, pulling her closer to drop a kiss in her hair. "The other piece was that when Lynda found out she was pregnant, the dad disappeared from their lives. Cammy needed a supportive family to thrive. When Mercedes was alive, I could do that and be a SEAL. But after Mercedes died in the car accident, what with Dad and Mimi's physical and financial worries, that changed. I needed to be around more of the time to fill the father role in Cammy's life."

Lexi reached up and tangled their fingers together. "I love that about you," she whispered.

The door slid open, and they all climbed in. Striker pressed the button for the Atrium. It was a quick trip down in a crowded space.

The elevator dinged, and they moved out into the bustle of the changing work shifts. Iniquus was fully staffed twenty-four-seven.

When Striker pushed the door wide, they moved from the cool comfort of Headquarters out into a wall of heat and humidity, Beetle and Bella trotting alongside.

"I parked all the way at the end under the trees." Lexi pointed. As they moved in that direction, she signaled toward the tree. "Go potty."

Beetle and Bella streaked off.

"Under Iniquus," Striker said, "that was all working out exactly as I'd hoped until Lynda got snarled with the wrong crowd. The kidnapping. The destruction to her body from the beating. And then she and Cammy moved home to Miami."

Lexi stopped to face him. "She needed to," she said softly.

"I agree. Lynda needed all the friends and help she could get. And I'm often out on missions. Still..."

Lexi looked up to catch his gaze. "It was a terrible crime. I know how much you're missing Cammy. She's obviously on your mind." Lexi turned to wrap her arms around him. "I checked in with your dad, by the way. They were getting ready to eat tacos. Hey, maybe when we get back from the Middle East, we can get her and bring her up to stay at my Silver Lake house. The neighborhood kids all just fold her into their pack. Lots of help if we were to get called into the field. Well, you. I don't do fieldwork. But if I were to have a long day at the office in support of you all, our neighbors are there for us."

Striker was dreading the conversation he needed to have with Lexi about Cammy. Honesty was paramount in their relationship. Trust was built over time and through life-and-death struggles for survival. He wasn't going to mess that up, even if this would make her feel like shit.

Maybe things would work out in Jordan, and then...*This* was about Angel; Striker reminded himself. And Angel was as myopic as the other black operations agents Striker had met along the way. He was all about the mission and zero about domestic fallout.

"Hey, what's going on?" she asked. "Is everyone okay?"

It was impossible to keep something from Lexi. But Striker wasn't quite ready to hash this out with her. "Let's talk about it when we get home." He sent out a whistle. "Bella, no! Leave that squirrel be."

"Come on, girls," Lexi called. "We're going home. Find the car." She looked over her shoulder at him. "Do you mind driving? I'm feeling distracted, and I'd like to close my eyes."

Striker reached for the driver's side handle, pressing the button to unlock the doors. He watched her as she waited for the hatch to open, then loaded the dogs into the back. She slammed the door shut and stood in the same posture as she'd had in the parking lot earlier when the whole team looked at her and realized something bad was brewing.

And now, with three challenges unfolding at once— Saadiq in Iraq, Angel in Jordan, and Cammy in Miami— Striker couldn't tell which threat was the most dangerous.

When Lexi was settled in beside him, Striker pushed the button to start the engine and asked, "Talk or don't talk?"

"Talk, please." She leaned back and shut her eyes while he adjusted his seat to accommodate his six-foot-three frame.

Striker hoped to get her on the subject of "*Three Blind Mice*" to see if there was anything new to share. "That was interesting what you said about generational family trauma, the mice."

"I felt like I was nattering when I was talking about that espionage-murder case they handed me. I don't communicate like most of Iniquus do. And in the end, I don't have an answer for them. I just think they have the wrong guy, and I explained from the things I've got rumbling around in my brain."

Striker reached over and squeezed her hand. "I love you. And I love what comes out of that amazing brain of yours. Nattering is never something I think when I listen to you."

"But you don't do that, Mr. Stoic."

He put the car in reverse and backed out of their spot. "As Marcus Aurelius wrote, 'Don't overdress your thoughts with fine language.' But you and I have very different job titles."

"Yeah, well, I'm not letting you get away with that. The next line in that quote is, 'Don't be a person of too many words or too many deeds.' You are a cornucopia of honorable deeds. As was good old Marcus. *Ergo,* if you're a plethora of good deeds, you should also be allowed the use of more good words."

Before shifting into drive, he adjusted the mirrors. Lexi (a mere five-foot-six) and he did not physically see eye-to-eye. "If I spent my time with good words, I'd have less time for good deeds. On the other hand, you require good words to find your way to good deeds. As I said, our jobs are not the same."

"Opposites. You know you have many of my father's attributes. Including his stoic philosophy."

"A huge compliment." Striker drove to the front of the Iniquus campus, rolling through the security gate with a wave at the guard, then waited at the top of the drive for a break in traffic. He turned to her with a grin then edged onto the road. "What's running through your mind now?"

"While General Elliot commanded that I get the situation with Angel over with—and I'm fine going to Jordan to try because...well, for oh so many reasons. I wanted your take on it."

"My take is that I love you, and I only want what's best for you. And ultimately, you're the only one who knows what that means."

"Impossible to know, right?"

"Is that a philosophical question?" Striker asked as they inched forward with a long line of cars. "If you're asking if we ever know for sure how our decisions will impact us? Absolutely not. That's why ethics is so important. You work for a place of clarity and consideration. Sometimes you depend on your gut. And the kicker is that you will never ever know what would happen had a different decision been made."

"Exactly. When I map out my life, I think this was bad, but then something unexpected comes of it. I mean, we met when I was undercover as a teenage boy named Alex. It took an attack—a very particular and unique attack—to bring us back together without my disguise. "

"Oh, Chica." He glanced her way. "I don't believe that for a second. We were destined. And one way or another, my soul would have found you." She wrinkled her nose at him, making him laugh. "Too sentimental?" he asked.

"Gooey, you mean?" She leaned over to kiss his cheek and let him know she was teasing.

"Listen, though, would I choose that attack?" Striker asked. "Hell no. Would I choose for you to arrive at my side for me to love openly as Lexi? Absolutely. Could I have had the one without the other? We will never know."

She twisted her head to look at the rearview mirror, the habit of spy craft. "Despite your optimism about your soul's homing capabilities, I can jump on that wheel and run on it ad nauseum like a rodent."

"Back to rodent imagery," Striker pointed out.

"Yeah, so let's talk about the CIA."

He flashed her a glance. "You put the two together in your head?"

"They can be rats. But that wasn't where my head went. An article I read just popped into my mind. The CIA is to the R&D spy game as DARPA is to the R&D military security game. So not rats but cats. Did you know that there was a weird CIA plan called "Operation Acoustic Kitty?" She grinned.

"Acoustic kitty? I'll bite. What the heck does that even mean?"

"Someone at the CIA thought: Wouldn't it be amazing if we could train a cat to go and sit next to our mark and transmit their conversation to our waiting officers." She skated a hand out. "Granted, this was a long time ago, even before my father's time with the agency. Tech is what it is today, so trying to fathom the need for this seems absurd. But back in the day, CIA officers tried to be out-of-the-box thinkers for ways to spy on conversations."

"This doesn't bode well for Mr. Whiskers."

"Sadly, no." She frowned. "The scientists tried to turn the cat into a feline-android mix."

"Like a certain billionaire wants to do by implanting chips in brains?" Striker eased out of the congestion as they reached the highway on-ramp.

"Basically, yes-ish. But for this, they implanted a microphone into its ear and attached the radio transmitter to its skull. Then they developed an antenna to weave into the fur."

"I get that part—the how. What I don't get is the training of the cat."

"Yeah, that didn't go so well."

"Why? What happened?" Striker didn't press down on the gas pedal; he could see the highway was a parking lot of stopped cars up ahead. "Someone was petting the kitty and could feel the transmitter on the skull?"

"Worse." She looked down at her lap and brushed her hands over her skirt. Lexi called this a "self-soothing gesture." "Do you really want to know?" she asked, then tipped her head to see his response.

"My guess would be some medical event?" Striker speculated. "Did they shock Fluffy?"

"They deployed the cat in a park, hoping it would go get scritches from a Russian diplomat having a very private-looking tete-a-tete with a scientist. But instead of going to the bench, the kitty saw a family of mice and chased them out into the street." Lexi's body froze as she looked out the front window with a thousand-mile stare. "And that was the end of that experiment," she said, her words painted with defeat. "You'd think that before they wired up Mittens, they'd test the theory of training cats. But the CIA seems to like to jump without weighing ramifications."

Chasing mice, again.

"Learn something new every day. About cats and the CIA, that is. The CIA jumping is an observation. And I get it. They can get blinkered. Hero-complex that they alone can save the world. Just not with kitties."

"Yeah. They moved on from cats to cyborg beetles. Did you know that DARPA could move beetles via neural stimulation with a remote control?" she asked.

"To what end?"

"The most I know is that they could get the bug to start, stop, and even make it turn. But living creatures die. I guess that's one reason the rogue agents went after Zoe and her robotic WASPs."

"Have you heard from her lately?" Striker asked.

"She and Gage are heading over to Hawaii to see her folks, and a cousin is getting married. Low key, family in the backyard kind of thing. I think, otherwise, she'd come up with an excuse not to go."

Striker reached for Lexi's hand and brought the back up to his lips to kiss. "Our wedding is coming soon enough."

"Yeah, I hope so." She was obviously no more convinced that her mission to Jordan was going to end up with signed divorce papers than he was. And Striker worried about the wasps' nest that would be kicked if Lexi failed and General Elliot and their legal team steamrolled ahead.

Striker let go of Lexi's hand as he flicked on his direction signal and slid between cars to the lane that had a little speed. Once they were moving forward, he said, "When you start in on some story from left field like 'Operation Acoustic Kitty,' I've found that tracing your thought process back to its origin is a good tactic. So, cats are natural predators of rats, and before that, rodents on a wheel when you're not sure about right actions. The simple answer is that you're trying to figure out what to do about Angel being in Jordan. But then, you've got that woo-woo channel. And you've been dreaming about rodents, tunnels, and *Three Blind Mice*. I'm going to run through the list again. Are you experiencing any heebie-jeebies? Knowings? Anything pinging on your psychic network?"

"Nada." She lifted her hand and waggled it on the side of her head. "Well, not on my psychic network, but from the point where I saw you pull up over at Cerberus, *your* body language is off. *You're* keeping something from me. What's going on?"

17

Striker

Washington, D.C.
    Thursday

STRIKER FLICKED ON HIS DIRECTIONAL AND HEADED THEM OFF the highway onto the ramp that was just a couple blocks from Lexi's house. He wasn't sure how to approach the subject.

"Okay, let's start with a different question," she said. "How'd it go with Hoover?"

"He was a miracle dog. Sonny was in Heaven. I've never seen a kid so happy."

"Aw, yay!" She clasped her hands to her heart.

"Thank you for your help. A child in danger is a terrible thing."

She leaned forward so she could see his face. "Funny sound to that sentence. Are you thinking of Cammy?" She sat back and readjusted her seat belt.

"Can't hide anything from you—not that I'm trying. It's

just I was waiting for us to be in the same place at the same time when I brought this up." He kept his speed on the low end. The neighborhood kids liked to play outside after dinner in the summers. Kids chasing balls into the streets were expected. "Okay, well, now is as good a time to tell you as any other. While I was in New York, I got a call from Mimi."

She swiveled in her seat to face him. "Is everything okay with your family?"

"No, not really. The call was about Lynda, but ultimately about Cammy."

"Why? What's going on with your sister?"

"After Lynda survived being beaten nearly to death, all of the things that she went through psychologically, physically, all of the surgeries and pain, all the years of painkillers—"

"She's addicted?" Lynx whispered.

"Yeah. Lynda's spiraling downward."

"Is this something she's accepted? Is she interested in rehab?"

He shot her a quick look, then pulled alongside the car in front of their house and threw the gear into reverse so he could go back in and parallel park. "She won't go until she thinks Cammy is safe."

"Wait," Lynx said. "Lynda thinks that Cammy is safe around an addict? Go back. How did Mimi figure it out?"

Striker nudged the car up next to the curb, then put it in park. "Dad's back surgery." He unclasped his safety belt and turned her way, wanting to keep this conversation in the car and not in their home. She had that pretty pink skirt on, and he wanted to enjoy his evening with her. He didn't want to bring the energy from this conversation into the house. "Mimi discovered that Lynda was swapping out his pain pills for over-the-counter meds."

Lexi was wide-eyed. "Oh, wow."

"Mimi's beside herself. She's livid for all the pain Lynda caused Dad—you know, not just physical pain but emotionally. To think that Lynda would do that to her father after all they'd done for her. There are a lot of bad feelings, especially from Mimi, because, in the end, it's her biological daughter. Dad stood with Mimi over all these years, caretaking Lynda through her medical battles."

"Yeah." Lexi exhaled.

"Mimi says she's exhausted taking care of Dad and can't do it all. She doesn't have the capacity to mother Cammy too. And Lynda's not doing it."

Lynx reached out and laid her hand on his knee. "Of course, Mimi can't do it all." Her voice was painted with concern. "Just have Cammy come here to live with us."

It was exactly what he'd anticipated Lexi would say.

Yeah, this was the part he didn't want to tell her.

When he took too long to answer, Lexi's brow furrowed. "Is the problem that Cammy might need to be here, and you're taking off for Iraq, and I might be in Jordan? We can work through that." She lifted a palm and gestured toward the neighborhood. "We have so many people who know Cammy and would make her feel stable and welcome. We could hire a nanny. There are lots of possibilities. And neither of us will be gone long."

"I wish it were that simple."

She pulled her chin back. "How is it complicated?"

Striker wrapped her hand in his, feeling the grace of her delicate fingers. She was so soft and gentle; all he wanted to do was protect her. "Lynda has been leaning on prayer to get her through these last few years."

"Of course." Lynx nodded.

Striker added slowly. "And she's embracing more traditional morals."

It took Lexi a split second to get where this was going. "And we're living in sin? She doesn't know Angel's still alive. She has no clue you're coveting thy neighbor's wife."

"Not just coveting, I'm an adulterer," he said softly, "but no, she doesn't know that. She knows we live together. And sex without marriage is sinful."

"The bitter catty part of me wants to point out that's exactly how precious Cammy came into being." Lynx picked at her skirt, a deep frown pulling at her cheeks. "We should be married." Her voice was barely audible. "There should be no barriers to Cammy's having a stable home." She looked up and caught his gaze. "You weren't going to tell me any of that because you didn't want me to weigh your family into my decision-making about going to Jordan to see Angel."

"Angel isn't a barrier. I can go to court and fight for Cammy if it comes down to it. Temporary custody until Lynda is clean."

"Which would set off lifelong anger in Lynda and cleave your family apart. You've already given up so much for them, leaving the SEALs just as you moved from Green Team to DEVGRU. Moving to Washington, D.C. to be in the same city."

"I never felt like there was much choice in the matter. Family first. No man left behind. Especially when that man was a tiny pink baby girl. I could pay my own expenses when I lived on a SEAL salary. I certainly couldn't financially support Lynda at the same time. Under the circumstance, my move to become an Iniquus commander was a no-brainer. Granted, Iniquus isn't the SEALs, but I still get to work with Jack and Blaze. I make enough money to do the things I want and need to do. I'm available when my sister does what my sisters have always done—run after danger. First, it caught up to Mercedes, and then it caught up to Lynda."

Lexi held up a hand. "Stopping you there. That's not a sister thing. You run after danger, too. Only I guess there is a line of demarcation, the danger that attracted them was the dopamine hit of stepping over legal lines or at least hanging with people who did. And your kind of danger was to run at the enemy. The yin and yang of family dynamics."

"When Lynda and Cammy were in D.C., I felt like I could better protect them. But once Lynda was broken in the attack, she needed her friends, and I was glad she moved to Florida—"

"Where are her friends now? Can any of them help with an intervention?"

"Mimi said Lynda's been burning bridges, stealing from her friends to pay for pain medication. Lynda's angry, needy, and everyone around her is worn down."

"Your parents, too." Lexi raised her brows for emphasis. "They both worked labor-heavy jobs that beat their bodies to hell."

"They don't have it in them to push through anymore."

"I get that," Lexi said. "I was the sole caregiver for Mom after Dad died. It was an enormous burden. I bore it with love. I was so glad to be able to be there with her. But she wasn't manipulating and stealing from me. I can see how that would twist a relationship into a pretzel that couldn't be untwisted again." Lexi sniffed and straightened her shoulders. "What's the bottom line here?"

"If Angel would sign the divorce papers, we could marry the way we planned to do last June. If we were married, Lynda wouldn't have that argument to keep Cammy away."

"You heard yourself, right?" Lexi asked. "She's an addict who doesn't want to go to rehab, and she's anchoring herself to Cammy. If we were married, I'd bet she'd come up with another excuse."

"If I went in front of a judge," Striker said, "they'd see me as a single male who has to travel at the drop of a hat."

"Health or prison? If something were to happen to Lynda, what then?"

"Social Services would probably ask Mimi and Dad to take Cammy, and Mimi told me, in no uncertain terms, she will refuse."

"The universal timing seems impeccable then, doesn't it?" Lexi asked. "Your getting a phone call about our needing to be married to protect Cammy is coming in right about the same time as my phone call giving me the address and date for Angel. What was that?" she asked. "What's going on in your head?"

"Nothing is black and white. Sometimes I wish it were. It would make everything that much easier. But also less interesting. Little to learn if everything's already packaged up for us."

"Says the man who likes everything in its precise box."

Striker leaned in to kiss her. "I think I've evolved past that. Right now, I focus on the thing that's in front of me."

She gave him that hungry look that made his body stir. "Which is?"

"You. I have you here with me until morning, and I plan to take advantage of every second you're willing." He leaned toward her to press his lips to hers, letting them linger. "Do you want to play, Chica?"

When they heard 'play,' Beetle and Bella barked happily from the back of the vehicle.

"Simmer down back there, ladies." Lexi lifted her chin to call back to them. "You're not invited. This is a private playdate."

18

Lexi

After dropping her keys onto the entry table, Lexi turned to shut the door.

Striker sidled up behind to wrap her in his arms. "Do you know what the Stoics say about pleasure?" he whispered against her neck, then laid a gentle kiss just behind her ear.

The way he said pleasure, his voice warm and raspy, conjured pictures of how good their bodies felt when tangled into one.

Striker was obviously in a mischievous mood, and Lexi knew from experience that this conversation was about to take them on a journey. "Stoics on the topic of pleasure?" She smiled as she paused with her hand on the deadbolt. "Well, in my mind, they're all cold marble busts, so I would say that doesn't immediately bring up *pleasurable* thoughts. But as I remember my lessons on the topic, a Stoic might say something like, 'Pleasure is *not* to be sought. Pleasure is a drug. When you experience pleasure, you just want more of it.' I hope you're not going to try to convince me that pleasure is bad." She leaned her head back to rest on his broad chest.

"I like pleasure." His voice was warm and sexy as he drew a finger down the side of her face. "I like to pleasure you."

She melted against him. The stress left her body as it warmed to his intention. "Mmmm, so do I. I really, really like it when you're pleasuring me." She grasped his arms to keep him from moving away. She liked being right there, just like that. "And I like pleasuring you in return. So what is this about the Stoics? Are you saying that my wanting you makes me a poor philosopher?"

Despite her hold on him, Striker grasped her hand and gave it a gentle tug as he led her to the sofa. "I think that it entirely depends." Entwining his fingers with hers, he sat down sideways so they were face to face. "Let's take sex," he said.

"Oh, yes, please." Lexi adored Striker's soft, moss-green eyes, flecked with gold. His eyes, the way he looked at her, taught Lexi to trust his love.

"Sex with you is mind-blowing," He pulled her hand to his mouth and kissed the pulse point on her inner wrist. "Amazing."

"Why, thank you." She batted flirtatious lashes at him. "Same."

"But true happiness comes from contentment."

She stilled. "Are you saying we're *not* going to have sex? Because that would be so disappointing."

And there, the softness left his eyes as they turned dark and lusty. Her body responded by sending a wave of desire from her imagination down through her organs to settle hot and needy between her legs.

"I'm saying, Chica, that you're about to head to the other side of the world to meet a goal that has been set out for you by the general. But I want you to clearly grasp," he laid his free hand on his heart, "that I am happy with our relationship no matter what happens with our legal status."

Lexi opened her mouth to speak, but Striker moved his hand from his heart to signal to wait. "I know you're not. And I know you're juggling ethics and emotions that are not part of my experience. From my own point of view, I'm telling you that I am *content*. When I am with you, I feel peace. Even when things are hinky—"

"Hinky." For some reason, that word tickled her, and she laughed.

He leaned forward to drop a kiss on her nose. "Hinky." He leaned back again. "When you were injured—all the times you were injured—when I was drugged by the crazy person, when we didn't get each other and were trying to work through the logical and the irrational parts of loving someone, even in the chaos and pain, I was content. I feel a certain peace in knowing that I found you and we belong together. And in my arms or not, I just want to be part of your world. That you found your way into my bed is one of my life's most valued miracles."

Her heart pounded in her chest. She needed to hear this. Striker knew her so well. "Yes. Trust and love."

"And when I find *pleasure* with you, which I most certainly do, it's not the hit of dopamine that gets me high and then drops me back to earth only to seek it out again like the addictive drug that the Stoics warned against. Pleasure with you is something I savor. It's like floating in warm water, rising on the crests of the wave, and gently lowering again to an equally wonderful place. I like both. Both make me content."

"Like otters." Lexi lifted off the cushion and moved between Striker's legs to rest her cheek on his chest, scrunching her fingers into his soft rusty-blond hair. "Did you know that otters hold hands when they sleep so the tide doesn't pull them apart?"

He chuckled. "I *otterly* love you, Chica." He curled over to drop a kiss on the nape of her neck, letting his fingers softly paint along her clavicle, making her feel delicate and very female. "We weather the storms, but even that feels positive somehow. Fighting for the same goals feels good. And I like how we play without any agenda other than to have fun."

She lifted her head and looked toward the kitchen when Beetle and Bella barked at the back door. "And we float," she said, turning to smile at Striker. He looked uber sexy, and yes, she absolutely was looking forward to a long night in his arms. "You set the girls off when you said 'play.'" She pushed off the couch to stand. "Hold that thought. I'm just going to let the pups out into the yard." She threw a kiss over her shoulder for him as she left the room, calling, "And I'm coming right back."

After shutting the door behind her dogs, Lexi moved past the dining room table to the living room, where the first notes of dance music swelled. The lamp had been dimmed.

Seduction it was.

Her whole body tingled in anticipation. "You're pulling the curtains closed? What have you got in mind, Striker?"

He didn't answer, just turned and wrapped his arm around her, moving them in a slow dance to the beat. After a moment, he reached for her ponytail and gently tugged the elastic free, letting her long blonde hair fall down her back. His hand glided down the length as he lowered his forehead to hers, and Lexi felt the stress of the day ebb. "You said something about playing?" she whispered.

"I did." He kissed her. "Are you up to a game?"

"I don't know. What are we talking about here? Tennis? Backgammon?" She cuddled herself in, cheek to chest. "I don't think I'm up to the tennis."

"Have you ever played strip poker?"

"I have not." She tipped her head back to kiss his jawline. "Have you?"

"I, uhm." He cleared his throat, "You're familiar with the concept, though?"

"That was weak sauce that feint you just did" She tucked back under his chin. "But yes, I am familiar with the concept."

"And you're familiar with political bingo?"

"When a politician says a catchphrase on your BINGO card during a debate that you drink?" She pulled her hand from his so she could warp her arms around his waist and hold him a little tighter. "That one? It's one of Washington, D.C.'s favorite sports."

He reached for Lexi's hand, lifting and spinning her until her ass pressed against him. Bending, he whispered in her ear, "That's the one I'm thinking about."

"So, what I'm picking up here is that you're not looking for a checkers partner."

"I am not." He spun her out and tugged her hand to spin her back into his arms, where he dipped her low. "I thought up a *new* game."

"A new one, huh? Okay, I'm listening."

"A dancing game." He lifted her back to her feet. When he released his hold to change the music to a rumba, her body felt coldly deprived of his touch.

When he stepped back toward her with a slow smile,

Striker slid his arm around her waist and held up his left hand.

Lexi moved into place, and Striker stepped off into the hip-swaying box step. "I don't know that I've ever heard of a dancing game. What has this to do with Washington drinking games? I'm not playing a drinking game with you. You're twice my size."

"I would never put you in that position, Chica."

Lexi dropped her voice to low and seductive. "What position would you put me in, Striker?"

He spun her out, then tugged her hand to have her spin back until her breasts pressed into his chest. "Oh, so many. But first, we have to play the game."

"The dancing word game?"

"Exactly, so I'll play a song, and we'll dance. And when they say 'beauty' or 'beautiful,' you have to take off a piece of clothing. And when they say 'love,' I have to."

"You specifically chose this song in advance?"

"Throughout my life, I have discovered that advanced preparation leads me to the outcomes that I desire."

"That's a lascivious gleam in your eyes," Lexi said.

"Mmm, There's more to this game. So, when they say 'kiss,' we kiss, and when they sing 'caress,' we caress, and we simply follow their instructions."

"A game of strip dancing and Simon Says?"

Striker winked. "The adult version."

"How did you come up with this?"

"Oh, I was in my hotel room in New York, feeling lonely, wishing you were there. And I entertained a few fantasies about having you in my arms, holding you close."

"Well, I think it's worth a try. Thank you for thinking of me." Her whole body hummed, knowing Striker's love for her was an action word.

To Striker's credit, he didn't run over to his phone to change it to his game song.

Today, had been a lot—Saadiq, Angel, and Cammy. She needed a bit to let that go and relax. She wanted to kick off the kitten heels pinching her toes, but then she wouldn't have that much left to take off for their dance game.

"What are you thinking about," Striker asked.

She exhaled happily. "How much I love you." She turned to kiss his chest. "Thank you for making a new game."

The song changed, and Lexi knew immediately by the look of anticipation in Striker's eyes that it was game on.

I SEE YOU THERE, A BEAUTY SO RARE, I CAN'T HELP BUT STARE.
My heart's racing.

LEXI CHUCKLED AND TOED OFF A SINGLE SHOE, LIFTING ONTO the toes of her bare foot, so she'd be even.

When I look in your eyes, your inner beauty shines.

"AGAIN?" SHE BENT TO TUG OFF THE OTHER SHOE, TOSSING IT toward the door.

Striker opened his arms to her. When Lexi moved in to snuggle against him, he closed his eyes to revel in their connection.

MY HEART DANCES AT EVERY CHANCE TO LOVE YOU.

"YOUR TURN," SHE SAID.

He took a step back and started to bend to unlace his boot.

"Uh-uh." Lexi slid her hands down to his hips and pulled him tightly to her, feeling how hard he was already. "Shirt first."

"New twist to the game?" He canted his head. "We get to choose for each other?"

She smiled. "Shirt, please."

He reached over his head and tugged off his work shirt, tossing it onto the back of the couch. Mmm, bare-chested Striker was an Adonis of a man.

BEAUTY, DRESSED IN WHITE LACE.

"YOUR TOP, PLEASE."

When Lexi lifted her hands over her head to let him do the honors, Striker shimmied the summer sweater from her skirt waist. Slowly, slowly the silken texture glided over her heated skin, awakening her nerves. He bent and kissed along the lacey edge of her pink bra, leaving her panting.

OUR LIPS MEET, AND OUR HEARTS RACE.

HE KISSED HER LIPS. AS SHE FOCUSED ON THE SWIRL OF sensation, Lexi lost the words in the song. She grasped his head between her hands to direct his kisses to her neck. "I can't hear past my pounding heart," she gasped. "I have no idea…" She pressed her lips into his, sliding her tongue between his lips for just a moment, her message that she wanted him to take the kiss deeper.

Lifting her in one arm, Striker moved to the table and reached for his phone. With a tap, he switched to one of their favorite lovemaking playlists.

"The game was good in theory," Striker said, setting Lexi back on her feet. "But I'm feeling rushed when all I want is to spend the whole night savoring you."

19

Lexi

Lynx opened the door to Reaper Hamilton, who lived on the other side of her duplex. Reaper worked with them at Iniquus as a Cerberus Tactical K9 trainer. At his side, his K9 Houston sat expectantly, tail thumping. "Good morning." She held up her mug. "Are you done with your run? Can I get you a cup of joe?"

"No, thanks. I'm heading out to the park now and wondered if you'd like me to take Beetle and Bella on the trail with me."

Beetle and Bella flew down the stairs, and both plopped their behinds under the coat rack that held their leads.

"I think that that would be a yes from the girls." She walked over to get their safety vests—that held their water bowls and poop bags—on. "Come on in."

"Ash and Hoover went with Strike Force over to Iraq at zero dark thirty this morning. He said you were heading overseas. What part of the world are you heading to?" Reaper asked as he stepped inside with Houston and closed the door against the muggy Washington heat.

"The Middle East, but not until tomorrow. Margot's my battle buddy."

"Battle buddy?" He folded his arms over his chest, leaning into the door. "You don't do field work."

"Battle buddy is hyperbole. Wingman might be better." She clicked both clasps on Bella's vest and reached for her lead. "But then that connotes picking up someone in a bar. So, I'll just say that Margot is going with me. Now, the positive thing for us versus the rest of the team," she laid Beetle's vest on her back, "is that they're in the back of a military cargo plane for twenty hours. Margot and I are in business class on a direct flight." Click. Click. Reach. "Half the time and a hundred times the luxury." With Beetle prepped, she picked up both leads and walked them over to Reaper. "While you're gone, I'm heading to the store. If you have a list, I can pick the things up while I'm there, save you all a trip."

"I went last night on the way home," Reaper pulled the door wide for the dogs and then followed them out onto the porch. "We're all good. I'll see you in about an hour and a half?" he asked over his shoulder. They loped off, warming their muscles for a good hard run.

LEXI'S PHONE RANG AS SHE HEADED TOWARD THE STRIP MALL to do her errands—Striker.

Pressing the button on her steering wheel to open the

Bluetooth line, she was safe to talk. Even here in her car, everything was encrypted end to end. "Hey, there."

"Are you driving?"

"I have a few errands. I need to go by the salon and get my hair dyed so I can blend better in Jordan, pick up some snacks for the trip, and get some things at the dry cleaner. What about you? How are we talking?"

"Layover. I wanted to have you all to myself on Thursday night, but today, I'm thinking strategically."

"You and your boxes," Lexi said as she cruised slowly through the neighborhood, her eye out for kiddos.

"Not so much my boxes as you were doing it again last night." His voice was his typical calm and steady. It didn't give her any clues about the topic at hand.

"You're going to have to be more specific." Lexi pulled to a stop at a red light.

"You were singing *Three Blind Mice* in your sleep."

"And that freaks you out?" She glanced up at her rearview; she was alone on the street.

"It's just that I wish I had some context. Do you think it has anything to do with *him*?"

So even on this secure line, Striker didn't want to mention her husband's name. Maybe he was afraid that someone in the vicinity would hear.

"I don't think so. The only thing I'm worried about when it comes to my mission is interfering with the work that he's doing."

"Yeah…I'm not worried about you blowing *his* cover. You won't be standing in the middle of an arena yelling about your situation. You'll be behind closed doors. Frankly, this mission should be as easy as pulling up a secured contract and having him digitally sign it if he doesn't want to sign the paper copy. Iniquus legal already set that up for you."

"I'm missing something. There's more to this from your end." She pressed the gas to cross the intersection. "Too much tension in your voice with that last bit. I'd really prefer not guessing."

"It's about Gator. I pay attention when the two of you start pulling up the same themes in your conversations. He was talking about groundhogs this morning, and then he flipped to how it's interesting, timing-wise, that we'll be across the border from each other. He thought it was good that we wouldn't be on opposite sides of the globe if you and Margot ran into any trouble with Angel. That you have us at your back."

"What about groundhogs?" Lexi asked.

"Something about their warrens. Chica, I wish the timing was different. Command would probably insist that the whole team go to ensure the contract was finalized and this effort gets done. Gator also brought up not just timing but players, the last time we worked with Ash and Hoover, Color Code's White was along for the ride and—"

"Interrupting. Do you remember that Colonel Grant said Color Code worked a specific elliptical? How did that fit together with the Seychelles?"

"That working group has been in Africa, too. Not knowing more than you do, I'd speculate that it has to do with *where* the intelligence was uncovered. I bet they run it down from point of origin to wherever it takes them. But I agree with Gator. We do keep running into the Color Code officers. And the general is correct. There is a thick layer of distrust between them and you." When Lexi didn't respond, Striker added, "Rightfully so on your part. But trust is a mutual thing. If I distrusted you, I might work in specific ways to protect myself, and those ways might serve my interests and not be mutually beneficial. Everyone in a life-or-death needs to trust everyone is playing on the same team. And that dynamic has been part of our interactions. It was getting out of hand on the Seychelles mission from their end, not yours. I felt it, too, that White thought we were going to stab her in the back."

"We didn't because we wouldn't. That's not the Iniquus ethos."

"But they don't trust that. It's the old saying, 'When you point your finger at someone, three fingers are pointing back at you.' They were projecting. It needs to stop. So, it's not just Angel that you need to pay attention to, not if Grey is going to be on hand."

Lexi slowed again, waiting for a car to maneuver into a parallel spot. "Nope, that's not it. There's more in your voice."

"It seems to me that particular dynamic with Color Code not trusting might come from a place of experience. They're protecting Saadiq's family while Saadiq rolled the dice with Numbers, Saadiq goes missing, and he's held for ransom. Where do the numbers fit into this? Are the two teams working for the same outcome?"

"Which would be?" Lexi asked, motoring on.

"Keeping America and her people safe. Yeah. I guess in the end, I'm just calling to see if you learned anything new in your sleep about those mice. And as I say that, they're starting the engines. Tell Deep if you have any insights," Striker yelled past the noise. "I love you! I can't wait to say that when you're in my arms."

And the line dropped.

I was singing Three Blind Mice again?

20

Lexi

WHEN LEXI TRAVELED, SHE ALWAYS WENT WITH PLENTY OF food. Even if she was traveling first class, shit happened. Food and water to get her through was a habit. Once, Lexi's Kitchen Grandmother, Nana Kate, sat on the tarmac for eleven hours in the early two-thousands. People didn't have their medications, T1 diabetics didn't have enough carbs, mothers hadn't toted on sufficient diapers, and the poor people with a fear of flying or claustrophobia who thought they could muscle through the flight were having meltdowns. Regulations changed, and it wasn't supposed to happen anymore, but why chance it?

Lexi tossed her grocery bags of snacks into the back seat, moving down her to-do list. Once home from the laundromat, she needed to finish packing, get Beetle and Bella to the Cerberus kennel, and head to the airport to meet Margot.

Lexi climbed in behind the wheel and tugged her belt into place.

Margot was an interesting woman in that Lexi knew just about zilch about her. She lived on the Iniquus campus in the women's housing area, which meant she didn't have a family. Long black hair, and liquid obsidian eyes, she had the classic French features of Catherine Deneuve. Command recruited Margot from the CIA as Iniquus's only female field operator. Though, Command said that they were pulling her from her team as they deployed to a training mission in Madagascar to go with Lexi to Jordan, Lexi wasn't aware of Margot ever going out on a field mission before.

"Super top secret, maybe," Lexi said to herself as she pulled out of her spot and rolled through the parking lot.

Up ahead, a middle-aged man and what looked like his teenage daughter strolled smack dab in the middle of the lot. Lexi glanced at her rearview mirror and then gave a little toot-toot to let them know that cars were piling up behind the pedestrians.

The girl looked over her shoulder, held up an apology wave, and scuttled off to the side.

The dad did not.

He turned until he could glare directly into her eyes. He spread his feet as if declaring that spot was his forevermore. His body seethed with acidic how-dare-you energy.

Hands. Hands. Lexi thought as she lifted her foot off the gas peddle and rolled up to the man's shins.

Things in the news had been nuts lately. People were shot and killed for no reason—a delivery person who turned into the wrong drive, a child playing on the wrong lawn. People with no moral compass got pissed—the man who was out on a date when he realized he'd been scammed, went outside, shot a man dead, and returned to his date. Day after day, on the news, people didn't discuss. People simply shot. And the more people that pulled the trigger against the innocent and got away with harm or death, the more people decided that was an acceptable way to conduct themselves in public.

This guy felt like someone just itching for an opportunity to draw a gun and shoot.

And Lexi had given him more cause—though a toot of the horn shouldn't have been a cause to begin with—by pulling up as if antagonizing him.

That wasn't what she was trying to do. She needed to be close enough to see what his hands were doing. If he reached for his belt and pulled a firearm, Lexi was going to stomp down on the gas pedal and run him over, hoping his finger wasn't on the trigger so an errant bullet might fly toward a different innocent person.

There he stood, seething with anger that she, *SHE!* would have the audacity to ask him to move out of her way.

He screamed the F-bomb at her.

Lexi was pissed. This kind of man ruled his life with threats and violence. Lexi was sure that his daughter was watching this. Even if it upped her own danger, Lexi decided she wasn't letting this man bully her. She was going to stand her ground and let the girl see it could be done. And yes, a part of her brain said it was cheating because she was in a car with bullet-resistant windows and run-flat tires. But she also didn't want to go hand-to-hand with a man for no reason in the middle of a grocery store parking lot. She F bombed him back.

There he stood, calling out his F-Bombs like a World War II fighter pilot dropping death on the Nazi troops.

And there she was, meeting him bomb for bomb, looking thoroughly bored by his antics, trying to, anyway.

A crowd gathered on the sidewalk as they tried to figure out what the man was screaming about. And finally, he turned away.

That man is evil, Lexi thought as she rolled to the other side of the strip mall. I have met evil, and he is it. And then Lexi felt conflicted. Maybe she modeled standing up to the father for the daughter, or perhaps he went home with that anger and taught the women in his life how powerful and in charge he was.

Lexi wanted to cry.

That sense of doom was a grey cloud over her head as she got her clothes, and then it followed above her all the way home.

She was glad that Reaper had her dogs. She'd just stay for a chat until she felt better. Lexi put the food and clothes in her living room and went next door to the Hamiltons'.

Reaper came to the door with Little Guy clinging to the leg of his pants. Little Guy grinned his four-toothed grin, holding out a book to Lynx. "Buh!"

"A book?" Lexi said, taking the book from his hand, then scooped him up. "I love stories! Shall we read it?"

Kate lay on the sofa with her feet up. The dogs were scattered in curls of fur across their rug. As Lexi walked in, they all thumped their tails, but they were too worn out from their run and too comfortable in their little beams of sunlight to lift their heads.

Lexi squatted with her back to the sofa, and Little Guy balanced in the nest of her crossed legs. She opened the book, and Little Guy leaned in. His tiny finger moved around the illustration as he tried to identify the different objects that he recognized with his one-and-a-half-year-old baby babble.

"You look stressed," Kate said as Reaper disappeared into the kitchen. "Is that about your upcoming trip?"

"Lexi, can I get you something?" Reaper called from the back.

"Glass of water if you don't mind." She bent to smell the baby shampoo in Little Guy's hair and dropped a kiss. "No, not the trip. I just had a weird experience up at the store and wanted to bring it to Reaper's attention."

She waited for him to come in, balancing a sippy cup and two glasses of ice water. He handed them around.

"Listening," Reaper said as he picked up Kate's feet and rested them in his lap after he sat.

While he massaged Kate's feet and legs, Lexi told them about the incident in the parking lot.

"You?" Reaper asked. "Throwing F-bombs?

Kate frowned. "I get why that seemed frightening."

"Look, I had a gun on me when my stalker was on my trail. I have shot to kill. I understand the importance of the tool in my life. But, like all Iniquus employees, I had a doctor who signed off on my psych eval every year, and I have on-going physical and ethical training. I'm not shooting at someone because I'm in a bad mood. I didn't know the guy from Adam. Was he someone from a state with stand-your-ground laws? Did he and his buddies get online and talk about how they'd take down anything that looked like it was affecting their day? Best case scenario was he was a bully—by the way he puffed himself up with entitlement. There is little that scares me as much as a fake alpha male who thinks having a gun is a stamp on his man card. I live amongst people that have honed skills and a trained mindset. You, for example, Reaper. You aren't out posturing. Quite the oppo-site. The wannabes who have talked themselves up in the bathroom mirror then surrounded themselves with fearful, supplicating people to bolster their fiction are dangerous because they're running on a rancid combination of fragile ego and emotion."

"Agreed." Reaper was in his operator stoic mode. Taking in information. Processing. Data, not sentiment.

"And I could have made some kind of placating gesture, I guess. But the guy's daughter had to have been watching."

"So, you stood up to the bully to show her it could be done," Kate said.

"Exactly."

"And how'd that work out?" Reaper asked.

"I'll never know, will I? I'm just afraid I riled him up and sent him on home to go after women who had been beaten down, figuratively and literally. He had that serial rapist kind of energy with all his knife-blade anger and entitlement posturing."

"Sounds like a psychopath." Reaper dropped his chin. "You weren't teaching him a lesson."

"No, clearly not. So, he finally got out of my way, and I had to go into the dry cleaners. On my way home, I started freaking out. He could have been a cop, someone with cop buddies. He could have looked up my license plate and now knows who I am and where I live. Could have stopped and put some kind of tracker on my car."

"That last one would mean that he came prepared, and he'd have to do it in front of the girl," Reaper reasoned.

"He could have one of those trackers on his key ring and just used that," Kate offered.

"And adhered it to her car? I don't think so." He turned toward Lexi. "I can drive your car to Iniquus tomorrow and have them check it out. When we signed our lease with you, it was to an LLC. The house isn't in your name."

"No. And now that you mention it, Striker had me register

my car and get a new driver's license with his barracks address. If anyone came to look me up, they'd get stopped at the gate and their license plate registered."

"It might have been fun, though, if you had Beetle and Bella with you, and you all jumped out of the car." Reaper chuckled. "Yeah, that would have been fun."

"Speaking of the doggos," Lynx said. "I was hoping I could leave Beetle and Bella here with you tomorrow, and you could take them to the kennel with you in the morning. That would allow me to call a taxi and head right to the airport."

"Oh, no," Kate said, her hand resting on her pregnant belly. "If you don't mind, I'd like to keep them here with me. Ryan takes Houston to work with him, and I'd appreciate the company."

Lynx thought that what she'd really appreciate was two tactically trained, hyper-protective doggos by her side. "I would so appreciate it, either way. Thank you." Lexi stood. "And thank you for listening. I need to go get packed." She handed off Little Guy to Reaper.

"Hey," Reaper said. "I know you worry like Kate does when the team is down range. I don't know if this is going to make you feel any better about Strike Force or not, but in Iraq, the number of violent gun deaths per capita is significantly lower than violent gun deaths here in the States."

Lexi had not, in fact, been thinking about Striker and violent gun deaths until Reaper said that. With the Iraqi laws and the team's role, Strike Force had opted for stun rifles. They only had bullets in their ankle pistols to protect themselves in a life-or-death.

"No, Reaper. No. That does not make me feel any better."

21

Striker

Saturday

The noise in the holding area of the cargo plane was too loud for conversation. The men wore headphones to protect their ears and allow them to get some sleep along the way.

Striker was stretched out on a hammock that swayed with the turbulence, thinking Lexi was probably getting on her own plane right about then.

Lexi was an enigma that he enjoyed with no plans to try and solve.

He called her his 'surprise party,' never sure what ideas would pop out of her beautiful mouth next.

It was rare that Lexi allowed anyone to see her vulnerabilities.

Why did she look so delicate right now?

There was that big and bad that he had sensed gathering strength since before New York—was there a threat raising its head?

Bad timing with the team spread out.

Sure, she was skilled. But she wasn't invincible. Nobody was.

And if the team were facing something, she'd be there for them.

Loyal. Completely flawlessly loyal. And he'd admit that trait was of major importance to him. He remembered vividly the day his mom packed her bags, yelled at his dad, and left without a backward glance. He had just turned four.

Every detail of that moment had seared into his brain. Branded him. The cold on his bare feet, the blanket he'd shoved into his mouth to keep himself from screaming. A few days later, his dad hired Mimi to take care of him. She and her daughters moved into their basement. And later up into the upstairs bedrooms. And eventually, there was a wedding.

Mimi was a natural mom, nurturing and fierce.

But it hadn't driven the demons away, the ones that said if he'd been better, if he'd been the greener grass rather than what she had seen off in the distance, then she would have stayed and loved him. So, he pushed himself hard to live up to his potential and shine.

And to his salvation, in that quest toward excellence, in eighth grade, he'd found the Stoics. Marcus Aurelias, Seneca, and Epictetus counseled him. Soothed him. Got his head on straight.

And still, when he thought of a forever love, Striker had to weigh the possibility of future children. He needed to make sure that his kids wouldn't go through abandonment like he did, barring parental illness and death.

Of the women he'd dated, he had always kept an

emotional distance. He enjoyed their beauty and company, and that was about it.

Until he walked into the hospital room and saw Lexi.

Every cell in his body said she was his to have and to hold. To love and cherish. The only thing that was not decided was the form of that conviction, and that was completely Lexi's choice. Friend or more, her decision.

And she had decided to love him. Though, yeah, things hadn't been smooth at first. She had things to work through. At the same time, he was unwinding from past mental habits that weren't easy to release, lowering his barriers and allowing her in close.

Four years later, they were in a good place. Except for Angel's existence that rubbed Lexi's morals and ethics raw.

Children. He felt like he'd taken on the father role for Cammy since her birth. He had no idea who the birth father was; Linda had never said.

When Lynx told the story about the mice being shocked as they smelled cherry blossom, she'd looked over at him and said, "It's something to consider when planning a family." They planned on kids. At some point, they should probably talk about the idea that even though he'd done his work to understand his mother and forgive her in absentia, the trauma of watching his mother walk away without a word or a glance surely shifted his DNA.

He wondered about Cammy's biological father. What experiences infused that man's DNA?

WHEN THE BIRD SET DOWN, THE CARGO DOOR OPENED WIDE to a butter-colored sky. It was still the chilly part of the day before the summer sun's heat broiled the brains.

The team hung back out of the bustle of military activity. They were guests via Pentagon contract. But they all knew, from years in the service and out, that people could get testy when their job was interrupted, especially by someone who wasn't in their chain of command.

"Gentlemen, including you, Hoover," Striker said as they huddled up to keep their focus and to hear with all the commotion going on around them, "we're walking through this like a diplomatic mission. As Command said, we will be respectful of cultural norms and laws. No matter where we are or what the task is before us, we will get our job done without causing a negative ripple effect for Uncle Sam. Whether we're pulling a child out from under the tires of a car accident," Striker bladed his hand toward Jack to recognize his professionalism, "or we're pulling our friend Saadiq out of the trap he stepped in, we show up and do the job. I'm going to go ahead to the TOC to pick up our team's visas, so we're all nice and legal in the country. Ash, I need you to hand me Hoover's paperwork."

Hoover was panting with his tongue hanging nearly to the floor. He knew he was on a mission and was anxious to get going.

Ash knelt over his bag to extract a manila envelope.

Striker took it and tucked it under his arm. "I'll meet you back here when I've got us squared away. I want our equipment unloaded and triple-checked. The only bullets we're carrying are in the guns in our ankle holsters. They're a last resort. We are using our mouths to get us out of any situation we find ourselves in. If things go sideways, we're using non-lethal. Bear spray. Stun guns and stun rifles. We put them down, zip them up, move away. We're not here to make friends. We're also not here to create enemies. Jack, you're in charge." He handed the next part over to the team's number two. "Also, go ahead and pull out our outfits for the wedding. We'll be changing before we leave. All of us except for Ash, who will hang out with the vehicles with Hoover in the air conditioning."

"Yes, sir."

"Let's keep to ourselves and out of everyone's hair. Jack, as soon as our equipment is off the plane. I want you and Blaze to go to the motor pool for our vehicles. We have two somethings. Make sure that whatever keys they hand you, the vehicles are in decent repair, suit our purpose, and have plenty of gas in the tank and the cans. If we're running the AC for Hoover today, we need to have what it takes to get us out of here. There's only the one town between the two family complexes. Logistics indicates their station sometimes runs dry."

"Copy," Jack said.

"Here we go, gentlemen, this is personal. This is our brother. But remember, emotions get in the way of training. We're here as professionals. Are we all squared away?"

Fists reached into the circle until each individual joined together as spokes on one wheel.

The men shouted as they lifted their fists into the air.

"Let's get this job done." Striker gave them a curt nod, then headed out the back of the plane.

22

Saadiq

IRAQ
    Saturday

THE RASP OF RUSTY HINGES POPPED SAADIQ'S EYES WIDE. HE jumped from his bed as the door to his room swung open.

The elderly man who had brought the food trays earlier in the day arrived with a new person. Moving in a stuporous, zombie-like way, the new man was led over to the table where Saadiq's keeper pulled out the chair, then pressed on the man's shoulders until he took a seat.

He was in rough shape. Matted rust-colored hair hung to his shoulders. His beard frizzed from his face to mid-chest. A patina of filth, ground into his flesh over time, masked what was surely the fair skin of European descent.

The keeper caught Saadiq's gaze. He pointed at the new man and the bathroom and gave him a nod of what Saadiq interpreted as encouragement. This old man had never said a single word in front of Saadiq, and Saadiq didn't know if that was because he *couldn't*, or *wouldn't*, or *shouldn't* speak. Saadiq would really like the answer to that question. It would give him some much-needed information.

Right now, all Saadiq knew was that he had been locked in here except for a brief time when he was taken to a dark room.

Saadiq sat at the table at a loss for how to interpret that call.

It could be that these people were being careful to protect Saadiq from being discovered as staying with them. Perhaps the family was afraid that Saadiq's presence brought terrorist eyes to their compound.

It could be that Saadiq was being held for ransom and treated well in the hopes that the payout would be high— unlike the state of this man sitting dazed in the chair.

Was this man in this state because he had had no one to call? No phone number sitting on the tip of his tongue?

This whole situation was incredibly disorienting.

Well, the new guy's presence might explain the two sets of meal dishes brought in earlier and the two sets of clean clothes. And here, Saadiq had surmised that his keepers wouldn't be able to get in to care for him for a longer period of time, so they were loading him up like a family filling the cat bowl with extra food before they left for the weekend.

With another nod toward Saadiq, the old man walked out to join those waiting in the hallway with rifles held casually in their hands.

The door shut; the lock tumbled into place.

Saadiq squatted and offered a smile. "Well, here's a project." When Saadiq performed surgery, when he opened a body up and reached his fingers into the bowel, all the interior smells rose and assailed his nose. It had been twenty years since Saadiq had scrubbed up to perform surgery, but the smell of this man brought it all back.

"Let's start by getting you comfortable," he said gently.

The man didn't seem to have a mind of his own. When Saadiq pinched his sleeve and drew him into the bathroom, he shuffled along without emotion—an automaton. Saadiq left him standing there, then returned to the bed chamber, where he retrieved the chair, the waste basket, the broom, and the dustpan that leaned into the corner.

There were religious laws for different devotees of Islam about the length of hair and beard, but the felted state of this man's hair necessitated cutting. There were no scissors, but there was a beard trimmer. Saadiq decided to remove what was necessary for hygiene and trim the man's beard, leaving some of it in place.

Surely, this was humane.

Squatting in front of the man in the cramped bathroom, he said, "I am Saadiq. Saadiq." He flipped back and forth between English and Arabic as he repeated the phrase. He put his hand on his chest, then opened his hand to the man, "What is your name?"

Nothing. Perhaps drugged.

Saadiq said, "I'll just check your eyes." After washing and drying his hands, he pressed the man's eyelids wide. They were vacant and unflinching. But the man didn't seem to be sedated.

Saadiq approached him the way he would a child going into surgery. Kids had their own pre-surgery anxieties. Saadiq would sit with them and show them his instruments, explaining what he would do. He had a certain voice to share the information, it wasn't happy, but it was offered in an adventurous tone.

Holding up the clippers, Saadiq said, "I am going to cut your hair to make you more comfortable."

Starting front and center, Saadiq drew the beard trimmer over the man's scalp, leaving about two inches behind. The weight of the hair and filth was surprising. He remembered watching springtime sheep, with their heavy winter coats making them itchy and uncomfortable, being shorn by the shepherds. The animals always seemed so relieved after their cut—fresher and happier.

The removal didn't arouse any emotion of liberation in the man.

As the rusty locks fell to the floor, gaunt shadows under the man's cheeks became more prominent.

Saadiq turned to get some water running into the tub while he trimmed the man's beard, leaving it about an inch in length. It was patchy and thin. That could be from his DNA. It could be from illness or malnutrition. Saadiq didn't know whether this man had a naturally ectomorph body type or if his skeletal look was the result of whatever was happening to this man.

Saadiq faced the man and said, "*Na'eeman*" by way of polite habit. It was said after someone had showered or had a haircut, it meant "blessed." Though clearly, this man was experiencing some kind of torment.

This new arrival was such a shell of a man that Saadiq felt compelled to give him a name to humanize him. Saadiq said with as much dignity as he could offer, "Look, if you aren't going to share your name, I'm going to call you—if it's all right with you—I'm going to call you 'Chris.' You seem like you might be a Chris." Saadiq gingerly slid his hands under the man's armpits and lifted until the man balanced his full weight on his feet. "I don't want to be rude. I feel like I have to call you something." He carefully took

Chris's clothes off. "Please correct me as soon as you're able."

He threw the clothing right into the trash and hoped that the old man would come soon to take it out of the room. The garments were putrid with old sebum, dead skin cells, and sweat.

Taking Chris's elbow, Saadiq drew him to the tub. Chris mechanically lifted his feet to step in, then sat with the water coming up to the middle of his thighs.

Saadiq inspected the man's head for scabies and head lice, and finding none, he pressed a thumb under Chris's chin so he'd tip his head back. Using the faded-orange plastic pitcher, Saadiq scooped up water and poured it over the man's head. Not a wince, not a blink—it frightened Saadiq. He worked to keep his hands firm and compassionate, to keep the tremble from his fingers. "You're all damp now. I'm going to shampoo you and use some of this conditioner. When I'm done washing you, you'll feel like a new man."

Saadiq rubbed and scrubbed until the water turned black. He let that drain out and filled the tub three more times, repeating his efforts. The dirt was like a tattoo; it had been deeply ground into his epidermis. It would take a couple of weeks of bathing to allow that skin to shed and for new skin to rise to the surface. Would he be here that long? Was this his new roommate, or did the old man just want Saadiq to get him cleaned up?

His surgical eye assessed Chris. No exercise in a very long time; his muscles were atrophied. No sun. Little food. His skin was dry and hung from a bony structure. No bruises or contusions. No burn marks. No scars that would make Saadiq think of torture. If he were back doing his hospital residency, Saadiq would order a psych eval and one of the linguists at the university could call to see if the problem was a language barrier. But Saadiq had only seen that work when someone was vocalizing.

Chris was this side of catatonic.

Perhaps it was clinical depression.

Saadiq had so many questions, questions of curiosity, and questions that would help orient Saadiq to his present situation. Questions like: Why are you in Iraq? How did you get here to this room? Where have you been? Why are they holding you? Are you still being held? Am I?

Now freshly cleaned and dressed, Saadiq moved Chris to the chair beside the table, where he spooned mint tea into Chris's mouth to see how he swallowed, checking if the man had good use of his lips and tongue, trying to determine how much of a choking hazard the meal tray would pose.

Was this man's presence some kind of interrogation technique, some kind of cautionary lesson?

Saadiq wondered, then stopped with his banter and questions.

Suddenly, Saadiq stopped seeing the man as a human.

And started to see him as a trap.

23

Striker

Saturday

FROM STRIKER'S EXPERIENCE IN IRAQ, WEDDINGS WERE A days-long event that united a man and a woman and the families. The bride would have already moved through a day of ceremonial henna. The couple would have already met to sign the marriage contract.

Today would be the festivities.

As they drove up the road toward Naseem's family compound, Gator blared his horn along with the other cars arriving.

The more noise, the more joy, and blessings for the new couple.

Gator drove across the open dirt, past where others were parking, and off into the distance, half the team in their armored truck, the other half in the armored truck behind them.

He parked at a respectable distance where they could set up a campsite for the night like many of the guest families.

Without warning that they'd be working in this part of the world and having just come off of personal protection duty in New York, where they had been clean-shaven, Striker and his men now had scruffy faces and tight military-style haircuts. Ash, Randy, and Jack all had dark hair and deeply tanned skin from training under the summer sun, but Blaze was a redhead. Gator only got blonder in the sunshine, and Striker was somewhere in between.

No one was going to mistake the team for locals. Their height, muscular bulk, and how they held themselves set them apart, as much as their coloring and hairstyles.

Logistics had supplied them with the proper attire for a rural wedding so they didn't offend or pull attention away from the other guests.

The team's clothing was basically identical, a uniform that tried to bridge traditional and modern wear. Their collarless white shirts hung loosely and modestly, hitting their legs at fingertip length. Over that, a coat, each a different shade of tan, reached the same length of the shirt, much like a formal African *dashiki*.

Under this, the loose-fitting linen pants matched the color of their coats. The band around the hips worked like their tactical gear with pockets holding basic everyday carry items, pen, pad, flashlight, and multitool. The pants were wide enough to comfortably conceal an ankle holster for a stun gun on one side and a tactical knife on the other, should they be required.

Though male guests would fire off rifles to make celebratory noises, bringing weapons of self-protection would be an insult. And the last thing that Strike Force wanted was an embarrassed host to call off the cash exchange for Mahmoon's son.

Their pants were also wide enough to mask the fact that the men were wearing tan tactical boots.

The men had rejected the sandals that Logistics provided. Open-toed, with inflexible soles, the sandals were comfortable when the men weren't on the company clock. But they became a liability if the temperature of a situation got turned up high. They weren't running and gunning as their shoes filled with debris. Too much of a hazard. And that would be fine unless their host invited them in. When arriving at an Iraqi house as a guest, as opposed to knocking on the door as a soldier, traditionally, a guest removed their footwear and left it in the entry.

The only one not wearing the wedding gear was Ash. He'd be missing out. Sitting for hours on end in a car with a dog, guarding their equipment, monitoring comms, and watching the horizon with his binoculars was tedious business, so the team developed a rotation to hang back with Ash and Hoover.

Strike Force piled out of the vehicles and performed a comms check.

They'd stay in contact for this part of the mission via magnetic comms dropped into their ear canals and a push-to-talk button taped to their sternums.

Jack and Gator moved to the back of their vehicle and pulled out their hostess gifts designed to be an honor for their host but not so outlandish that they put the other guests to shame. It was a fine line that they walked as outsiders.

Striker was first through the compound gate. Behind him, Jack was to his right with an intricately woven basket filled with dried fruits, herbal teas, and sweets. Gator was to his left with a sturdy plastic basket of gifts for the children—the logistics person had chosen outdoor toys like jump ropes, hackie sacks, jacks, a collapsible basketball hoop and ball, baseballs with mitts, and various-sized bats.

Later, Striker would draw the small gift box from his jacket pocket, a gift of gold and diamond earrings as a traditional bridal gift.

Randy and Blaze brought up the rear of their group.

"Eleven o'clock," Gator said.

"Got it." Striker had seen it too. A spotter was on the roof with the ubiquitous rifle and a handheld radio to his mouth as he watched the team approach.

It was no surprise when Naseem el-Pars walked out of the compound's entryway with his arms spread wide. "My friends!" he called, striding forth beaming. *"Salam Alaikum"*

"Wa Alaykum as-salam," Striker said as he approached, reaching out his right hand. After shaking hands with Nassem, they continued to stand hand in hand. This custom had taken Striker a while to get used to when he first started working in the area. The handshakes continued as the conversation unfolded, or they walked along hand and hand with other men.

When he mentioned that to Lexi once in passing, she said she had a theory she'd developed. She said that people need physical touch to be healthy. In some countries, men and women were often physically separated into different spaces. It was entirely human to have the psychological and physical need for friendly and familial touch. The American culture had a stopping point at which children no longer held hands out of pure companionship—when the act of holding hands became part of what Lexi would call "pair bonding traditions" or sexualized. Lexi liked the way women in Europe walked arm in arm and that men held hands in the parts of the

Middle East. She thought that people in the U.S. lost out. And she thought that was why Americans were so bonded with their pets, companionable touch.

Striker turned those thoughts off. He needed to focus on the mission in front of him.

Hand in hand with Naseem, Striker gestured toward each of his teammates and introduced them.

Naseem switched to English. "Jack, I remember. And Blaze. They were on your team when you came to help us when Isis wanted to eat my herd. Welcome. Welcome, my friends."

"I'm glad that we were able to help. And it's an honor to be here at this auspicious time."

"The wedding. Yes. But you are also helping to bring calm between rivals. Thank you. Tonight, though, we will not speak of that. You will sing and dance. You will eat delicious food that we have been preparing for days, and in the morning, when the guests depart, we will exchange treasure for treasure." He gestured toward the building. "Come let me show you where you can sleep."

"Thank you, but knowing you would have a full house, we are setting up a camp just over there."

"Very well, my friends, please, make yourselves comfortable, And enjoy!" Naseem moved off to welcome other guests.

"Not like any kidnap and ransom mission I've ever been to," Gator said.

Striker started forward. "It's unique. I'll give you that."

On one side, there was a cluster of women. From his peripheral vision, he took in the palette of their bejeweled-colored dresses. The same rich hues that he liked to incorporate into his oil paintings. But where he liked broad bold brush strokes, the women were adorned in intricate beadwork and embroidery. He carefully averted his eyes and searched for a space where they could leave their gifts.

Jack said, "There under the olive tree, it looks like they're collecting things over there."

A young teenager looked like he was left in charge. He placed the fruit basket with the others. But when he looked into the children's basket, he called out, and very quickly, a swarm of boys came running.

The team stood in the shade as they watched the bride arrive in the bed of a festooned truck. The noise that accompanied her was clamorous. The traditional *Zaffa* played music, and the women ululated.

Disembarking, the bride and groom went up on the stage where a sofa had been placed and sat side by side.

As the party progressed, Strike Force did their best to honor their host by participating in the festivities. They danced with the other male guests, doing the steps that were part of their past times in Iraq. For each team member, some good memories mixed in with some recollections that they didn't welcome.

As the night wore on, the team gauged when they could move off and not cause offense. They made their way back to the camp that Ash and Blaze had set up with a tarp strung between the two trucks in such a way that should they need to dive in and drive off; it would just be left behind.

Their mats and sleeping bags ranged across the ground tarp.

"Y'all have fun?" Ash asked.

"You'd never guess who was partying hard." Jack squatted in front of the fire, splaying his hands toward the warmth.

"Who's that?" Ash asked.

"Mahmoon's son," Randy rounded Blaze with a camp stool and set it down.

"So why are we spending the night here?" Hoover's head rested on Ash's thighs, enjoying getting his ears scratched. "Let's give Naseem the money, get Mahmoon's son and head."

"The intelligence packet said it would be a breach of etiquette to try to affect a business interaction at a wedding. And Command said we couldn't break laws or customs," Striker said. "So, we wait."

"Just out there partying?" Ash asked. "Not locked in some back room someplace?"

"Nope. He was there in fancy clothes, laughing it up," Randy said.

"He's a dancin' fiend." Gator had shucked his boots and was lying on his sleeping bag with an arm curled under his head. "Big doin's," Gator said. "Sorry you missed out."

"That's all right. I got to eat the food, listen to the music. Hoover and I have been star gazing. Sometimes I miss the night skies. We have stars like this in Alaska." He jerked his thumb toward the campfire he had going just outside of the sleeping area. "I've got hot water on the fire for you to clean up. And now that you're here, I'll set out the infrared security perimeter."

As the men settled, they slid into their sleeping bags.

Striker would take the first watch.

Tomorrow they'd pay the ransom to Naseem, collect Mahmoon's son, drive him home, make the exchange for Saadiq, and head back to the American base.

Right now, Lynx was in the air flying from D.C. to Jordan.

In the best of all worlds, she'd walk in, hand Angel the paperwork, gather his signature with a couple of witnesses, and fly home. Freed from that part of her life, they could marry just like they'd planned. Cammy could come live with them while Lynda got the help she needed. Dad and Mimi could rest.

And yet, this was Angel, and Angel was nothing if not mission-focused.

Angel was glad enough when Lexi showed up to free his ass from enhanced interrogation, but Striker was sure that it was going to take more than a smile and an extended pen to free Lexi from the ties that bound her.

24

_____

Lexi

Jordan

   Sunday

Margot and Lynx walked side by side under the stunning arches of the Queen Alia International Airport. Their bags whirred and clicked as the wheels worked to find traction on the slick gloss of the floors.

Both women dressed modestly in long flowing dresses with loose sleeves clasped at their wrists. It was as much for the requisite cultural modesty as for the July heat. The heat here in Amman was a temperate eighty degrees throughout the summer months. But Lynx and Margot would take a paid car service southwest to Sweimeh. It was a resort town bordering the Dead Sea that filled with European travelers in the spring and fall when the temperatures were lovely. Before they left D.C., Margot had warned Lynx of the humid winds that blew across the salty waters and the daytime temperatures around a hundred in July. With salt and water in the air, it was challenging to thermoregulate. Honestly, Lynx didn't think it would be much different than July at home.

"Did you ever have a chance to get in the Dead Sea?" Lynx asked as they walked along. "I mean, I'm Irish-pale, so I'm not a huge fan of beaches. But I have been in ocean salinity. When I get out, my skin begs for a shower. How people lay out all day with the clinging sand and the salt drying on their skin is beyond my comprehension."

"I got a chance to get into the Dead Sea once, the saltiest and most mineral-rich natural water on planet Earth." Margot rearranged her headscarf, tucking it so it didn't flap in the air current created by the fast clip of their pace. "It was an unforgettable adventure. I got to tick that one off my bucket list."

"You have one of those, a bucket list?" Lynx asked.

"No. Not really. I guess I should say I ticked that one off my curiosity list."

Lynx nodded.

"It was a weird experience, both fascinating and awful," Margot continued. "The fascinating part was that I could stick both of my arms and legs in the air, and I didn't sink even a little. There were men out there, floating along, reading the newspaper. The papers never got wet. Also interesting was that I was in the water, but I couldn't swim—I take that back —I could swim only in a particular way. I'm used to freestyle swimming, plunging my hand into the water, and scooping back toward my hip. But I couldn't thrust my hand into the water. Even breaststroke was tricky. I ended up kind of resting my legs on the water and making little propeller motions with my hands."

"How cool was that?"

"Hot as Hades, to be honest. The air and the water. Now for the torture part, it was salt. Just wet salt. And everywhere the water touched, if I had even the smallest nick in my skin, that cut screamed. And the women had it so much worse than the guys who were with us. The saltwater went into our... hoo-has, and that was terrible. Terrible, especially for me because that morning, I had had a very aerobic game of sheet tangling with a very handsome friend. The pictures my friends took of me when I got my hips into the water were comical in retrospect but at the time..."

"Sounds awful."

"The other thing was that where we went into the Dead Sea was basically desert. There were no outhouses. No water sources. While we brought water, it was only enough to drink. By the time I got back to our hotel room, I was desic- cated. I had to soak in cool water, let it run down the drain with the salt, then more fresh water and more. It was quite the process. But we'll be right there at the hotel. You should defi- nitely go in and try it out."

Lynx lifted her elbow to bump Margot and veered to the side where a man held up a handmade sign that said, "Sobado."

While Margot, with her French features and dark color- ing, blended in naturally with the Jordanians, Lynx had to work at it. Part of yesterday's early to-do list before her encounter with Mr. Entitlement was to stop by the salon for temporary hair coloring to look like she had chestnut-colored hair and brows and a spray tan that hid her day-glow pale skin. While she passed through customs with the natural color of her blue eyes, Lynx slipped into the women's restroom to put in her deep brown contact lenses once she'd made it through customs and her passport check. She fit in if one didn't scrutinize too closely.

"Hello, do you speak English?" Margot asked.

"Just so," the driver said with a bow. "Mrs. Sobado?" he

asked of Margot, who was in her mid-thirties and looked so much more in charge than Lynx. They were traveling in Lynx's name since Margot was a single female in the Middle East, and Lynx had a "Mrs." in front of her name.

Margot opened her palm to indicate Lynx.

The driver offered Lynx a bow, "Very good, madame. I shall take your bags for you." He pushed them along in front of him. "We will be on the road for about an hour."

They moved through the sliding glass doors out into a breeze that swirled their silk dresses. Though it wasn't required, Lynx pulled a scarf over her head to keep the fine strands of her brown hair from tickling her cheeks and catching in her lashes.

Margot did the same as their driver opened the back door to the car. The engine had been left running; the air conditioning was fresh against their faces as they bent to climb in.

Lynx moved the bottle of water, with its sweaty label, to the seat pocket for later, then pulled her belt into place.

After their bags were safely stowed in the trunk, the driver rounded forward, shutting the door, and moving to the driver's side. "Not many people are down in Sweimeh this time of year."

"No?" Lynx pitched her voice to sound reserved. She'd always been accompanied by men when she was in the Middle East, and while this man seemed fine—nothing that got her antennae up—they would be traveling out on very rural streets for long stretches on the road. Lynx didn't want to seem overly friendly. She just didn't know enough about the culture and how to comport herself. She'd follow Margot's lead. And frankly, between Margot's skills and hers, a lone man without a powerful weapon would come out poorly from any kind of altercation. Lynx hated that dark thought that had bubbled up. Her guard was up.

Of course, it was. Lynx was about to confront her husband.

"The heat," their driver was saying. "The sea water is not good this time of year. 33.5 in Celsius, I don't know in Fahrenheit. You come from America, yes?" He didn't stop for them to answer. "Close to body temperature. This is like hot bath. Not hot tub with the bubbles, no. Salty hot bath. It can be very dangerous for the heart." He held up a finger and waggled it from side to side. "This is a bad time for the Dead Sea."

"Thank you for the warning," Margot said. And that was the last thing that was said until the car pulled up in front of the Dead Sea Spa and Resort an hour later.

Five stars. A very nice choice for Angel and Grey. Lynx guessed that Grey and Angel would want a little pampering to restore themselves after being out in the desert for long stretches.

Their driver placed their luggage on the sidewalk and bowed as he accepted Lynx's cash tip in Jordanian Dinar. Iniquus had a bank of world currency. When an operator traveled, they always had cash in their wallets, not that Lynx was an official operator.

Margot was, though, an ex-CIA field officer—a badass spook. Lynx's father and mentors were CIA or CIA adjacent, but they were men, which was a different world. Lynx would watch and hopefully learn from Margot on this trip.

Margot waved away the doorman. "We're fine thank you." Once he went inside, Margot turned to Lynx. "I wasn't given anything other than to be available to you. I have no idea why we're here."

"Weird, right?"

"Not really," Margot said. "Do you have a plan?"

"Get registered. Get to our suite. I'm going to do my thing." Lynx walked forward.

The doorman bowed as they passed into the towering reception area. "Too hot to be out and about," Lynx popped her brows. "It is called a spa. You should enjoy."

"I'll check that out."

As they stood at the reception desk and the concierge walked Margot through their offerings, Lynx looked around the lobby nervously.

She didn't know who gave Auralia this hotel's name and date. She definitely wasn't sure if she could trust the information, even if it were coming from Auralia.

Too many people now knew of Lynx's marital situation. Angel going black ops to protect his friends and family was falling apart. Auralia was just the newest person to discover the truth.

Some unknown figures knew the players in this situation. *Someone.*

Was it Grey? White? One of the other Color Code officers? Heck, it could have been Angel himself. Would that make sense?

Lynx had scratched around with her psychic senses and got absolutely nothing.

That wasn't true. There was something brewing on the horizon. It just didn't feel like it belonged to this. Whatever *this* was.

Keycards in hand, Lynx and Margot headed to the elevator bank.

"Fair warning," Margot said, "if I'm in a massage coma, I won't be available for your call."

"Nothing like that's going to be necessary. I'm here to say something to someone and listen to what they say in return. Friendly. The general thinks my age and my gender might draw unwanted attention. That's why you're here. Chaperone duty." Lynx sent her a grimace. "Sorry."

Having waved away the porter's assistance when they first entered the hotel, Margot reached for her luggage handle. She drew it along behind her as they went through the double doors into a comfortable reception room with vaulted ceilings. "If that's what you want me to know and that's what you want me to do, I've had worse assignments."

And there it was again.

Three Blind Mice—a hum that echoed as if it bounced off the rock. A dank smell curled her nose. A shiver of cold shook her in her sandals. Her mind reached for Striker.

Holy moly, Striker was right. This was a *knowing*.

25

Saadiq

Iraq
   Sunday

"Chris" hunkered in the corner. After the first taste of mint tea from Saadiq's spoon yesterday, the man had turned to the food, tearing at the bread, scooping the meat and rice, and eating like a train, with constant forward motion—shoving, chewing, swallowing, shoving. The man had found a place to rest his eyes between Saadiq and the plate so he could monitor the factory-like effort of consuming all the food and the possible threat of Saadiq removing the plate. His eyelids were stiff and unblinking as if any micro move needed attention.

Saadiq had sat very still, trying to project calm.

A cornered animal was the most dangerous, was the thought that skittered through his mind.

Even backing away might be seen as aggressive. So, Saadiq sat and breathed.

When Chris had finished his plate, he went to the corner, where he pushed himself backward as tightly as possible, drawing his feet toward his hips and his knees toward his ears. He wrapped his arms around his legs. His feet stuck out to the side like training wheels on a toddler's bike. Then, he tucked his head down, resting his brow on his kneecaps.

And that is where he stayed.

As the evening grew cool, Saadiq wrapped a blanket around the man.

In the morning, when the keeper came to bring their morning meal, Chris didn't uncoil.

Having been in one too many crates over the last month, Saadiq relished his ability to stretch himself long. But they had each, obviously, moved through different life experiences.

The keeper came out of the bathroom with the waste-basket full of hair and rotting cloth.

Looking toward Saadiq until their gazes met and held, he offered a bow as if thanking and possibly honoring Saadiq's efforts.

Bewildering.

Saadiq sat on the one chair, lifting one of the plates to place in front of himself. He gave thanks to God for the food, profound thanks that he didn't feel compelled to vigilantly protect this nourishment. He expressed immense gratitude that despite the crates and the cramps and the disorientation of this last month, he had never been hungry.

Exhausted? That was a whole other subject.

He'd had brief moments of sleep, but a whole night's rest? That hadn't happened since the night before the last trip in a crate. Saadiq had lost count of the days.

This morning's meal was bean paste with fried eggs, freshly baked bread, dates, and pistachios. And as Saadiq placed each bite on his tongue, he savored the experience, sending gratitude to his host for providing for him and the women who prepared the meal.

Afterward, he went and washed himself.

Coming out of the bathroom, he glanced at Chris, still folded and unmoving in the corner.

Saadiq was suddenly terrified that the man had died in the night and was held there, rigid with rigor mortis.

Saadiq put a hand on the man's back, feeling his lungs' slow expansion and compression working, alive.

Again, Saadiq was filled with gratitude.

Since the day's heat began to rise, Saadiq quietly removed the blanket, folded it, and placed it at the foot of the sleeping pad to the right of the folded blanket he himself had used last night.

With the sound of children calling to each other, Saadiq pushed the table under the window and carefully climbed onto it so that he might see the children at play. He missed his family. He missed his daughter. Saadiq drank in the sight of the children running and laughing, thinking that Iniquus knew of his family and knew that something strange was happening in his own life. And he hoped that Iniquus could render him aid, that perhaps he could soon be with his family again, only somewhere safe.

The door opened for the second time that morning.

The old man walked in, looking up at where Saadiq stood barefoot on the table, then down to Chris in his ball. As always, the old man was expressionless.

As usual, there were two men outside his door holding rifles.

This time a third man came in, a big grin on his face. "Saadiq?"

Saadiq put his hand on his chest. "That is me." Then he climbed down from table to chair to ground.

"I hope you were comfortable, my friend," he said in accented English, lifting a hand toward the window. "The children are playing soccer." After glancing at Chris, the new man held his hand toward the tray. "I see that you have eaten. Good. Listen, we had a call with Iniquus, and they have sent a man named Striker here to Iraq to collect you. So, I will take you to meet his team. The team will see you safely on your way."

"Striker?" Saadiq asked. "Striker is coming here?"

"Striker is flying to Iraq. Do you not wish this? You gave their name and phone number." This man's accent sounded like he might be from Afghanistan.

"Yes, I'm sorry. Yes, I did," Saadiq said. "I'm just confused about why Striker has a team flying from America to Iraq to collect me."

"I know very little, my friend. Your host has put your care in my hands. Shall we go? Do you have any things that you wish to gather to take with you?"

"No." Saadiq shook his head. "I brought nothing with me."

"Good, then we go."

And just like that, they walked out into the morning. They climbed into a truck and left, driving out into the desert. They stopped in a village around lunch.

"Where are we?" Saadiq asked as they sat there, obviously waiting for someone to arrive.

"This is where I live." His driver pointed toward the town. "My instructions said I was to bring you this far to meet Striker and his team. They should be here soon."

"Of course," Saadiq said, but something felt…off.

The driver pulled a sports drink from a small cooler. "A very hot day." He untwisted the top and handed the bottle to Saadiq.

Nervous energy had made Saadiq's mouth dry. He accepted the bottle and drank it, feeling the cool liquid soothing his parched throat.

The driver took out a bottle of water that he sipped.

As the four men sat waiting in the truck, the heat of the sun and the exhaustion of his sleepless days made Saadiq's eyelids heavy. He felt a strange sensation spread through his body. He tried but could no longer lift his arms or shift in his seat. He couldn't even pop the door open to tumble to the ground in sight of other people.

Too late, Saadiq realized that the driver had opened the top to hide the broken plastic seal and handed it to him in such a way that it would be impolite to resist.

Saadiq drank himself into a drugged stupor.

26

Striker

Sunday

"From the satellite images, the road is clear on the approach." Deep's voice came from the open comms speaker. "Once you get around the bend in the road, the land flattens. Fifty yards out from the compound are your welcome wagons. I'd say fifteen armed males."

"Striker. Copy."

This morning had been as simple as it could have possibly been. As the Strike Force team drank coffee around their morning fire, watching the daybreak, Mahmoon's son walked casually and comfortably into the Iniquus camp along with Naseem and some guy with a ubiquitous rifle. Striker held up his phone app, and it measured the son's features. With a positive identification, the son climbed into one of the

Iniquus vehicles, putting his head back and closing his eyes, looking worn out from last night's festivities.

Striker held out the duffle bag with the ransom cash.

"Thank you," Naseem said. "Many blessings." He turned and went back into the compound.

The doors shut.

Done deal.

Now for step two, switch Mahmoon's son for Saadiq.

This exchange should be as easy as the first.

As their borrowed armored military trucks approached the compound, Hoover leaned farther out the window to see forward of the car. The blue mirrored dog goggles protecting his eyes reflected the sunlight out into the desert wind.

From the desert I come to thee, echoed in Striker's mind. *On a stallion shod with fire. And the winds are left behind in the speed of my desire.* Those words were from Bayard Taylor's *Bedouin Song*. It was the poem Lexi chanted when she thought she was drawing her last breath after a plane crash.

Striker wasn't a man who swam in emotions. He had trained himself since his first days of high school to follow the path of the ancient Stoics. But Lexi wrenched emotions from him that he thought didn't exist.

Lexi had been lying in his arms, looking up at the sky, when she told him the story of how she had tried to fling those words through the winds to him as her last conscious thought of this lifetime. *I love thee, I love but thee, with a love that shall not die.*

He worked to convince himself that he suddenly remembered that night and those words because the landscape here was similar to where her plane had crashed.

But he knew that if he told Lexi those words suddenly came to mind, she'd start picking them apart, looking for why his subconscious was remembering that particular poem at this particular time. All he could think was that at the time she was telling him goodbye, he, along with the team, had been in the air frantically searching for her, knowing that every minute that passed put her in deeper danger, that she could easily die because they didn't get to her in time.

And he wanted to put that together with Saadiq's situation.

But Saadiq didn't need to be found. He was at Mahmoon's compound. They had handed Naseem the suit-case of bills. They had Mahmoon's son sitting in the follow vehicle driven by Jack.

Now, all they had to do was make the exchange.

"One o'clock," Ash said, pointing in the direction of Hoover's snout.

Striker pushed the grief and horror of the poem's personal meaning up and out of his mind, letting the words drift behind him as they drove forward.

"Got'em," Jack said through the speaker.

"We're here by invitation, gentlemen." Striker's voice was calm. "Just another day in the life."

The team knew that walking in with one dynamic didn't mean that it would hold. Back when Striker led a SEAL team with Blaze, Jack, and Ash among his men, they had gone in as a friendly and had to shoot their way to freedom as they left.

"Listen up," Striker continued. "We have the compound on the horizon. Iniquus has asked that we use the new communications system on this mission. We've tested it in our training, and it looks like a game-changer for our line of work. This should be an easy practice run. Go ahead and get your systems in place."

Iniquus used cutting-edge equipment, often handed to

them by DARPA for use in the field to gather operator feed-back. Iniquus replaced their standard compression uniforms with high-tech fabrics with monitors entwined with fibers to help those on oversight keep track of the operators' locations via GPS and their wellbeing with biometric sensors. And apart from the tedium of Deep continuously telling them to drink more water, the shirts had been a good safety addition.

The newest fancy tech came to them as comms units. And it was futuristic as hell.

Typically, Strike Force dropped a magnetic audio commu-nicator into their ear canals, where they were invisible to the adversaries. On routine security assignments, like the one they'd just returned from in New York City, they had a button taped under their shirts that they could depress to speak to their teammates. And until this mission, they also wore a unit that wrapped their throats, allowing the system to interpret the air pattern over their larynx as they mouthed words without sound.

This was beyond.

With the placement of the apparatus at seven contact points on the head and face, the device was able to pick up the micro-neuromuscular movements in the jaw and face that were stimulated by thought. Not all thoughts transmitted over this device. Striker and his men could think through a situa-tion with those thoughts remaining privately in their brains. But when the team turned their inner thoughts into thoughts of speaking the words, the system detected the microscopic jaw movements. It translated those movements into vibrations that moved the tiny bones of the inner ear. This technology didn't impede the team from being situationally aware or hurt their ability to hear anything they would usually hear.

These words were then picked up on bone-conduction headphones that vibrate the bones in the inner ear.

This meant the team could communicate without anyone seeing their mouths move, not even a lip-twitch. It looked as though they were standing there silently when, in effect, they were communicating.

It took practice to get to their level of proficiency. It had to come naturally to the team, or it might pull their focus away from a threatening situation. If it worked in the field, it was a game changer. The force operators at Iniquus, like the special operations forces in the field, depended on stealth for safety. Any sound could make a dog bark or pull eyes to a window. When operating during a mission, communications often get lost in environmental noise, especially when working in a hot zone. In both of these circumstances, the teams turned to hand signals, but hand signals could be hard to see through night vision goggles or missed if someone was watching their six.

With the specialized flexible plastic wrapping his head from around his ear, down the side of his face, and around his jawline, Striker was hands-free. He didn't need to press his comms. He merely thought about saying, "Gator, hold back while we come around."

"Copy." Gator was in Striker's ear.

The follow vehicle slowed to a stop, circling until they were broadside to the compound wall. This gave that half of the team cover and a faster retreat if an exit became necessary.

Striker's truck drove forward a few more yards.

Striker held up a hand. "Okay, hold up here, Randy. This is close enough."

Randy focused on his rearview mirror. Once he assured himself they were out of the dust cloud that the follow-vehicle had kicked up, Randy pulled the steering wheel around, so they had a tactical position. He softly applied the brakes to keep the road from stirring up too much dust and obscuring their view.

The team twisted in their seats to keep eyes on the vehicles parked up ahead.

Deep was correct. About fifty yards from the compound's main gate, two pickup trucks with wooden guardrails waited. In the beds of the trucks, men stood with rifles in hand.

Striker had given them a buffer zone from the compound's men of about fifteen yards.

His practiced eye saw nothing unusual in this setup.

After performing a comms check, binoculars came up.

"Jack. Fifteen by my count, including drivers," he said from his place in the follow vehicle.

"Randy. Copy," he said from his place beside Striker. "I have the same, fifteen."

"Striker. Two to one, easy day, gentlemen." Striker panned the binoculars. "No, Mahmoon. All right," Striker said. "Gator, you stay in the driver's seat. If things pop off, Gator, you take our guest and get the hell out of Dodge."

"Gator. Copy."

"Striker. Blaze, you stick with Gator. You have control of our bargaining chip."

"Blaze. Copy." Blaze's response was in Striker's head. So far, so good with the new tech.

"Striker. As for the rest of the team, here's how we'll move forward," Striker reached for the door handle, "when I say go, the rest of us jump down, range out. Jack and Randy, halfway, you'll take a position. Ash, you'll stick to my shadow with Hoover on a short lead. Three, two, one. Moving."

The men advanced like water, fluid and sure as they exited the armored trucks and swirled to a V formation, leaving the doors open wide for a quick exfil.

At the halfway point, the men took a knee to get a lower profile and harder to hit, should bullets, for some reason, start to fly. They had pistols with short magazines in their ankle holsters, a double tap stun gun on their hips, and a stun rifle in their hands. None of those weapons, even the pistols, had a long gun's range or human-liquifying power.

Distance was their friend.

As Striker moved forward, his hands open and slightly out from his side to show that he wasn't going to draw arms on them, Ash and Hoover stayed to his right with enough of a gap that Hoover had full range. Hoover was a fur missile and had a trained eye. If a gun was directed at any of them, that was an acceptable move. If a finger moved into the trigger guard, Hoover would fly into action, mouth wide, joyous to take a bite and exert enough pressure to crush the assailant's bones.

In Striker's experience, the scream that went up when the would-be assailant felt the teeth of a tactical K9 was enough to freeze the limbic system of anyone not accustomed to hearing it. Just shut them flat down. It gave the team the luxury of about five seconds to make a tactical decision and act.

No one from either truck moved. The Iraqi men held their rifles in loose hands pointed toward the sky. One guy was on his radio.

The compound door slid open enough to emit three men. The trio walked out of the front in a horizontal line. The men on either side looked like family members dressed traditionally for a farmer or herdsman. The one in the center with no head covering was a man with red hair.

Absolutely not Saadiq.

27

Striker

Sunday

When they were about five meters apart, the redhead squinted past the sun, focusing on Strike Force. His eyes became wild in his head. "I...I...I'm not Chris!" he shouted as he wrenched his arms away from the men escorting him out. He couldn't seem to coordinate his legs underneath himself and pitched forward, falling to all fours.

The men on either side reached down to help him up, but the man threw elbows left and right, finally flopping on his back and kicking at them like a child in a fight with his brothers.

Striker could feel his men flick their gaze his way, looking for a signal. But Striker wasn't clear on how to proceed.

He stilled, taking in the scene.

The escorts didn't look tense or watchful. They actually seemed to be presenting Striker's team with a present, something of value. It was much like the puffed chests and pleased faces at the wedding last night when the bride received a particularly lovely gift that brought honor to the family.

One of the escorts backed away from the flailing redhead. He opened his hands toward the man and made a kind of shoveling motion like, "This is for you!"

The redhead turned over, posting his weight onto his elbows so his torso lifted from the dirt. "I'm not Chris." His foot swung around, and he came up on a knee, patting the flat of his hands onto his chest with an insistent hand.

"Who are you then?" Striker asked.

"I'm not Chris!" he called in response.

"That's not Chris," Ash said.

Striker commanded silently, "Blaze, reach out to Deep. Apprise him of our situation."

"Blaze. Wilco."

Striker pulled his phone from his pocket, tapped the Iniquus app open, and spread his fingers on his screen until the man's face filled the rectangle. He took the picture. Then he angled until he got a good shot of the man's ear. "Randy, come up," Striker thought.

Striker didn't take his eyes off the situation in front of him. But when he heard Randy's boots behind him, Striker held the phone up for Randy to grab. "Get the computer fired up. Get a satellite connection so Deep can process the images," he said quietly. "And let's see if the Iniquus system can give us workable intel about this situation."

Randy jogged back to the truck.

Striker signaled what looked like the leader over. In Arabic, he said, "How about you run get Mahmoon for me? I think we need to have a talk."

The man shook his head. "It is I who will make this exchange."

"So, here's the deal." Striker stood wide-legged and immovable, his bladed his hands on his hips. "I have Mahmoon's son in our truck. And we want Saadiq."

"We give you the English speaker." The man, who was about as thick as Striker's left leg, opened his hand toward the redhead.

"What's his name?" Striker asked.

"I don't know." The escort shook his head and opened his hands to show he had nothing to share.

"Right, well, here we stand. I came for Saadiq. I will leave with Saadiq. I suggest you go get Saadiq or you get Mahmoon. And I suggest you do that now." Striker knew that this guy had been given an important task. And he recognized that this man thought it would be a cake walk. In Striker's experience, there was no such thing as an easy mission. As they say in the SEALs, the only easy day was yesterday.

The leader commanded his men to stay put and not let Strike Force leave.

The men looked none too pleased that this was going south. Sure, his team was holding Stun rifles, but they didn't know that. If they were looking at these rifles, they probably thought they were some new high-tech plasma shooting weapons that could blast them into particles. Striker was beginning to appreciate their futuristic design.

Randy came around from behind the truck, thinking into his comms. "Randy. The guy's name is Rupert Shaw. He's a British journalist who disappeared on assignment eighteen months ago."

Striker looked Rupert over for a clue of what had happened to him. His clothes were clean, his face gaunt. "Rupert Shaw?" Striker called.

The man's face crumpled. He was a Greek tragedy mask. Gripping his hands and holding them to his trembling jaw, Rupert nodded his head continuously and sobbed.

Striker felt compassion for the guy and wanted to move forward to collect him and assure him that he was safe now.

But fifteen rifles pointed at the team. Strike Force was in a foreign country with their own laws and their own sense of justice. And Saadiq hadn't shown up yet. As hard as it was on the man lying there uncomfortably, this needed to play itself out.

Striker watched puffs of dust rise as another vehicle approached the compound's gate. It pulled up right beside the escort who had remained beside Rupert.

Mahmoon stepped out of the passenger side of the vehicle.

Arms wide, robes flowing as he rounded toward Striker, he shouted, "*As-Salaam-Alaikum.*"

Striker reached for the handshake that Mahmoon was offering. "*Wa-Alaikum-Salaam.*"

"My friend," Mahmoon switched to English. "Welcome."

Striker tightened his grip just enough to make the point that he wasn't feeling friendly. "Mahmoon, cut to the chase. Where is Saadiq?"

"Come, you are my guest." Without letting go of Striker's hand, he turned and walked toward the compound. "We will talk, leader to leader."

Striker silently gave his commands. "Ash, you're with me. Randy and Jack, you have control of Rupert. Gator and Blaze, you will not let them get control of Mahoon's son until we have the story on Saadiq."

"Sir."

Randy and Jack ran forward to stand with Rupert.

Their small group—Mahmoon and his guard, Striker with

Ash and Hoover—walked in silence through the compound gate and across to the main building.

Striker stopped at the threshold of their home and indicated his boots.

"Yes, this is fine," Mahmoon said. "I have known many American soldiers, and they are all terrified that they will become separated from their boots. We have learned to adapt."

"Thank you," both Striker and Ash said.

"This morning, before the rooster crowed, I received a call from Naseem," Mahmoon said as they walked into the main salon. "He said they had a wonderful celebration at the family wedding and that you and your team were impeccable guests."

"May their family be blessed by the union," Striker said, lowering himself to the cushion that his host indicated.

"Yes. Yes." Mahmoon touched his heart and bowed his head. Then squatted to find a seat on his own cushion. "The ransom they requested was paid, and they told me you left with my son. How is he?"

"He was kept comfortable but bored in a room by himself. He lacked company. So, he was quite happy at last night's wedding. We saw him dancing and enjoying the other's company."

Mahmoon laughed. "He can talk, that one. Yes, a great talker."

"We are here to exchange your son for Saadiq. That was the deal that Iniquus agreed to." Striker paused until he had his host's full attention. "Where's Saadiq?"

"Yesterday, we had visitors." Mahmoon inched forward on his cushion. "You do not know of this?"

"I do not."

"They weren't your advanced team?" His brow pulled together in distress.

"They were not." Striker swept his arm toward the front of the compound. "My team is here now. We have done as you asked. Iniquus gathered the ransom for your son. We delivered it and collected your son from your neighbors. We have brought him home, where he belongs."

Mahmoon glanced toward Hoover. When they'd come in, Ash and Hoover had stopped where the tile floor met the carpet. Hoover rested on the cool surface in a down stay between Ash's legs.

"Saadiq is no longer here," Mahmoon said. "I will tell you the story."

"Please." Striker shifted to ensure that his boots' soles did not face his host.

"Visitors arrived on the day of the wedding. They had the man you called Rupert with them. He was in terrible shape. We put him in Saadiq's room with him to help care for the man as my men only speak Arabic, and we felt Saadiq could communicate with him. Saadiq cleaned Rupert up very well. He looks a hundred percent better than when he arrived."

"Yesterday," Striker clarified.

"This is so."

"They didn't tell you who the man was?"

"I have found that it is sometimes best not to know. But the visitors were obviously not Iraqi. The men said that because you were here, they would hand this man to your team to take with Saadiq."

"These foreigners knew Saadiq's name, and they knew my name?"

"This is so. These men went to the wedding at Naseem's, then returned to stay as my guests overnight. As I said, this morning, I got a phone call from Naseem that my son was on his way back. After this call from Naseem, the men came to me. They said, 'Striker has called and asked that they go forward with Saadiq to take him to his family. That you were on your way.'"

"And you just let these strangers go?" Striker asked.

"No, my friend, I said I would not do this as I had already negotiated with the Americans."

"They said that if they did not leave immediately, they would miss Saadiq's ride to his wife and child."

"They said, 'wife and child?'"

"Even so. They said that the Americans had been missing this man Rupert and that he was a treasure that the Americans would prize. That you would be very pleased that not only had you secured Saadiq's freedom but that you also had brought this man—they did not use Rupert's name—to you."

"You're sure these men weren't Americans or Iraqis?" Striker asked.

"Neither. A hundred percent sure," Mahmoon responded. "They spoke Arabic with heavy accents, but I could not tell what kind of accent. My guess is that they were from Afghanistan."

Striker's mind went immediately to Zero-One. "And you agreed to let Saadiq go."

"Rightly so. However, I should add Saadiq seemed comfortable as he left. He smiled as he thanked me for his comfort while here. And he walked with ease next to the men who had come to collect him. He climbed, unhindered, into their truck."

"This was not our agreement, Mahmoon. You have verified that we did as we said we would."

Mahmoon flung a hand into the air. "I give you Rupert!"

"We are glad to have Rupert and help him to get home if that's what he wishes. And we are grateful for your hospitality and for bringing Saadiq to our attention. But I came from the United States for Saadiq. I paid a ransom to get your son so that I could have Saadiq. I hold your son to exchange with Saadiq. *This* was our bargain, my friend."

"I see." Mahmoon changed his tone. "What is it you wish to do to Saadiq? Do you wish to take him away for interrogation? To torture that Iraqi man?"

Striker wasn't playing that game. "You would think such a thing of me, Mahmoon?"

"This has happened before. And Saadiq is a countryman. I will not give you a fellow countryman. I will give you an English countryman."

"Ah, that was your calculus. Now consider, Mahmoon. Saadiq gave you my name and phone number and asked that I come and help him. I was not searching for him. He asked for me."

"This is true." Mahmoon leaned forward so his mouth was close to Striker's ear. "Saadiq was brought to my home by accident. He was not the man we sought. Once here, my men put him in our guest room while they consulted with me. There was a group of American men who arrived at our gates. They had the physical bearing of men with dangerous capability, you know of what I speak. Men like you and your team." He spread his arms wide. "This is my home, my children, my flocks. These men said that they had come to help Saadiq, but we have a code of honor. Saadiq was under our protection."

"So, Saadiq was with you?" Striker asked. "You recognized him?"

"How would I know this exactly?" Mahmoon shrugged. "I saw a man. He stays locked in my guest room until we can decide what to do. He said his name was Saadiq. From there, I have no idea."

"Tell me about these American visitors."

"On their caps, I saw the patches. I recognize the design. They are for DZ. I know the DZ can be dangerous men. Should I hand over a fellow countryman to the DZ? I don't know. I ask them to wait. I have Saadiq brought to me. I ask him who he trusts. This is how we call Iniquus. And I will tell you, at this time, when I speak with your Honey, I saw a way to get my son back."

"Why the ransom?"

"Naseem says that I poisoned his flock so they do not eat the vegetation, and my flock has more forage. He said I should pay. They take my son until the flock is replaced. I did not have this kind of money. This is the money you paid to him. Now Naseem and I are brothers again."

"DZ was here. You had Saadiq. Saadiq said he trusted me. You arranged for the exchange."

"Even so."

"Then what happened with the DZ?"

"I told them that Iniquus was coming for Saadiq, and Striker would pick him up. And that I had given my word that Saadiq would remain my guest."

"And DZ was comfortable with that?" Striker asked.

"No. They went outside and made a phone call on their satellite phone. They were asking for orders."

"Do you know whom they called or what was said?"

"I do not, but I am sure the person gave them orders. They came in, thanked us, and left."

"Left without seeing Saadiq?" Striker clarified.

"We would not show them where he was within our compound."

"Just left." That didn't sit right with Striker.

"Even so. At the end of the day, Rupert arrives with the foreigners. I received a call from Naseem's brother that you and your team were at the wedding. I think all is well. Again, this morning, I got a call. All is well. So when the men have all the correct names and timelines, and Saadiq seemed comfortable going, we let him go be with his family."

"Then we showed up."

"To collect Rupert."

"Saadiq. We are here to collect Saadiq."

Mahmoon stroked his beard. "I can no longer help you with this."

"DZ didn't return?" Striker asked.

"No."

The team had been able to hear this conversation over the comms. But now, Striker silently said, "Striker. Jack, I need you to contact Deep and ask him to find out what kind of story Rupert Shaw was chasing when he disappeared."

"Jack. Wilco."

"I will not give you the Englishman without receiving my son," Mahmoon insisted.

"Mahmoon, I am not holding your son against his will. I have provided him with transportation from where he was staying to you," Striker qualified. "I have no intention of causing harm to your son or keeping him with my team. Your son's well-being is not at risk. I thank you again for the hospitality you provided to Rupert. But I am very worried for Saadiq's safety."

28

_____

Striker

FIRST THINGS FIRST, STRIKER NEEDED TO VERIFY THIS STORY as much as possible.

Iniquus knew that the kidnap and ransom phone call had originated from this compound. But from there, things were murkier.

Striker's thoughts transformed from an idea into a vibration that his team could hear, "Randy, go back to the truck and get a plastic bag and a new shirt for Rupert. We need the one he has on for a scent source. Once you have that properly packaged, bring that to me."

"Randy. Wilco."

"Deep, when Randy comes into the compound, can you direct him to me?" Striker thought. Deep would have used the

GPS information from Striker's shirt to map where he went in the building so there was no difficulty in trying to meet up.

"Deep. Wilco."

In his ear, Striker heard Ash's AI voice, "Ash. Sir, I need to do a 'track back' if Hoover is leading us to Rupert's room. I need to go retrieve the scent source from Randy."

A track-back skill was very useful in certain situations. In a search and rescue, if someone ran to get help but couldn't put a pin in the map where they'd left their injured friend, having a K9 follow that trail was lifesaving. If Ash were only to have the "find it" command, Hoover would sniff the scent source, walk over to Rupert, and sit down. Ta-da!

"Copy," Striker said. "Go."

Ash and Hoover left. And Mahmoon leaned to see where they were going.

Waiting, Striker turned to focus on Mahmoon. "Have you heard of artificial intelligence?"

"I have not. What is this?"

"Many things. But in this case, I'm concerned that perhaps Saadiq was never here with you."

"Ah, my friend, I know that you know better. I know for a fact that Iniquus has the ability to listen to recorded voices and assess if they are true or not." He placed a hand on his chest. "I know that my voice is on record. And I believe that someone like Saadiq, who has memorized the phone number of the honorable Striker that Iniquus would have a recording of his voice, as well."

"This was true when I knew you last," Striker said. "Time passes, and things have changed."

"In many ways, this is true. Things changing with time," Mahmoon agreed. "But in the case of the phone call where Saadiq spoke before I did, proving in real time that he was with us, what would the passage of time matter?"

"There are now computers that, with just a few words recorded in passing, could mimic that exact vocal frequency of an individual. Someone could approach Saadiq on the street and ask, 'Excuse me, but do you know where the pharmacy is?' Saadiq's reply would be enough to teach a computer to mimic his voice."

"The computer is not a thinking thing, it might mimic, but it could not respond," Mahmoon said.

"This is incorrect. Artificial intelligence can do one of three things. One, the computer could respond as if it was a person. Two, the computer could read words that someone typed onto a keyboard in the artificial voice. Or three, a real person could speak into a mic in real-time. As the voice goes into the mic, it is then fed instantaneously through the computer system. On the other end of the line, we would hear it as Saadiq's voice."

"But this is something of futuristic novels and Hollywood," Mahmoon asserted.

"I assure you it is not." Striker placed a hand on his heart. "This is what we're going to do. Ash went to get a scent source from Rupert. When he comes back, he and his K9 will be taking a little tour of where you held Rupert. And see if the K9 agrees with what you have said." Striker put his hands on his knees and leaned forward. "For now, I need to make sure my men are safe and no accidents happen. Tell your trucks of men to come back into the compound and shut the gates."

"But you have my son," Mahmoon stammered.

"This is true. And you will have Ash and me with you. Do you think my men will leave without us?"

"No, I do not." Mahmoon lifted his hand, and the man hovering in the corner ran toward the door. Soon, engines turned over, and the sound came closer.

"Striker. Jack are the trucks inside and the gate closed?" he asked silently.

"Jack. Affirmative."

Striker rose and extended his hand to Mahmoon, helping the older man to his feet. They walked hand in hand as friends out to the courtyard.

There, they watched Hoover approach, his legs wide, his snout to the ground.

Mahmoon and Striker fell in behind the working dog.

Iraqi families typically lived in a collectivist culture. Households were multigenerational. "Family" was a term that extended past the nuclear families in American culture and included a much broader idea. Coming together to share their abilities and provide the strength of unity, these family compounds, especially in the rural farming areas, always had interested Striker.

Briefly, Striker's mind went to his sister's addiction. What happened to the broader sense of family if one person churned the waters of an otherwise placid existence?

Mahmoon gestured toward a corridor.

"With your permission," Striker said. "It's best to follow the dog. Once we have seen Rupert's accommodations, we can continue on to where Saadiq slept."

"Ah, well. The men were together in the same room. This direction was merely the way that remained under a protective cover. The sun is hot today."

Striker thought, "How's it looking to you, Ash?"

Ash's lips were closed as he held tight to Hoover's lead. "Body language says we're getting close. Of course, if Rupert just walked out this way, the trail is fresh, and that might be why Hoover's having so much fun."

And just then, Hoover turned to a door and sat.

"What's on the other side of this door, Mahmoon?" Striker asked.

"This is a room where our guests stay." He released Striker's hand and reached into the pocket of his *dishdasha* to pull out a ring of keys. After sorting through the selection, he picked one and inserted it into the lock. He turned the knob and pressed the door wide. "Please," he said by way of invitation.

Hoover spent a lot of time sniffing a corner.

Ash took him into the bathroom, then over to the table where a book lay, making an equilateral triangle of the corner table. Striker stared at the book for a moment, reaching back in his memory to recall a mission where that was the sign that all was well and the team should proceed. He thought, "Ash, distract our host."

Ash pointed at the bed mat. "Sir, did two people sleep on this bed at the same time?"

As Mahmoon turned, Striker lifted the book and opened it to the dog-eared page. There in English, it said, Pediatric Surgery Maryland.

As he'd learned from Lexi when she had her puzzler hat on, one can't assume. The book could have been laid like that by happenstance. And the book with Saadiq's writing could have come from anywhere. They needed more information, and frankly, the idea of AI interference just made this situation all that much cloudier and more complicated.

What does one believe when human eyes and ears can easily be manipulated and deceived?

"Ash," Striker thought, then quickly explained, "This may be a scent source. Saadiq touched it at one point, but Rupert could have as well."

He heard back. "Copy, sir. Put it on the edge of the table." Striker did as told.

Ash opened the bag with Rupert's *dishdasha*. "Scent. Scent. Scent," he commanded Hoover.

Working away from the corner that seemed a rich scent source, Ash signaled Hoover to "find it." They approached the table, and Hoover sat in front of the chair. Put back on task; he walked right by the book. Over at the bed, Hoover sat in front of the blanket on the right.

Next, Ash offered Hoover the book. "Scent. Scent. Scent," he commanded. And once again, Hoover was chuffing as he worked to understand that particular combination. The scent seemed to be all over the room. But the place where Hoover smelled it the strongest was on bed and on the blanket on the left.

"Is that Saadiq's scent source?" Striker asked silently.

"Grain of salt, Commander." Striker heard. "It could also have been someone who handled the book and lay down on the bed and wasn't Saadiq. For example, your scent is now on that book since you lifted it. Hoover wouldn't be able to make that distinction."

Aloud, Striker said, "With your permission, Mahmoon, we will take this blanket with us."

Ash pulled a plastic bag from Hoover's working vest.

And here they were. DZ had made contact, and a foreign group had used Striker's name. The wayward son had been returned. The team was plus a Rupert but still minus a Saadiq.

That the foreign group had mentioned Saadiq's wife and child told Striker that they knew specific information about Saadiq's family. That this group left before Iniquus arrived boded poorly.

Had the group captured Saadiq's family?

Well, there was one way to figure that out.

29

Lynx

PRESSING FORWARD ON THE GENERAL'S COMMAND, HERE SHE was on her Jordanian mission to gain her freedom.

The general was right; her baggage was something that Iniquus had to stumble over.

In her room, Lynx had popped in a video contact lens so Deep could see what she saw. She was also wearing a cami that fed information to Deep, just like the Strike Force operators wore.

She thoroughly expected a call at some point that day telling her to drink more water.

Now changed out of her traveling clothes into a pair of loose trousers and a blouse, she fit in with the few other women she had passed as she moved around the hotel. With a confident stride, Lynx walked down the corridor toward what Deep told her was (probably) Angel's room.

Deep had hacked into the hotel's system. Since John Grey was his code name, surely, he had some other name on his passport and travel documentation. And Angel being "dead" and all, he could hardly travel on his real passport.

While Lynx and Margot were en route from the airport to the spa, Deep got hold of the hotel's security feed and watched as the two men checked in about a half hour apart this morning. Following along, Deep tracked Grey to room 10260, John Addams. Angel was 10256, Omar Azar. They had each gone into their rooms upon arrival with their suit-cases and, moments later, left again with their hands free. They left within ten minutes of each other and took separate taxis.

So far. So good.

At 10256, Lynx took in the "Do Not Disturb" sign hung from the knob, written in different languages. As she tapped lightly on the door, her eye scanned for any signs of a camera that had been placed to monitor the entry, though surely, Deep would have watched for that and warned her. She saw a piece of white thread seemingly draped over the latch bolt. "Old school," she murmured. If Angel had set up surveillance inside the room, he wouldn't have needed to leave a string to warn him that someone had entered. The Do Not Disturb sign meant that if the string was gone, the staff hadn't opened the door.

In researching this hotel, Deep had discovered that the door locks, though modern key card devices, were made by the company that had been on the news channels because they were so simple to bypass. It took simple wiring stored in a magic marker case inserted into a hole in the bottom of the lock, and boom, you were in. While some hotels corrected this security risk, the lock company mostly sent out plastic plugs to cover over the problem. These plugs were easily popped free with a screwdriver.

Lynx felt along the bottom of the device and found the hole was still open. Out of her pocket came the magic marker. She popped the top, slid the prong into the hole, and before she opened the door all the way, she caught the thin white thread.

In.

Whew.

Before she shut the door, Lynx carefully placed that thread across the latch bolt. Since Angel had put it in place from the hall, Lynx licked the end of the string so that it would cling to the outside of the doorframe. As her saliva dried, the thread *should* drop back into place with the pull of gravity.

She shut the door. Locked it. Spun and looked around.

The only sign that anyone had been in there was the suitcase sitting in the closet.

She pulled out her phone and called Deep. "I'm in his room."

"I saw. Well done. I'll keep an eye on you. Put your phone on vibrate, and I'll buzz when I see him in the building and again when he's in the hall. Don't pick up. Just swipe the call, so I know you got your warning."

"Will do. Thank you."

Lynx scoped out the room, wondering where she should be when Angel first saw her.

In the bathroom, she considered lying in the tub and rejected that as uncomfortable and unnecessary. She briefly imagined hearing Angel at the door and throwing the door wide to an "I Love Lucy" style "Honey, I'm home."

Doing something like that to a black ops guy might just get her shot.

She walked over to the window and peered out.

Perhaps she should hide behind the curtains? Well, that was silly. She could shadow walk and hide from sight. Besides, he'd notice a change. Any change.

Modern technology made it easy for spies to tell if anyone had touched their things.

Sometimes, they needed to tell if someone had entered the room and searched it. Sometimes, they needed to know if the false information they were trying to feed the enemy had been seen.

Cameras were easy enough for a pro to find. They had apps for that. Download a Wi-fi scanning app to your phone, and every device that connected to a network showed up. It would take a little more time to find if the device didn't connect to the Wi-Fi and stored data on a memory card instead. Still not hard.

That string, though, and the brief time the men were in their rooms told Lynx that probably the only other thing that Angel would have done was to place his suitcase and take its picture. When he got back, he'd pull up that photo and hold the camera lens over the same area until the read-out said the camera was lined up identically to when the photo was first taken, then it would show the present image as a ghost. If the suitcase had moved even a millimeter, the app would flag the object as having been moved.

Fascinating stuff.

But it meant that Lynx couldn't dig through his bag.

Lynx held her hand over the case. It contained her husband's things. Mundane things. His underwear and socks. The deodorant that kept him from having B.O. A toothbrush and paste. Anti-diarrheal and his daily vitamins. The things that mortals used.

Not *an* angel. *The* Angel.

A man who risked his life daily to protect the vulnerable.

Lynx let her jaw drop as she exhaled.

This whole situation was a mindfuck.

Her phone rang, not buzzed. She looked at the screen, Striker. "Hello?" Lynx gasped into the phone. "Are you okay?"

"FUBAR, Chica. We got here, went through the wedding, paid the ransom, and returned the guy to his family."

"Saadiq? Is Saadiq, okay?"

"He's not here. They handed us a British journalist."

"What?"

"Rupert Shaw."

"Shaw?" Lynx put her hand on her forehead. "He disappeared over a year ago. Auralia knows him. They worked on a project together." And Auralia had told Lynx to be here now. So very interesting the connectivity of things.

"He's found," Striker said. "We're going to need a military medic to pick Rupert up. We don't want to get too far away from this area until we can track down Saadiq."

"What happened?" Lynx asked. "I'm confused."

"So is everyone else. Except for the people who have Saadiq, I guess."

"What does Rupert say?"

"Nothing. He's not in good shape mentally."

"I'm so sorry. So, when they gave you Rupert instead of Saadiq, you let Mahmoon have his son?"

"What would we do with him?" Striker asked.

"Nothing, I guess. And there's the whole 'don't break the laws by kidnapping folks' to worry about. Did Deep see anything? Is there anything on the satellite feed?"

"He's working on that."

"Okay, how can I help?" she asked.

Striker took the time needed to bring Lexi up to date on what had happened and the possibility of Double Zero and Zero-One's involvement. "You're going to be in a room with Grey and Angel. Color Code has been working in this area for a very long time. I think we need to back burner the personal agenda. We need these guys to help us figure out who might have grabbed Saadiq and where they might have taken him. But most importantly, we need the biggest weapon they could wield against Saadiq removed."

"His family."

"Exactly," Striker said. "I need you and Margot to implement a plan to get Saadiq's family out of Iraq. Though, it's possible that someone already captured them." Striker went through Mahmoon's story with her so she'd have a clear picture to paint for Angel and Grey.

"Wilco." Her phone buzzed. "Deep just signaled that Angel and/or Grey are at the hotel. I'm on it. I won't let you down."

30

Striker

STRIKER WALKED TOWARD THE VEHICLES AS GATOR OPENED the door, and Wayward Son jumped down. Passing one another, Wayward Son lifted his hand and said in English, "High five."

Striker ignored the man. Spinning his finger in a loop to signal his men into the vehicles, they jumped in and drove off, with Rupert clutching a bottle of water and sobbing in the backseat of the follow truck.

"Deep for Striker. I have an update."

"Striker. Go."

"Iniquus Command reached out to both the Pentagon and the State Department. I told Command that you must stay in your area to complete your mission. An Army medic is en route to a designated village to meet you and take control of

Rupert Shaw. I've loaded the waypoint into the GPS systems."

"Striker. Copy. Do you have an ETA on their arrival?"

"I'll get that to you as soon as I know."

"Striker. Out."

Striker had a lot to process. And one of those things was the safety of Saadiq's family. With DZ's involvement, reaching out to Langley on that seemed problematic. It wasn't like Iniquus could dial up Color Code. Their contacts were all field officers and a poorly timed text ping could mess things up. On the other hand, Lexi and Margot would be right there, face-to-face with Agent John Grey.

Striker had to weigh that ask. If Lexi was unsuccessful with her mission, Command was taking control of her divorce. Things could get all kinds of messy. Messier than they were now. The personal stuff—Lexi and his relationship and his niece's current status—weren't life or death, whereas Saadiq and his family might just be in mortal danger.

"Striker for Jack. How's Rupert doing? Is he ready to talk about his experience?"

"Jack. That would be a negative. I'm considering giving him a little calm juice from my syringe to help him hold it together until he's got people to help stabilize him." Jack's voice had the mechanicalness of the AI response, meaning he spoke silently through his comms.

"Striker. Your call, Jack. But since we don't know his medical history, I'd try to hold off unless he becomes volatile. Team, you can remove your comms units. We'll speak through an open line for now."

"Sir."

After about forty minutes on the road, Strike Force pulled up in the shadow of a building on the outside of town.

Ash said, "See those two trucks in the back of the next

building over? They were at the wedding last night. Hoover and I walked past them a couple of dozen times while we were stretching our legs and keeping near camp. I watched them pull out and leave last night around twenty-two hours or so."

"Your sure?" Striker asked.

"Of the time? That's a guess. Of the trucks? Affirmative. One looks like it was in an accident, and the dent looks like my grandma. May she rest in peace. The other one had that flag sticker peeling off just like that."

Gator's voice rose over the radio. "We passed those trucks this morning. Hang on, let me look at the map." A moment later. "We were leaving our camp. And they were at the crossroads where we turned left to get to Mahmoon's."

"Striker. Gator, that looks like your granny too?"

"Gator. Nah, it's just that as we were passing, everyone looked to the right. I looked out my window to see what caught everyone's attention. All I saw was dirt. When that happened back when I was with the Marines, it meant they didn't want us to clock their faces."

Striker turned to Ash. "How about you take the two scent sources over and have a good sniff on those two vehicles? Open them up and get inside if need be. Randy and Blaze, take your weapons and watch his six."

"Wilco."

Striker got down from the cab to help keep eyes on the area. He watched Ash work with Hoover. When they finished up, Ash taped GPS units onto the undercarriage of both vehicles. While Deep could follow them on the satellite, this redundancy was important if the drivers entered a parking garage or the satellite's angle was off. In this way, the vehicles could still be tracked if their sky-eyes failed.

The team gathered.

"Striker. Deep have you got two new units on your map?"

"I do. I'm putting boxes on them for the satellite, too. Everybody drinks."

"I'm not sure how much I like my shirt tattling on me," Gator said as he reached into the cooler and tossed water bottles around.

Rupert had pulled his knees under his chin, dropped his forehead onto his knees, and cradled his water bottle against his chest.

"I used the blanket scent source and Rupert's," Ash said as he poured water into Hoover's bowl. "I got hits for both on the second truck. So, the people who had Rupert also had the guy who slept in the bed. The one that might be Saadiq."

"I wonder if we do a walkabout if we couldn't pinpoint anyone we saw at the wedding," Blaze said. "Maybe ask a few pointed questions."

Striker shook his head. "We have no leverage. If they have DZ in their corner, and DZ is watching them the way Deep is watching us, our team can end up in a black hole instead of our team finding our brother. We need to walk softly here." Striker turned to Ash. "What did Hoover say about a trail? Did either scent get out of the truck?"

"I mean," Ash brushed the sole of his boot back and forth in the dirt as he thought that one through, "it's possible. Hoover sniffed air and terrain. Neither Rupert nor scent-two got out of the truck here recently."

"How long would the scent linger in this heat?" Randy asked.

"Hard to say. The reliability of tracking decreases over time. In extreme heat like what we've got going on today along with the low humidity conditions, yeah," Ash squinted at the trucks, "the scent trail may only be detectable for a short period of time, a few hours if we were very lucky."

"Deep might be able to see the vehicles pull up on the satellite feed," Jack said, "but he won't be able to see people getting out of the vehicle. We'd need a drone overhead for that."

"If these trucks delivered Rupert to Mahmoon and picked up scent-two, came here, and then everyone jumped out and is hiding in the village, we're too late to use Hoover to track it," Ash said. "The other possibility is that they transferred scent-two at a different location." He scratched at his three-day-old beard. "So, we're back at zero."

"Here's my question, why would Rupert's kidnappers be at the wedding?" Randy asked.

"Good question." Striker leaned his hip against the door. "My guess would be that they were making a payment to Naseem in exchange for those very well-timed phoned calls. Let's sit tight here. The first step is to get Rupert to the medics."

"Deep. Striker, you have Army vehicles to your location in fifteen mikes."

"Fifteen mikes, copy." Striker used the term mikes to mean minutes.

Striker had his eye on Gator. He stood, hands bladed on his hips and his head on a swivel. While that might be reflex in this terrain, this was something different. He'd squint and tip his head. Then a shiver raked down his body.

"What've you got, Gator?" Striker asked.

"I swear I've been here before." He pointed his finger down the road. "See that shop there with them baskets hanging from the awning for sale? A couple'a doors down is a shawarma shop. Woo-whee! Was that roasted meat good. It'd like to curl your toes in ecstasy and make you think you'd gone straight on to Heaven. I'd like to go down there and get me a plate right about now."

"What happened when you were here before?" Striker asked.

Gator wrapped a hand around the nape of his neck and leaned back, seeming to gather his thoughts. "I was here with my Marine buddies. We were celebrating one of the craziest missions I've been on in my entire life."

"How's that, princess?" Blaze asked.

"This was after Fallujah, obviously. But y'all know what went on back then. The jihadis they'd be there in the American gun sights one minute, and poof, disappeared the next. And you know, it was a tunnel system that did that for them. Under the streets, around the houses, they popped up like groundhogs to hunt, then they'd slide back underground where they were safe from bullets and explosions."

"Yeah, a buddy of mine in boot joined up because he lost his brother down there," Randy said. "When the jihadists pulled out of the city, they booby-trapped the tunnels, and he stepped on a wire."

"Fallujah is forty miles west of Baghdad," Jack pointed out. "We're nowhere near there. Not stop for a shawarma close anyway."

"Nah," Gator said, "this is another system out in the middle of nothing. So we get called out because the CIA thinks they'd tracked down a high-value target. Getting to this high-value target was a fight like nothing I'd seen before."

"Why?" Jack asked. "What happened?"

"We came up on a ruin, stack of rocks, but they were guarding it good. We had to fight our way in. A lot of them fell. We were coming around the other side of the rocks, and the rest of the fighters disappeared. Poof." He mimicked a magician's gesture. "Then we found the entrance to the underground place."

"Place like a cave?"

"I don't rightly know what to call it. In the end, we got our HVT out, but a good fifty of the jihadis disappeared. We figured they were farther back than we were, but it wasn't our assignment to run them down. In, grab, and out. That's it."

"Near here?" Striker ran his thumb along his jawline.

"Near enough that when we came up from underground, we drove to the nearest town to eat."

"Tell us what you remember you saw down there," Striker said.

"It wasn't laid out at all like them tunnels in Fallujah that were kinda like an underground road system. This one, we couldn't rightly figure it out. I mean, some of my buddies thought it was ancient, and the jihadis were taking advantage of the existing structure. Others thought it was a crazy person that put it together. Best way I can describe this place to you was like one of them science experiments you see where they're trying to teach a rat."

"Set up like a maze with dead ends?" Blaze asked.

"First, it was deep underground. Pitch black. Cool even on a day when the temperatures hit a hundred and ten. Cold even, 'cause when you get that hot under the sun, and the temperature is in the sixties in the cave, it's a shock to the system. The ceiling overhead was easily eight feet tall. I didn't need to crouch in any part. It seemed the walls were carved out of rock, and they were black."

"Black?" Randy asked. "Why?"

"I'm guessing decades of soot. We all come out of there lookin' like coal miners," Gator said. "When I said this was deep underground, it started as just underground, and it seemed to get deeper and deeper the longer we were in there. Radios weren't working down there. We tried setting up a relay, leaving a man every so many yards so the radio waves could pass from one to another. But the turns were confounding. We were so deep under that the GPS was useless. And we didn't have no night-vision goggles with us. It wasn't a night raid. We couldn't see much of anything in there. It seemed to swallow our light. And I ain't gonna lie. It was spooky. There we were, rats in a maze, no idea where the cheese was hid."

"You said rats?" Striker was hard-focused.

"It's how I saw this place." Gator took a swig from his bottle. "So there we were, deaf to the outside and mostly blind. We started out using normal clearing tactics. One guy peels right, the next hooks left, but once I went into that room and searched the corners, I got turned around. We'd go through what we thought was the door we went in, but the rooms weren't square. We couldn't count walls. Five-sided, six-sided, three-sided. Sometimes a doorway on each of the walls. Sometimes there was only the one entrance. Remember how I said it was all colored black? That seemed to swallow our light. With our headlamps, it was hard to tell where the doorways were. You ended up running a hand along the walls. Time-consuming. And in the back of my head, I kept thinkin' how the tunnel system was all booby-trapped up in Fallujah. Every step I took, I was surprised I was still in one piece."

"That's nuts." Blaze leaned to the side to look into the truck and check on sleeping Rupert. "So what happened?"

"The panic set in. We tried to be quiet to surprise our mark. But after a while, trying to catch up with our squad, we were calling out. Now, we got a bunch of Marines' voices echoing around. It was like to make you crazy. No information other than up and down. No way out."

"No shawarma," Jack said.

"Which was the worst of it." Gator grinned.

"So, how did you get out and get your dinner?" Ash asked.

"I found my way back out. I think out on the bayou, where it's easy to get yourself turned around when you're out on a cloudy night, you just develop a sense for the right way to turn. I tell you, the sun was a torch that day, and I have never been that excited to be that miserable. We had posted two men at the entrance, and they were freaking out from the noises coming out of there."

"So that's when you guys left to get the shawarma?" Blaze asked.

"The guys guarding the entrance had called it into the TOC. Operations said they were sending in another squad for support. And that was something that harmed a man's reputation and honor."

"Couldn't have that," Randy said.

"Not when I found out it was the Army coming."

"Oh, shit!" Randy broke out laughing. His Army days were spent in the Rangers, and he knew exactly what would have happened if the Marines had to be rescued.

"So what I did was I loaded a pack with chemlights—then grabbed me three rolls of line, tying it off outside, right? There I am movin' through the maze. A light got thrown into each room that I went in. I tied a chemlight to the line at the door and kept movin.' First guy I saw, I handed off the chemlight duty, made me twice as fast. Second guy I saw got to carry all the crap. Fourth guy I saw followed the trail back to the exit. And so we worked until I counted off everyone in my squad. We were three dozen." Gator rubbed his stomach. "Then we all decided we were hungry and deserved something a might better than an MRE and hot water. So we came on to town."

"Wait, you were in there looking for a high-value target," Jack reminded him, "and you said the intelligence was good."

"Oh, yeah, yeah, we found him all right. He was lost in the maze. Near as we could figure, they had a group of jihadists living down there where they were safe and hidden. And they must have gone off to do some terrorist crap, and they just left him down there on his pallet. So there he were, just layin' on his mattress with a little oil lamp burning. When they told him they were taking him out, he walked along, glad to see the sun. We bought him some shawarma, then handed him over to the CIA to have a talkin' to. Later, a CIA agent came to ask us about that place. That's when they said the spookiest damned thing. The HVT said the terrorists let prisoners loose to wander around. They felt like they were free if they could just find the exit, and they could never ever find the exit. That he had been left there with a bunch of water and MREs, and he'd gather 'em up and carry 'em along, spending days searching with their little oil lamp. The terrorists would find him and lead them back to their section of the maze and laugh like that was their big entertainment."

"Can you imagine?" Blaze asked. "It had to be torturous to think you're free and yet be held prisoner. So much easier when you were in a cell with bars, and you knew that that's where you were. A shitty head game."

"The CIA knew all about that place?" Randy tipped his head toward the vehicle. They could see Rupert's red hair mashed up against the window as he slept. "You think that's where they put Rupert? You think that's why his skin and eyes look like they do? Why he's having trouble processing?"

"I hope we can find out," Striker said. "Remember when we came in from New York, and Lynx was standing in the parking lot with 'the look.'" He used quote fingers.

Ash glanced back and forth as his teammates nodded. He wasn't looped in.

Striker wasn't about to try to explain it to him. "Yeah, well, she's been having a series of dreams about something in tunnels."

"Shit," Randy said. "How bad was it? Like aliens from outer space with mile-long tongues kind of something?"

"Nothing that spectacular." Striker grinned. "She said maybe voles."

"Voles have weak eyesight. They can't see. Don't need to when they're underground," Randy said.

"Here comes the Army." Striker pointed toward the road. "Gentlemen, if we can find this black hole of a cave maze, I think it warrants our checking it out." He turned back to Gator. "Any chance you can find it on a map?"

"It wasn't visible on a satellite image," Gator said. "It wasn't on any map. Could I pinpoint it in a stretch of desert? To be honest, I don't think so."

"Fine," Striker said. "Plan B, then."

31

Striker

Sunday

"We're sliding right past Plan A?" Jack asked.

"'A' was using a map." Striker squinted toward the road. "Deep, you with me?"

"I'm here. Is the medic on scene?"

Striker leaned to the side. "I can see them coming up the road. Before they get here, you have us pinpointed on the map?"

"I do," Deep said. "I also have your vitals up. All of you need another bottle of water."

Striker called out. "More water, everyone."

Blaze went to the cooler and started tossing bottles to the teammates.

After quickly bringing Deep up to speed on Gator's

adventures underground, he asked, "Can you see anything on the satellite?"

"I can task the AI system to do a search. Give me a second. Let's make it a grid from outside of Baghdad-proper down past you to Naseem's compound. Give it a minute to churn. How's Rupert doing?"

"He's asleep in the vehicle with air conditioning on high," Striker said. "He wouldn't drink from his bottle, so Jack put an IV of saline in his arm on slow drip because we know how you like to keep everyone moist."

"That's my job. And the AI system isn't finding any entrances to underground bunkers. I can contact JASOC. If Gator can give me as many details as possible, they might be willing to give me the coordinates."

"Let's make that our Plan C. Most everyone at the Pentagon has gone home for the day."

"You were saying there's a Plan B?" Deep asked.

"There's always a Plan B. Can you call Dr. Sophia Abadi? She's got use of Geographical Imaging Systems-based space archaeology to make archaeological finds. With GIS, she can look at the images and get an idea of where ancient peoples had towns, now covered over by land and new buildings. She might be able to spot this thing."

"Yeah, man." Deep sounded hesitant, "Brainiack hates it when we involve Sophia in any of our doings at Iniquus. He doesn't want her caught up in anything that will direct any more stress into her life."

"Okay, that's Brainiack, and he's entitled to his opinions. I'm more interested in knowing what Sophia thinks. She doesn't seem to mind when Lexi works with her."

"Sophia doesn't seem to mind," Deep agreed. "Her thing is saving people and ancient artifacts."

"I get Brainiack's point. I really do. Sophia went through

a hell of a lot. I'm not interested in burdening her. But I can't imagine how this could endanger her in any way. She's looking at a map and reading off a coordinate. She does more dangerous things while she's drinking her first cup of coffee for the day. So why don't you call her and see if she's available or even has the time or interest in helping? If she says no, we move on to Plan C and JSOC. If yes, I'll tell Brainiack what we asked and why we asked. And he can share his feelings with me."

Deep laughed.

"I want there to be zero pressure on Sophia to do this," Striker said. "But if she's able, that might save us a lot of time, and—I'm saying this between you and me, not to Sophia—time may be of the essence."

"Panthers are in Madagascar. So it'll be a while before you have that convo with Brainiack. Do you need anything else while I'm on the line?"

"I'll be back in touch. Medics are here. Out." Striker moved forward to introduce himself to their lead.

After shaking hands, Striker brought them to the armored vehicle. Rupert slept, pressed against the window. Striker opened the front door to rouse the man from his sleep so the medic team could get to Rupert for their checks.

A groggy Rupert sat up, looking around in bewilderment. The vehicle doors stood open wide as the air conditioning continued to blast cold.

The medics introduced themselves as "here to help you" instead of actual names, while their leader accepted the page where Jack had been documenting Rupert's vital signs and interventions taken to make Rupert comfortable.

Rupert seemed to come around as they did their own assessment and became a bit more lucid.

Striker pulled the lead away and explained the need for

what intel they could gather, and finding Rupert stable, the medics all took a step back.

Striker sat sideways in the front seat, twisting around so he was face to face with Rupert, but he had the barrier between them. "Rupert," Striker began.

"I'm Rupert. Rupert Shaw."

"That's correct," Striker said evenly.

"I'm English."

Striker smiled. "That's correct.

"Your American."

"American." Striker pointed at himself. "From Washington, D.C."

"But you're taking me home to my family now." Rupert clenched his hands at his chest, rocking back and forth to self-soothe. "I'm going home?"

"Yes. That's right. Home to your family. Rupert," Striker said, holding up his phone with Saadiq's picture, "do you recognize seeing this man yesterday?"

"I don't know." Rupert's voice was raspy. "I was rather blind there for a bit. I had been put into this very dark place."

"How long were you in that dark place?" Striker kept his voice gentle.

"Hard to tell. I had no night or day. I had food and water. I had a waste bucket, and I had someone who came in with a glow stick to resupply me. I tried to count how many times they came, but my body rhythms were off. Did they come twice a day? Every three days? I tried to count meals, but I wasn't hungry. So did I eat three times a day, or did I eat once a week? I have no idea. I can't tell you how disoriented I became in the dark without the clues that even a profoundly blind person would have—an alarm to wake up in the morning. Voices. A calendar. Expectations. Goals."

"Do you have any idea how you got to the dark place?" Striker asked.

"None at all. I was at my hotel. I ordered room service and woke up sitting on a sleeping pad in the dark."

That wasn't a normal terrorist MO. "What did you discover about your environment? What was the floor like? The walls?"

"Dirt and rock. Tall, I couldn't reach the ceiling even when I jumped."

"You were able to jump?" Striker was checking if Gator's account and Rupert's lined up.

"I wasn't tied up or anything, but I knew I wasn't being physically hurt in that space. Food and water showed up. I was always taught to stick with my vehicle if you were lost because that's how I'd be found, and in there, I was nothing if not lost. My cousin, Cliff, died because his canoe flipped over. Instead of swimming up next to his brother, he turned and swam down. His brother, my other cousin, was almost out of air, so he had to get to the surface. By the time he got back down to turn Cliff around, Cliff had drowned." Rupert continued to rock. And now his teeth chattered, making it harder to understand what he was saying. "Surely, the British government was looking for me, right? I thought I should stay put. I think it's been a few months, though. Five? Maybe six? How long was I gone?

"Eighteen months," Striker said softly as if trying to ease the blow.

"What?" Rupert thrashed out in agitation. "What are you saying to me now?"

The medic stepped forward. And Jack gestured for him to wait.

"I've lost a year and a half in the dark sitting like a monkey on my haunches?

"I'm sorry to press you," Striker said. "We believe that our friend was traded for you. We think that his captors took him to this dark place. Can you tell us anything to help us track him down?"

The startled look on Rupert's face turned to terror.

"Rupert, listen to me. The medic standing right there has come to take you to the American base. We're not trying to trade you back. You're on your way home." Striker swept his arm to take in the Iniquus operators. "My team just needs to know where to go and look. When you *left* the dark place, what was that like?"

Rupert nodded. Swallowed. Seemed to wrestle himself into control to help another human from experiencing the fate from which he'd just found release.

"I remember sitting on a sleeping pad. The food man came with some others. Three of them, I think. They had a light." He wagged an open palm in front of his face. "I couldn't properly see. My vision… They put a bag over my head, and then with someone holding either arm, they led me. It was a gentle leading. They weren't trying to harm me. But they never said a word. It took a while, but, as I've explained, my time frames are askew."

"You walked in a straight line?" Striker asked.

"No, we turned ninety degrees, then several paces and another turn. Always turning."

"What else did you notice?" Having fought in mines before, Striker had a sense of the disorientation and claustrophobia that could be felt under such circumstances, and that was with night vision goggles. What would it have been like with no light at all? This would explain the strange color of Rupert's skin.

"I was winded. And I know that's probably because I had no exercise in." He shook his head in disbelief. "*Eighteen* months? I was winded from the walk. But also, it felt to me like I wasn't walking flat. It was rather like going up a gentle slope. It was the same in the space where I stayed. One end of the room was slightly higher than the other. I could go to the top of the space—there was a kind of entryway without a door—and could lay a water bottle on its side, and it would roll down to the back wall. I amused myself in that way."

"They had the hood over your head. You walked through the turns, then what?" Striker asked.

"I was in a vehicle, and we were driving."

Striker rested his hand on the back of the headrest. "Still with the hood?

"Yes. They took it off when we got to the compound. When they pulled the hood off, I could see the basic geometric shapes of the buildings, but my eyes were quite weak. All of that movement to get to that compound, all of the anxiety from moving to that place, I was exhausted to the point that I couldn't speak."

"Who cut your hair?" Jack asked from beside Striker.

Rupert turned his way, "Excuse me? What?"

"If you were gone for eighteen months, somehow your hair and beard were cut."

Rupert put his hand on his head. "Yes, a man in my room did that. He was very kind. But the emotional exhaustion and my lack of clear sight. I didn't speak to him. He spoke to me, though. He called me Chris. He said he had to call me something, and I looked like a Chris." He put his hand to his chest. "I'm Rupert Shaw."

"Yes, you are," Striker said. "And you're going home, Rupert. It was an honor to bring you this far. Thank you for your information."

And with that, Rupert covered his face with his hands and sobbed. "Rupert Shaw. Going home."

As the medic walked Rupert to their ambulance, Striker looked over to Gator. "Sound like it could be the place?"

"I don't know of any other place like that in this area," Gator said. "And the ones like they have in Falluja are all monitored by the police. I think there's a good chance they put Saadiq underground."

32

Lexi

LYNX'S NERVES FIRED AS SHE HEARD THE MURMUR OF TWO men's voices approaching the door. She felt her heart clutch when there was a swipe of the key card.

There was the sudden illumination as, with the press of a button, the lights turned on.

A pause, then Angel's voice, "Just checking." He opened the bathroom door; the light clicked on. "Do you think we should be worried that she isn't at her hotel?" he asked as the light clicked off.

"I don't think so." That was definitely Grey's voice—he sounded tired. "Airlines being what they are. She's not working in Afghanistan anymore. They kicked all the female NGOs and foreign workers out."

"All the better for us," Angel called. "Once she's got her Iraqi contacts back in place, it'll be gold."

Lynx sat very still in the hotel's occasional chair that had rested in the shadowy corner. But now, with the lamp lit, it shined down on her lap as if she were a traveler enjoying an evening's read. Next time, she'd remember to unscrew the lightbulb or unplug the lamp from the wall to maintain control.

Grey was the first one in sight. He stood as if frozen in time and space, staring at her. Then he cleared his throat and turned to Angel. "You have a visitor." And back to Lynx, "How do you do, Mrs. Sobado."

"A little weary, to be honest, Mr. Grey. It's been a long and tedious journey."

Angel stalked into the room, blinked at her, then shook his head. "How did you find me?"

"Hello to you, too." The nerves had fallen away now that the point she had dreaded—coming into each other's sphere for the first time since she saved him in Syria almost two years ago—was over. "How could I *not* find you is probably an easier question to answer. How about you cut the ties that bind, and this won't keep happening for you?" She angled her chin. "But actually, I'm here for Grey."

Grey sat on the lowboy. "Langley sent you?"

"They did not," Lynx said, trying to figure out the best way to approach the subject.

"You're in Angel's hotel room," Grey pointed out. "Not mine."

She lifted her hands and brought them down on the arms of her chair, pressing herself to stand. "Plans change. I don't have time for this. To be honest with you, we have a clock ticking." Lynx walked closer so she wasn't projecting her voice across the room.

The two men huddled up as she explained the timeline from when Saadiq handed Striker his family's documentation a month ago to the Iniquus call from Saadiq, the negotiation done by Honey, the ransom, the trade, and the Rupert surprise.

"Rupert Shaw, the journalist that disappeared?" He turned to Angel. "—year and a half ago?" He pulled out his phone and texted someone.

Lynx was both alarmed and curious about what he'd sent and to whom, but there was nothing she could do about his actions, done deal.

"The general said it was like a shell game, and so it continues. We don't know who has Saadiq, though we have a good guess."

Grey's phone rang. He checked the screen, held up a finger as a sign for one minute, then disappeared into the bathroom. The spray of water in the sink drowned the sound of his words.

Lynx turned to Angel. "Divorce papers?"

"Problematic," Angel answered.

"Obviously. Let's take care of that problem."

Angel said nothing.

"Angel?" She brought her brows up as she lowered her chin.

"I have superiors."

She crossed her arms over her chest. "You're a smart guy. Navigate them."

Grey came bursting out of the bathroom.

"What did they say?" Angel asked.

"There's another CIA working group involved—"

"Double Zero, from the Numbers Group," Lynx turned to Grey, finishing his sentence.

"You know about them?" Grey stared at her unblinking,

then shook his head to release himself from whatever thought-trance that had sucked him in. "Okay." He looked from Lynx to Angel. "Okay. DZ lost contact with Saadiq after he had accompanied them on a mission as their interpreter. That was roughly a month ago. They've been looking for Saadiq ever since. DZ finally tracked him down to a family compound south of Baghdad a couple of days ago. Where in that compound they didn't know, they approached the patriarch, hoping to offer him something in exchange for Saadiq."

"Why do they want him?" Angel asked.

"I'm being told that they need to be sure he is still functioning as a free agent and that terrorists haven't captured him."

"Do you believe that?" Lynx asked.

"My belief or disbelief doesn't really play a role here," Grey said. "Langley would like to make sure that Saadiq is safe. And they have authorized me to work with Iniquus in any capacity necessary to ensure that Saadiq isn't endangered. Now, to continue with my information on Double Zero. The patriarch told DZ that Iniquus was en route the next day and would take control of Saadiq. An agreement negotiated, the patriarch said he would not change the deal. DZ thanked him and left. Langley confirmed with Iniquus that this was an accurate picture. As far as they were concerned, Iniquus became responsible for Saadiq's safety. That Saadiq is back in the wind is—it's—"

"Problematic?" Angel asked.

Lynx sent him an arched brow.

"It doesn't line up with Iniquus' experience and the sudden appearance of Rupert Shaw, now does it?" Angel asked.

Lexi moved over to the chair and sat. "I have a theory."

"I told you," Angel said to Grey.

"What's that?" Lynx leaned back and crossed her legs.

Grey said, "Angel has told me about you over the years, and one of your many attributes is that you're a theory generator."

"Well, there are worse things, I guess." Lynx smiled at Angel. "So, Grey, you're telling me Double Zero lost sight of Saadiq after their mission, they spent the last month tracking him down, found him at Mahmoon's—that's the patriarch of the compound's name—and left without Saadiq in tow?" Lynx felt her phone buzz and pulled it from her pants pocket. "I guess that could be the case. But it occurs to me that isn't how things panned out." Lynx read Deep's text: "Rupert Shaw's last journalistic assignment was to follow Zero-One assets from Afghanistan to Iraq to find out why they made the move."

As both men sidled over to the bed to sit across from Lynx, she tapped her voice-to-text button to record and send her thoughts to Deep so he could get them to Strike Force.

"Why would Zero-One go to Iraq?" Angel asked, looking at Lynx for an explanation.

"Are you asking for me to guess?" Lynx asked. "I'm nothing if not a theory generator."

"That was meant as a compliment," Angel said.

Grey held a hand between them. "Okay, you two, I know there's baggage, but let's focus on this issue, please."

"Fine." Lynx folded her hands in her lap, glancing down to make sure that the app transcribed her information. "I'm glad to share my thoughts. Ready?" When the men nodded, she continued. "Numbers spent a lot of time vetting and training a group named Zero-One in Afghanistan. These men worked as black ops for CIA Numbers and did extremely helpful things for Uncle Sam and also extremely bad things. When the US left Afghanistan, and we no longer had a presence there, everyone who helped America along the way became a potential target. We know how that's turned out for our allies in Iraq, right? Like Saadiq, these men have essential information about how US Special Forces work. With that knowledge, terrorist groups can be that much more effective. What do Numbers do with these men? Why not move them to Iraq, give them some language skills, and use them here for the same purpose, using their training to stifle terrorism? We do have a presence here. As we speak, the Army medics are packaging Rupert for his trip back to the base."

"If Zero-One exists in Iraq," Grey said, "I'm not aware of that program."

"Why would you be?" Lynx asked.

Grey nodded his agreement. Projects were classified for a reason.

"Based on the story I told you about Iniquus' involvement on this mission, the puzzle pieces *can* fit together," Lexi continued. "Let me paint a hypothetical picture for you. Rupert is tracking Zero-One. DZ doesn't like it and disappears Rupert. Doesn't kill him, black holes him. Why? Because they can't let this project come to light, but Langley isn't signing off on the murder of an ally's reporter. If that became widely known, imagine the fallout. That was eighteen months ago. A month ago, DZ hired Saadiq to accompany them on a mission. Something about that mission freaks Saadiq out, and he runs. Many of our interpreters, who found themselves left behind without visas for themselves and their families, tried to set up safety nets of safe houses should they become terrorist targets. We can assume that someone as smart as Saadiq, who has run with special forces and intelligence for two decades, would have that in place. Off he goes. DZ tracks him to Mahmoon's to get him back. Mahmoon won't give him up freely. DZ doesn't want blowback and doesn't have the same freedom to do whatever they want whenever they want as they had in a war zone. They leave."

Grey scrubs his hands down his face. "Oh shit."

Lynx gave him a nod; he was getting it. "DZ got information from Mahmoon. They learned about the wedding and prisoner exchange. Maybe, they even know about the ransom that Iniquus was paying. And from that, DZ would also know that Naseem—the name of the man collecting the ransom for Mahmoon's son—was probably not a very honest man and might well enjoy a way to get some easy cash."

"They didn't have Saadiq," Grey said. "Mahmoon did, right?"

"That's right," Lynx clarified. "My guess is that Zero-One —the Afghans—went to the wedding and offered money to Naseem in exchange for phone calls from Naseem to DZ with information about Iniquus' movements and Mahmoon with a scripted communication."

"Why do you think it was Zero-One?" Angel asked.

"Because Striker said that Mahmoon knew the men weren't Iraqi because of their strong accents and suggested that he thought the men might have been from Afghanistan."

"Right," Grey said. "And they know this will blow up bigger if Strike Force isn't given someone of value. They can't just pull their stealth act and take Saadiq."

"That and they don't know where Saadiq is within the compound," Lynx added. "DZ knows they have an ace up their sleeve. They pull Rupert Shaw from his black hole and make the trade, knowing that Rupert Shaw is addled and has no idea who took him from his hotel room or put him back on the grid at Mahmoon's compound. Anyway, that's how this makes sense to me. And if that's true, Rupert had to have been held somewhere fairly close. And if *that's* true, it might just be that Saadiq has replaced Rupert in the hole. And if *that's* true, and Saadiq is uncooperative or is threatening them in some way—"

"DZ will be going to get his family." Angel leaned forward, looking at the floor, thinking. After a moment, he turned to Grey. "Because they are under CIA protective status—"

"Langley has a record of the safe houses and who is in them," Grey continued. "It is very possible that DZ has that information, and they're on their way to collect the family now."

"Exactly" Lynx swiped a finger through the air. "Before we can possibly get there. Grey, these are Color Code people protecting Saadiq's family, right?"

"Yes, that's right."

"Can you have your gatekeeper secretly move the family to a hotel and then have that agent take their own vacation, so they can't be found and questioned until Saadiq and his family have all been accounted for?" Lynx reached down to tap the send arrow, knowing that Deep would have her information and know what to do next.

33

Lexi

GREY WAS BACK IN THE BATHROOM WITH THE DOOR SHUT AND the faucet running.

While he was in there, Lynx texted Margot to come to Angel's room. When her phone rang, she swiped it immediately. "Yeah, hi."

"Striker. Checking progress."

"I'm in Angel's room with him and Grey. I'm waiting on Margot to get here."

Angel flung himself around to glare at her, spreading his information around so freely. Lynx ignored him. If he had followed through, she wouldn't be here. This was completely on him.

"Sorry, Chica." Voices from nearby murmured in the background. "Hold for a second."

Lynx truly believed in odd twists to timelines to line things up the way they were supposed to be. That she and Margot were an hour and a half flight to Baghdad to be helpful, yeah, that felt like the hand of the universe moving known pieces around the board.

Just like when a stalker's attack brought her into Striker's life wasn't her druther but had been the silver lining, just as being kidnapped and held in a foreign prison was torturous but probably saved her life. When viewed in a rearview mirror, major shifts in her life were bad but better than the alternatives. And it was an interesting thought experiment. Could it be that Angel's recalcitrance when it came to their divorce was there to play a role in "right place, right time"?

As Striker had said when they were talking before they flew off on their missions, the interesting thing about decisions is one can never know the ramifications of making other choices. That left one with making their best, most ethical moves, and then accepting what happens. It meant putting another foot forward, then another, and another.

"Chica?"

"Here."

"Sorry about that. The medic is getting ready to head back to base, and they needed to have me sign off on some paperwork."

"Do you need to call me back?"

"Jack's handling it," Striker said. "You said that you're with Angel and Grey? Did you bring them up to speed?"

"They understand the stakes. Grey is in the bathroom with the water running. So, he's either trying to wash his hands of this mess, or he's got logistics to work out. I think he's getting the family moved from the safe house, so if DZ shows up, they won't be available."

"Good. Thank you."

"You're turning your attention to the hunt for Saadiq?" Lynx asked.

"Unless Grey says that DZ already has Saadiq in hand. And even then, we need some assurance that he's safe and acting on free will."

"Oh, wow."

"Iniquus Command is already trying to get that information from Langley." There was a beep-beep, then the rumbling sound of an engine in the background on Striker's end. "The CIA is aware that we're in play and working toward the same goal, making sure Saadiq is safe. But I'm not sure they will tell us the truth. I'm hoping that since Color Code has a hand in this pot, they can get the information."

"Grey contacted Langley." Lynx slid her hand over the phone and angled her chin up. "All Iniquus calls are encrypted end to end." As she turned back to her conversation with Striker, she saw the muscles in Angel's jaw visibly release their tension. "They were under the impression that Iniquus had Saadiq in hand. I guess DZ is either not keeping up with their paperwork or they don't need to report in. Any ideas where to go next?"

"There are two vehicles here that we recognize from the wedding at Naseem's. Ash and Hoover gave the trucks a sniff test. Rupert and someone's scent that likely is associated with Saadiq were in one of them at one time."

"That's a pretty broad statement."

"And all we have." Striker's voice was professional and steady, as usual. "Question for you. *Three Blind Mice*?"

Lynx rounded over to put her elbows on her knees, tucking her head so she could concentrate better. "I have nothing more than I had before."

"Dreams of voles?" Lynx could tell that this was not a conversation that Striker wanted to have. Something was up.

Lynx thought *Three Blind Mice,* but when she opened her mouth to tell Striker that it had morphed into a "knowing," doing that felt wrong. Instead, she said, "Voles? Affirmative. All night long. I felt so cold and dirty that I longed for a shower when I woke up. But I was on the plane. I just haven't had a chance to settle in my room yet. From the minute we stepped into the hotel, I've been in go mode."

"Sorry."

She smiled at the warmth of his voice. "Oh, a little dream-land imaginary dirt never hurt anyone."

"Another question," Striker said, again with that friction of hesitation. "What comes to mind when I say Gator Aid Rochambeau and voles in the same sentence?"

Lynx let the words brush into her awareness. She closed her eyes, saying, "If I were him? It smells dank. The air around me is stale. I'm instantly dizzy and disoriented. There's a mild sense of panic in my gut. The sensation is growing, and I want to talk myself down. What I'd imagine he'd say is, 'Now, come on. How many times have you been lost in the swamps on a moonless night and found yourself back by the fire by breakfast?'"

"Good. That's exactly right. Now let me say another name. What comes to mind when I say Saadiq and voles?"

"Oh, wow. I… I wish…" Lynx got sensations, but she didn't understand them. They weren't part of an image vocabulary she was familiar with. "I don't know the man in any sense beyond what I learned in mission development."

"Because you know Gator so well in the ether, is that why you were able to do the first part of that?" Striker asked.

"Probably." She lifted her palm to form a rest for her head. "I'm going to reflect on this and see what I can get."

"No, you're not," Striker countered. "I mean, *please*

don't. I don't want you psychically attached to any of this. None of it. Will you promise me?"

"I already have. We all agreed I stay out of the ether unless I'm protecting myself or a loved one."

"Right. Thank you. But if you were to take a nap and wake up with an 'ah-ha!' we wouldn't mind hearing about it." Now there was a smile in his voice. "Got to go. I love you."

When Lynx swiped her phone closed, Angel twisted in his seat to look her in the eyes. "What's this about voles?" he demanded.

Grey's reappearance from the bathroom saved her from the need to answer.

"Lynx, did you come here on a mission to bring Saadiq's family out of Iraq?" Grey asked as he strode farther into the room. Stress was a crease across his forehead.

"No, as I told you, I came here to talk to Angel." She tipped her head in Angel's direction. "That I happened to be in the same place same time with a member of Color Code is helpful if not serendipitous."

There was a knock, and both men swung their gaze from the door to Lynx.

"That's probably Margot. She's partnered with me on this mission. Ex-CIA, by the way," Lynx said as Angel went to the door.

Grey leaned in. "What mission is that?"

"Mission Divorce Signature. Iniquus legal is done play-ing. They feel that my ongoing marriage to a dead guy is detrimental to their business model and insist that Angel and I arrive at a resolution. That resolution is that I am no longer married to a poltergeist."

"Iniquus hunted Angel down?" Grey's voice rasped as his eyes held unblinking.

"If true, would that startle you?" she asked.

"Absolutely. That would…" Grey leaned forward, his body banded. Posturing to intimidate was a side of Grey that Lynx had never seen before. "How did Iniquus do that?" His voice was gravelly with an implied threat. That tone was a shocking switch from Grey's usual professionally comfortable countenance.

Lynx offered Grey a smile, then stood as Margot moved ahead of Angel into the room. "I didn't say they did," she said for Grey's ears only.

"I got your text saying that I should come up." Margot was smooth as silk. No signs that this was never the plan. "How can I help?"

"Strike Force is in Iraq, and the exchange didn't go as planned." Lynx got up, gestured toward her chair, and sat on Angel's bed.

Margot held out her hand to Grey. "Margot."

Grey shook. "John Grey."

Margot then extended her hand to Angel. Angel shook it with a "Glad to meet you, Margot," but he didn't offer his name. *Interesting.*

"The team was given Rupert Shaw instead," Lynx continued.

Margot adjusted herself in the seat. "The missing British reporter?"

"Exactly. Strike Force is handing Shaw off to an Army medic unit as we speak. They'll take him back to the American base. Strike Force feels that, as things are going sideways, this is a dangerous inflection point for Saadiq's family."

"Why is that?" Margot turned to Grey, then back to Lynx. "My understanding is that Color Code has the family in a safe house."

"Saadiq, too, was in a safe house," Lynx said. "And then

he became the hidden treat in a shell game. When Strike Force showed up to make the prisoner exchange—for lack of a more precise word—Strike Force found out Saadiq was gone. Saadiq's kidnappers offered Rupert Shaw to our team as a consolation prize. This is fortunate for Rupert and those who love him, but that leaves Saadiq in the wind." She pinned her gaze on Grey. "If intelligence is that gossamer in this region, we can't assume that Saadiq's family is safe. If the person holding Saadiq was also able to capture Saadiq's family, it's game over with the intel. As you already know."

"And who has Saadiq now?" Margot asked. "Does anyone know?"

Lynx glanced down at her phone to read the text that just pinged from Deep. Her head came back up. "Whoever it is that has Saadiq declared to his captors that they were there to take custody of Saadiq at the behest of Strike Force. They had the players' names, the places, and the times. So not your run-of-the-mill terrorist. At this point, our conclusion is that the shuffle organizer in the shell game was Double Zero."

"The CIA? That would be a good thing," she turned to look at Grey, "wouldn't it?"

"As Lynx indicated," Grey said, his voice tight, "that's the working model of what's happening."

"Working model," Margot repeated. "Do you have a working *plan*?"

Lynx waggled her phone. "Iniquus Logistics needs Saadiq's family brought to the American base by tonight. From there, they will get the family rehoused in a different country. Iniquus will take control of their security. Times ticking."

"Langley agreed to this?" Grey asked.

"Doubtful," Lynx said. "But again, you have the power to ask."

Grey worked his jaw as he looked from Margot to Lynx.

Margot had zero idea what was going on, but she was sitting there, looking like she was placidly holding her cards to the chest as the possessor of every detail. Lynx was taking mental notes.

Lynx decided that she needed to make a play to keep Margot and her not only in the loop but eyes-on, so they'd know what was going down in real-time. "When Saadiq gave Striker his family's documents, Saadiq told Striker that his family of women, who only spoke Arabic, were unwilling to go by themselves to a foreign country. And as they surely wouldn't go with men when the head of their family is not with them, it's very good that Margot and I are here. Women with Arabic skills willing to escort them." She held up jazz hands. "Serendipity."

Grey dragged his phone from his pocket as he stood. He caught Angel's eye and held it in silent communication, then he moved into Angel's bathroom, shut the door, and turned on the faucet again.

If they were going to be working as a team, Margot needed to know everyone's name. Lynx weighed an introduction to Angel, then decided she wasn't making things easy on him anymore. It might be her circus, but he was no longer her monkey. "Margot, this is my husband, Angel Sobado." She gestured in his direction. "Not, in fact, a ghost."

Margot turned her focus on him. "Well, there's a surprise," she said without any surprise in her voice at all. Then she added, "I always thought you'd be taller."

Angel turned a glare on Lynx.

She popped her eyebrows to let him know for sure that she was done playing. "I'm sorry. Did you think I hunted you all the way to Jordan because I missed your charm?"

"This is a dangerous—"

"Game. Yeah, yeah." Lynx swiped the air with her hand in dismissal. Anger simmered in the pit of her stomach, but this was not the time. Her mission had shifted at Commander Striker Rheas' request.

Right now, she wasn't here for Angel. She was here for the man striding out of the bathroom with his phone to his ear. "Grey here. Look, I need four tickets to Baghdad ASAP. We're an hour away from Amman. We're on the road now. Find me tickets on the next plane out."

Lynx and Margot stood.

As he swiped to close the call, he caught Lynx's eye. "You can bring Margot up to date as we move forward. Langley wants Saadiq's family out of Iraq, which is now my mission as a Color Code agent. We do not have a contract with Iniquus, but there's no reason to be working against each other. I would greatly appreciate it if you and Margot joined me."

"I will," Lynx said, looking toward Margot.

Margot turned from Lynx to Grey. "I'll call Iniquus Command for my orders but assume I'm on board, and I'll act *as if* unless and until I'm told to stand down."

"Good enough. Grab your things and meet me in the lobby." Grey extended his pointer finger and swept it across the three others. He turned away from them, shoving his phone back in his pocket, then grabbed the handle to jerk the door wide and was gone.

Margot looked at Lynx as they both stood to leave. "Good thing I haven't unpacked." She turned to Angel. "Good thing you didn't either."

Lynx stood and headed out the door, impressed that on the way into the room, Margot had seen Angel's bag resting on the luggage support in the closet with the airline tape across the clasp, meaning no one had opened the case since his last flight. Subtly observant.

Lynx was glad to have someone with Margot's background allied with her.

Working with Grey and Angel alone always felt like she was tiptoeing through a minefield.

34

Saadiq

Sunday

Cold, Saadiq thought as he roused himself from blank to aware.

The cold squeezed him until his bones ached.

He remembered being in the crate hidden amongst the vegetables as the truck rumbled through the night to his safe house. His protectors gently turned the box over, and he had imagined himself as a turtle, helpless on his back. Kind hands had stretched him. And he had eaten the food that tasted of motherly love.

He remembered turning out the solar lamp and falling almost instantaneously into a nightmare.

It must have been a nightmare with the shaggy giant and the strange rooms decorated in his confusion.

He was lying on the thin bed roll, hidden behind bags of

onions and apples. As he peeked from the slit in his eyelashes, he could just make out their form in the dim pink light.

Pink…

Maybe his protectors would come soon. It would be nice to talk to another human being, for them to take a moment and help him to reorient himself.

Saadiq felt the echoing ache of his joints. He often felt this way now. Decades of physical abuse from trying to keep up with the men running and gunning. The uber-dedicated. The mountain goats. The gazelles.

And these aches were his old friends that greeted him in the morning. It had to be morning. Maybe that explained the pink…

Right now, more than anything, Saadiq missed his wife, Zahra. Her soft round body was warm and smelled of cooking spices. Sleeping with her was comforting. Her smile settled his soul. If he were lying with her in their bed, he wouldn't feel the hard floor bruising his hip bone or the cold stone sucking at his body heat.

But she was off with the rest of his tiny family. Hidden by the Color Code, the only CIA agents that he trusted anymore. They were the only group that Saadiq knew that had safehouses dappling Iraq. He would leave her to try to get a bite out of the carrot Double Zero dangled in front of him, the visas. He needed his family to be safe now and in the future.

He liked to think of Zahra with her long black hair splayed across the pillow, how her face softened when she slept. And how she had begun to gently snore at night.

That last morning in their marital bed had been a lovely memory.

That morning, too, had been pink.

He lay there and wondered about his decisions over the

last years. How would life have been different if he didn't accept one contract after another from the American government?

Maybe he should have contacted Iniquus earlier, should have called his friends, and sought their counsel, Colonel Grant or Striker Rheas. Striker was astonished when they ran into each other in Baghdad. Striker had been sure that he was living the good life in America.

Not so.

Saadiq had about a dozen Iniquus names in his phone. Men whose lives he had helped save time and time again. Names that he knew he could count on because he'd seen their ethos in the field. They believed in no man left behind. They *believed* he was one of their team. He, in his heart, had been their brother. He'd proven this with his mind and body.

And now his body ached.

Where would he be now if he had called Striker or one of his other friends earlier? Certainly, without his Zahra. And without his wife, he would not have his daughter. Yes, looking back, he had made good decisions. He had been in the right place to fall in love, and that was worth any torment that he'd been experiencing this last month.

"What is this stench?" he wondered. It reminded him of something he'd smelled recently.

When he awoke from this dream, he should find Striker had arrived. Wait. Was that part of his dream, or did someone truly say they were taking Saadiq to meet Striker? Was Striker in the plane, flying to Iraq, coming to help him?

That stench...

The cold.

Saadiq tried to pull his legs up into fetal position to keep his body heat in. But his legs wouldn't respond. Not paralysis, he could feel them, could feel the rough weave of the sleeping pad beneath his feet.

He reached for a cover, but his arms didn't move.

Blinking, he looked at his sleeve and traced it down to his hand.

Another blink, and he could make out the shape and color of a pink chemlight lying across his fingers.

Saadiq breathed in again and remembered the stench of Chris before he was sheared and washed.

Adrenaline and panic washed through his veins and bloomed like a hothouse flower across his chest. The sweat that coated his skin cooled his temperature more. And though he couldn't move, he trembled.

Saadiq forced himself to focus on the chemlight and trace the glow to the edge where it lapped at the darkness beyond. He was able to make out the color brown. Soon, he was able to define the shape as a corner piled with old cardboard on the floor and up the sides in a triangular form, imprinted with the silhouette of a man.

And now, the last few days flooded back to him. The confusion of where he was and his status. The phone call to Iniquus. Chris. Then the smiling man. The energy drink with the date rape drugs.

He had traded places with Chris.

He was destined to be Chris.

Saadiq tried to pry open his jaw to release the scream that blew through him like a tornado. But his muscles, imprisoned by the drug, would not comply. Flapping lips muffled the shriek of horror that roared from his lungs.

35

Striker

I<small>RAQ</small>

Sunday

"G<small>ENTLEMEN</small>," S<small>TRIKER SAID</small>. "I <small>SUGGEST WE MOSEY INTO</small> town and get some of Gator's toe-curlingly good shawarma. Now, grain of salt, we've all been out on missions where we thought maybe we drew our last breath. The food after that is always glorious, even if it's MRE peanut butter smeared across a cracker that could break your teeth."

"Agreed," Jack said, "if Zero-One or anyone else that might have laid hands on Saadiq is in the area, they probably already have eyes on us. We need to make it look like our handing over Rupert was the end of our task. We don't want them to think we're gearing up to search for Saadiq. That might harden their perimeters. It wouldn't be unusual for us to grab something to eat and look like we're off duty."

"Head on a swivel, looking for familiar faces," Gator said. "We don't need no surprises."

After setting up an infrared system that would ping their phones and put camera lenses on activity, the men felt safe that Zero-One or whoever belonged to the trucks with Ash's grandma's face dented into it wouldn't return the favor of adding tracking devices to their vehicles.

The men walked into town as if they had no agenda or timetable in front of them. They stopped to look at items displayed along the main road.

People turned to them with curiosity. They were big. They had dressed in tactical clothing. And they had Hoover with his beautiful shaggy red coat, a spectacle for this small village.

After ordering their meals at the window, the team dragged chairs from under the table to sit and wait. Under an awning that stopped the sun from beating on their heads, there was still little to no protection from the heat. Laughing and having fun, the team sat at specific angles looking over each other's shoulders, scanning the area for the men they'd seen at the wedding.

They got nothing.

A ping from DEEP: **I have information from a private source. When ready, call.**

"GATOR, GO TELL THAT NICE COOK TO PACKAGE OUR FOOD IN a to-go bag," Striker said. "I'm going across the street to the hotel to see about rooms for us. A little privacy is in order."

Striker and Blaze went across where they rented out the top floor. It seemed as if they were getting a room for each team member, but the goal was to guarantee no one had their ear pressed to the wall listening.

Besides gathering information from Deep, they'd be able to rest in the relative cool. Heat saps the body of energy and the ability to think and process.

Striker headed up the stairs to scope out the situation while Blaze went to gather the team.

Once they'd settled on the floor, their meal in front of them, Striker got Deep on the line.

"I have information from Sophia," Deep said.

"That was fast." Striker tore off a piece of flat bread to gather his chicken dripping with aromatic juices.

"It was an ancient kariz that dried up. Kariz—kilo-alpha-Romeo-India-Zulu." Deep made sure the men got the term fixed in their minds. "Reading from my notes. A kariz is a water system that dates back to ancient times but was still in use in northern Iraq. As well as other places in the Middle East and Africa, but those are under various names. The kariz keeps water deep in the ground, stored safely from natural disasters and evaporation. Sometimes a kariz is defunct, which happens for a variety of reasons. Typically, the village that grew up around the water source dies when the population moves to a livable environment. You can't survive without water, right?"

Striker wiped his mouth. "And Sophia thinks that's where Gator was trapped? You told her he said it was like a maze."

"As soon as I told her about it, Sophia knew exactly what I was talking about. She searched the one she was thinking about on her computer and gave me a GPS coordinate not far from where you are now—ten mics. She said archaeologists didn't understand the middle area design for a long time. The reigning theory is that the families would go underground in times of strife for safety. Each open area might have been a living space for a family unit, hence the soot-coated walls. Archaeologists modeled this kariz to test the theory. When the rains fell, they wound down a specific path past the room-like structures to a pool at the very back.

"Why is it set up like it is with crazy turns?" Gator asked.

"It slowed the current and kept the space from flooding, Sophia said."

"You said pool," Jack said. "How deep are we talking here? Like a swimming pool?"

"Deep enough that if someone wandered back in the dark and fell in, they'd die," Deep explained. "The archaeologists found bones, mostly animal bones, and a few human skeletons, lying at the bottom where the front lip falls off. The theory is that once that bed was dry, and the animals or people couldn't see, they died on impact when they landed. That's about all she knows from people going in to investigate. Most of the studies are conducted on computer models. Geologists found this kariz in the early nineteen eighties. Archaeological studies stopped soon after when Russia wanted to overthrow Saddam Husein, and they put boots on the ground there."

"Did Sophia have a sketch of how this is set up?" Striker asked.

"Better," Deep said. "I have a 3D schematic. How does she have that mockup, you ask? When the team's back in D.C., we'll have to take her out for a fabulous dinner and ask for details. But the short answer is muons. That's Mike-Uniform-Oscar—"

"I know what muons are," Striker said. "They make up most of the cosmic radiation reaching the Earth's surface."

"Yeah, I forgot you wanted to be an astrophysicist." Deep laughed. "Okay. They beamed those muon puppies into the ground and got a picture, and she sent it on to me."

"Perfect," Striker said, clapping his hands and rubbing

them together, knowing in his bones they were on to something good.

"Not if you're seeing what I'm seeing, it's not," Deep said. "I'll send it on now." He added, "That's the end of my notes. I've uploaded that map to your computer system, including the entrance coordinates, as a file. I also added a recent satellite photo. Basically, it looks like a ruin, a pile of rocks. That blends into a hill. That hillside is the highway-facing side. It's not discernable from the surrounding landscape. There will be nothing that'll catch your attention as you drive down the road.

"It's on the road?" Striker asked.

"Seventy-five meters off the road. No turnoff. You go until the GPS says turn west. Drive up to the rocks, and there you are. And when you're there. That's where you are. You'll be visible. Nowhere to hide. If you're going to check it out, I suggest you make that drive after dark tonight using night vision. Once you're in there, the sun wouldn't help you anyway."

The men ate, then pulled up the information Deep had sent from Sophia.

"Look, if they're there," Randy spiraled his finger over the topo map, "they're not all guarding the entrance. Two trucks. Let's say they're both full, twelve on their team. Six on ours, seven when we count Hoover."

"Hoover is definitely a force multiplier," Ash said.

"Maybe they're here in the hotel with us," Gator said, "and they send out a couple of guards to keep watch. Maybe they're setting up camp, hiding their fire behind the hill."

"If it's as bad inside as Rupert and Gator say, no one is going in there for funsies," Blaze said. "It didn't sound like Rupert had a guard over the last eighteen months, just someone who showed up to resupply him. I'd bet that if

Saadiq is in there, they'd keep an eye on him for a couple days and watch his behaviors. If he's like Rupert, they can go back to that care schedule."

"Why keep him alive?" Jack asked.

Their phones pinged. Deep: **Both trucks on the move. I'm tracking them heading north.**

"Saadiq is a formidable asset for this area," Striker said. They might need him in a hole long enough to make him pliable so they can shape him into a DZ asset, possibly to run with Zero-One. Maybe they need some time to gather his family, so they have leverage."

"So they put a guard or two on them," Ash said.

"Tonight? The trucks are gone. I bet they're camping out and making a plan."

While they waited to find out where the trucks went, the men evaluated the 3D plan. It would be easy to tell if that was where they held Rupert because Hoover could search for his scent. "Once we've confirmed the theory," Striker said, "the next step is to search for Saadiq or any other unfortunate soul held in there."

Deep: **Bingo, the trucks just drove off the road and stopped at a coordinate behind the hill near the mouth of the kariz.** Randy sent the coordinates.

"Knowing where those trucks are positioned will be helpful." Striker put a dot on the topo map. "Maybe they're just doing a check. Maybe they're switching guard. Maybe they're camping, as Randy suggested."

"I wouldn't sleep in there if only because I hate sleeping on any kind of slope," Blaze said. "And it can't smell good, all that stale air. Problems with smoke if they're trying to use a fire for heat. Without any rain, the most comfortable spot is this flat place in front of their vehicles. See where they are? You've got that rock wall to the north, that outcropping to the south, they blocked the east, and to the west is Never Never Land. No one to harass them."

"Okay," Jack said. "One scenario says they're sleeping. In that case, we step up and wrap a choke hold around anyone standing guard. We make damn sure to let off the pressure as soon as he passes out. We're not committing murder tonight. We just need control of the guard. Take sleeping beauty back to the truck and truss him up. Go in the cave while everyone is asleep around the coals, grab Saadiq, and leave."

"That scenario says that everyone is sleeping," Ash pointed out. "They know we're in the area on the hunt for Saadiq."

"You don't think Langley told DZ to hold off?" Randy asked. "Color Code is in play. We're in play. The goal is to make sure Saadiq is safe and not in terrorist hands."

"Zero-One are subcontractors. They might not have up-to-date information. And DZ might want to pull some crap like show up as the protectors, seemingly rescue Saadiq so he trusts them, and make a play for his loyalty."

"A lot of scenarios to put on the board," Striker said. "But I think that after their experience with Rupert, they're not worrying about someone jumping them tonight."

"Why do you say that?" Blaze asked.

"I'm assuming that British intelligence was looking for Rupert Shaw up until State contacted them with our find," Striker explained. "This sight is known to a finite number of intellectuals and hasn't been studied since Russia rang Iraq's doorbell. Rupert had no idea where he was and was non-communicative the last they saw him, twenty-four hours or so ago. This group here," Striker pointed toward his red dot on the map, "thinks they're off-grid. They would have no way of knowing about Gator's time in the mines."

"So we wait for zero dark thirty, we show up and scope

the scene. We bring doggo into the maze, have him check the scent source, and track Saadiq down. Cold temps, no wind. The trail should be good."

"True that," Ash said. "Only we're not a hundred percent that we have the right scent source for Saadiq."

"But we are sure we have a scent source for Rupert," Jack said. "If I were exchanging man for man in a maze, my habit would tell me to put Saadiq right back in the same place where I plucked Rupert. So if scent-two isn't exciting Hoover, we try Rupert's. We use night vision. We use our silent comms."

"Gentlemen," Striker said. "Zero-One are arguably CIA assets. And even if that's wrong, we're visitors in a foreign land with no special protections. We will not permanently harm a single hair on their chinny-chin-chins. If we encounter resistance, we have our non-lethal means of handling it: stun rifles or Hoover's teeth. I think we show up and see what intel we can gather. If the situation presents itself as work-able, we work it. If it doesn't, we back off and regroup."

36

Lexi

JORDAN

    Sunday

THEY HAD BEEN A QUIET GROUP IN THE CAR ON THE WAY TO
Amman, quiet on the plane that flew them to Baghdad, and
now, with visas in hand and their suitcases in tow, they
walked silently through the airport.

The goal was simple, collect Saadiq's family at the hotel
where they were waiting, drive the family to the American
airbase, and then wait until Iniquus Logistics gave Margot
and Lynx a directive or Strike Force showed up with Saadiq.

These four didn't need to be friends.

They simply needed to take the steps together to ensure
Saadiq's family's safety.

As they passed through the automatic doors on the way to
the parking lot, a man raised his hand in a wave, came over,
and said, "Amazing seeing you here," as he shook Grey's

hand. "I'm late, but call me, okay? We need to catch up." And off he bustled.

Lynx watched the exchange, and she saw the tip of a keychain.

Grey's phone pinged. When he tapped, a pedestrian map showed on his screen, leading the group to a white passenger van that could seat twelve. Four escorts, four family members, plus space for the luggage they would bring—all the possessions they would take with them to set up a new life.

Grey fobbed them in, then climbed behind the wheel.

Angel called shotgun.

"Grey," Lynx asked as she settled onto the bench seat, pulling the safety belt across her lap. "Do you know anything about tunnels between Baghdad and Bashrah?"

"Tunnels like they used in the Battle of Fallujah?" he asked. "There are some in city centers. The police and Iraqi Forces control them. Why?"

"I don't know—just a passing thought," and that was the last thought she shared for almost an hour as they snaked their way through traffic snarls.

Finally, she leaned forward and pointed at a store front. "Grey, see that pharmacy up ahead?" She sat back in her seat. "I need to run in there for a minute."

"Now?" he asked, glancing into his rearview to see her.

"Right now," she said insistently.

"Are you okay?" Grey asked as he clicked on his blinker and slowed to parallel park.

"Maybe you can do your shopping later," Angel said. "We're time critical."

"Wow, thanks for pointing that out, Angel," she said, gathering her handbag. "I was confused."

"What did you see?" Margot asked.

"I think we're the rabbit." "Rabbit" was a CIA term from training at The Farm in how to follow someone by watching them in various ways—from inside a store, walking past them on the sidewalk, and so forth—then passing information to teammates so the person being followed didn't know it, or couldn't be sure. By using the term, Lynx was able to convey that whole picture as shorthand to the others. She unclasped her seatbelt. "Hang tight. I'm going in to call Deep and apprise him of the possible situation. My shopping will give him time to develop a plan. Anyone need anything while I'm in there?"

With a general "no," Lynx slid the heavy door open and stepped out into the bright glare of sunlight.

She pushed through the door to the jangle of bells and wended her way into the aisles, looking for solitude. She slipped behind a stack of boxes piled on a dolly in the back. Standing there as if perusing the display of haircare items, Lexi quick-dialed back to Striker Force War Room.

"Lynx here. Deep are you following my shirt on the board?"

"Affirmative, you and Margot are both up. I have the computer following your vehicle from our satellite feed. You and Margot need to be sure to hydrate. You're both in the yellow."

Lynx reached out and fiddled with a hairbrush as if contemplating the purchase. "Do you ever get tired of saying that to people who are working in temps over a hundred?"

"Operators can get hyper-focused. It's part of my job to keep you all safe, so no. What are you doing at the pharmacy?"

"Giving you time to work on a puzzle and, if necessary, find a solution. I think someone is following our van. And if I'm right, it's a professional job—car, truck, motorcycle. The motorcycle has a guy wearing the same clothes but the helmet changes colors. Not sure what to do with that. At the last stop, he pulled up next to us. He had a ring on his pinky finger, and I saw that same hand with the same pinky ring as we were leaving the airport's parking area. That's what I've got."

"Pulling you up on satellite. Hold. White van?."

"That's us." Lynx read the back of a curling iron box as Deep worked through the situation.

"All right, the AI system has developed a route it suggests for observation. I'm sending you the map now."

Lynx's phone pinged.

"I want you to follow this exactly. It ends up at a grocery store, where you could pretend to shop. The street ahead is closed because of construction. There's a parking lot, but the road dead ends. That won't show up on most GPS readouts, so no one's getting around it except perhaps the motorcycle. Once you're at the shop, get out, go in to buy something—bottled water. I'll reach out and let you know if the computer finds anything interesting or not."

"Thanks, Deep. Okay, I'm going to buy a hairdryer. That'll give me a big enough bag, so it looks like I was actually in here for shopping purposes. If someone is following us, I want them to think this was an innocent stop. We'll head to that address."

Lynx adjusted the drape of her headscarf. Despite the summer temperatures, she wore a long-sleeved turtleneck. Fortunately, the Iniquus summer fabric worked with moisture to help the body thermoregulate.

When her turn came to pay, she put the box on the counter and paid with the beautifully colored Iraqi Dinar that Logistics had put in her wallet. Lexi had always loved the colors and designs of foreign cash and always thought that American money, in comparison, lacked imagination. "*Shukran*," thank you, she said as she accepted her bag and receipt. She walked out the door and wended past the stream of pedestrians as she climbed back in the van.

"Well?" Grey asked.

Lexi tossed the bag onto the bench seat behind her. "Deep gave me a map. I'm forwarding it to you." She pulled her phone from her pocket.

Grey handed his phone to Angel. "You navigate." He looked over his shoulder, and when there was a space, he moved back into the stream of traffic.

Everyone in the van was professional enough not to look around and give away the game.

After another twenty minutes, Lynx's phone pinged.

Deep: **You're being followed by a van, a car, and a motorcycle.**

Lynx read off the information.

"Is that what you saw, Lexi?" Angel asked.

"Lynx, please. Yes." She tapped the phone to bring up Deep on speaker. "Thank you," she said. "Should we continue on the designated route?"

"I'm going to reroute you. I need to know what you all want to do, evade or confront?" Deep asked.

"Evade," Angel and Grey said at the same time that Margot and Lynx said, "Confront."

"Confront it is," Deep said. "Our AI system says you can lead the car following you down a dead-end road into a compound. I'm adjusting your map. I can do that from here."

Angel looked at the phone. "New map up. Keep going straight for five klicks." Angel used klicks for kilometers.

"There is a gate at the end that protects the driveway," Deep explained. "The driveway is a semi-circle that takes you out. Right now, both gates are open. Get far enough up ahead of the car. One person jumps out and shuts the gate. It doesn't need to lock. It just needs to look like it is. Your van then circles and exits to block their exfil."

"Good," Margot said. "One person stays with the vehicle. Two approach from the front. One approaches from the back. We have a little conversation."

"I'll watch the satellite for the course of the other vehicles," Deep said. "I suggest, Grey, that when you exit the drive, you back up to limit the driver's maneuvering space. This will also position you to get out of there if and when necessary."

"Got it," Grey said. "Who's jumping out?"

"I am." Lynx released her safety belt.

"No, you're not. I am." Angel undid his seatbelt and unlocked the door.

"Fine, two in front, two in back," Lynx said. "Come on back here, hubby, and we'll jump out at the same time. I'll open the door, and then we'll walk out arm in arm."

Surprisingly, Angel complied.

As soon as they jumped, Lynx watched Margot slam the van door. The tires fought for traction as Grey pressed down on the gas to get himself in place and out of view.

"Coming closer." Deep's voice rose from Lynx's phone. "He would have definitely seen you shutting the gate. Have Angel pretend to lock it and pocket the key."

Lynx knew that Margot would have this over her comms as well and would be directing Grey to keep their van out of sight.

"Angel, I'm going to disappear and be the surprise." And with that, Lynx stepped into the shadow of the decorative entryway. She lowered her pulse. Her inhalation and exhalation were slow and deep. She knew that the driver in the car that pulled forward would focus on Angel and Angel's hands *precisely* as she had been hyper-focused on the guy outside her supermarket. He had pulled one hundred percent of her attention away from anything but his potential to draw a weapon and shoot her dead.

Angel stood in front of the gate.

He had his own kind of magic. He seemed to expand his size as he bladed his hands onto his hips. Taller, meaner, more formidable than she'd ever seen him before. *A shapeshifter,* Lynx thought with amusement, and then she remembered that he had a Canadian friend from the First Nations Peoples when Angel had first deployed and wondered if he had taught Angel how to stare down a polar bear. She might ask him about his technique later, but for now, she watched the car try to back up, only to see the van block its way.

The driver shifted gears again and inched toward Angel.

Angel crossed his arms over his chest, an immovable blockade.

When the man shifted into park, he opened his door. Brown hair hung to his shoulders. His bushy beard frizzed from his chin. He was small and wiry, like the gene pool that most special force operators pulled from. The massive size of the men on Strike Force was sometimes a blessing and sometimes a detriment.

This guy stood outside of his car using the door as a shield.

A bullet can go right through. A car door had almost zero stopping power. Obviously, Angel was the kind of man who would know such a thing. It must be an armored car, or the guy was bluffing, Lynx thought as she inched along the wall to get behind the man's peripheral vision. Lynx had heard stories from her team about how they would take the entire day from sunup to sundown, practicing getting across an open field without an enemy spotting them. Same task here.

"Dude," Angel called out. "You following me?"

"American?" the man asked.

"No shit," Angel said.

"Me too." The man touched his chest. "American." Big grin.

Everyone was pals, apparently.

The man was stalling, waiting for his team to arrive and cover his six.

"No, shit." Angel stepped forward. "And you just like to go around following fellow Americans so you can make friends?"

"That's right." He plastered that big grin in place. But he was feeling the heat. He was cornered, left his vehicle, had no ready weapon—though one could be on his body someplace, and had no allies. "I've met some interesting people that way." He looked over his right shoulder toward the van. And Lynx took advantage of that to move into place and quickly disappear. "You have friends in the van?" he asked with a lick of his lips and a thumb hitch.

Yup, sweaty. It could be nerves; it could be that it was over a hundred degrees standing out here.

"How about you tell me the real reason you're following us." Angel took a giant step forward without asking, "Mother, may I?"

The guy lifted his foot to step back, then glued himself in place.

"Cards on the table then." The man chuckled. "Your driver and I work for the same organization. Different working groups."

"Uh-huh. I know that. I'm well aware of who you are," Angel bluffed.

"We've been keeping track of your driver—"

"My driver's name is?" Angel interrupted.

"John Grey." The way he said it had the bite of acrimony

that convinced Lynx that this team meant to capture and inter-rogate Grey even if he was from the same alphabet. And her guess would be that they needed to know where Color Code had housed Saadiq's family.

"Okay, Double Zero, why are you watching him?"

When Angel said Double Zero, the guy's jaw dropped momentarily. He tried to pass it off by reaching up and drag-ging his finger under his lip, a thinking gesture. But Lynx read that body language tell quite clearly. He didn't like losing his anonymity. "He's sheltering a family," the man said. "And we lost track of the husband. Grey's group won't tell us how to get to the family."

"Imagine that," Angel deadpanned.

"But we're hoping that his wife has some secret way of how to contact him. We thought a face-to-face with Grey, since he's here in Iraq now."

"So you're saying you lost Saadiq?" Angel canted his head. "Saadiq, who has two decades of State, Langley, and JASOC secrets in his head. That seems bad."

"Do you know where Saadiq is? Is he safe?" The guy was pushing the concerned friend's pedal down hard. "We wanted to reassure ourselves that nothing bad is happening to him."

A van and a motorcycle roared onto the scene. The guy lowered his stance, turned, and took off running like a field athlete on the starting block for the hundred-yard dash.

Lynx stuck out her foot, tripping him, and he slid face down on the gravel. "I've got him. They want to take Grey. You can't let that happen!" Lynx yelled. She was in constant motion as she took control of the DZ guy, spreading his legs and then pushing his heels toward his rump.

Angel sprinted forward.

The man tried to flip, so Lynx reached behind his knee

and pressed an acupuncture point that sent fire up and down the nervous system. The man shrieked.

Lynx stood with her feet wide between his knees. And now that she was in a better position, the man couldn't flail himself free from her as she pressed on his heels, his leg folded up behind him.

There was a loud commotion ahead. Lynx focused on controlling the three-foot square around her the way Striker had taught her.

Untying the man's boot laces, tightening them down, and tying a knot that would not slip, she used the man's boots as shackles. She threaded the laces through the back of the man's belt and belt loop, then joined them with the laces of the other boot.

She had trussed him, and now she had to watch him carefully because tying people like this could lead them to suffocate and die by their weight compressing their lungs.

Lynx wondered if they needed her forward. She was deciding that maybe she should help when the motorcycle took off, then the van.

Angel made his way back to her. His face showed signs of fists landing hard.

"Are you all okay?" she asked.

Angel reached up and scratched his forehead, looking over his shoulder as Grey and Margot made their way over. All were disheveled. The others didn't have the same visible bruising.

"Gone?" Lynx asked.

"Momentarily," Grey said. "What did you catch?"

"This is a DZ snake." She pointed at the guy. "Rare, and I'm told, quite lethal."

"I've never seen anyone hogtie a snake before," Margot said with a smile. "Now, what are we going to do with him?"

Angel pointed to the man's car. "I'm taking him out to the desert at a good distance and dropping him with a bottle of water to find his way home. How about you three finish our task?"

After loading the DZ into the car and taking Angel's shotgun seat, Lynx watched out of her side mirror as Angel drove behind them. Yeah, maybe DZ was the snake, but so was Angel, and Lynx didn't love the idea that they were going in different directions.

And after Angel insisted on privacy to deal with the divorce papers, she still had a mission to accomplish.

37

Striker

Sunday

This might well be where the captors put Saadiq; it was also entirely possible that Strike Force chased a mirage.

Could be that this place felt safe and familiar for the men who most probably pulled Rupert back to the land of the living, a kind of a reverse Charon—the ferryman who took the souls across the river Styx. Instead, they pulled Rupert from his hell and brought him back to the land of the living. Familiarity was a soothing drug; maybe that was why they decided to camp here and went about their chores with a relaxed posture and jokes.

The team could wait and gather intel.

They could wait for the number of men below them to thin, though that might take days.

They could get Langley involved.

They could wander in with an extended hand of peace and an ask.

They could drop down with a war whoop and just see how the dice rolled.

What they didn't know—what they'd never know—was if there was a better way.

And as Striker and Lexi had talked about before they split up on their separate missions, there was a decision—to act or not—and there were the ramifications of those decisions. There were no do-overs. And even in the rearview mirror, there was no clarity. No alternative reality to test a theory.

The weight of those decisions rested squarely on Striker's shoulders. The men sprawled on the ground below them were allies at cross purposes. Friendly fire was a hell of a way to leave this world. How do you fight family when walking away isn't a possibility?

So here they were, belly down; rocks grinding into their flesh. Ghillie cloths hid them from the naked eye. Hopefully, the curve of the hill's crest would mask their heat signatures from night vision as the heat absorbed throughout the day dissipated with the cooling evening temperatures. Though, he didn't see any of the men pull out binoculars to scan or even set out a sentry.

"Jack. I count ten on the exterior." Jack's AI voice was in Striker's ear. No worries that the wind and rock would carry their echo down to the men below them.

"Blaze. Same from this angle."

"Randy. No one's at the mouth of the kariz. That tells me that *if* Saadiq is inside, they can't imagine him finding his way back out."

"Gator. That doesn't stretch the imagination." Even with his voice produced with AI, the pacing was different. That made Striker think the stress of that earlier mission was revisiting Gator. Striker would try to keep Gator from going back in; Gator could be overwatch.

"Striker. One thing I know, gentlemen, is Saadiq is not Rupert. It might have been the best choice for Rupert to sit tight while rolling water bottles down a sloped room. Rupert is, after all, a reporter. A damned brave reporter working in a damned difficult terrain. That doesn't mean he has survival skills. It means Rupert attached to people who did."

"Jack. Rupert could have been correct to sit tight and hope for the best. Remember the bones at the bottom of the abyss at the back of the kariz. Rupert could have simply stepped off into oblivion."

"Striker. Agreed, Saadiq, on the other hand, ran beside the best of the best in the U.S. military and then the CIA." He had a wiry body type that special forces appreciated, the men with a steady stream of go-juice. He had an amazing memory. If he heard it, saw it, read it, Saadiq owned that knowledge. Like a book on the library shelf, Saadiq could easily access the information. When Striker first met Saadiq, he was a strategic thinker, but he honed his skills to a razor-sharp military edge by participating in decades of missions. He would turn to actions of self-preservation now. "There's no way in this world that Saadiq would sit and wait for rescue. And as Jack said about Rupert, there's a non-zero risk of his falling to his death."

The men lay there as the sun disappeared, and the night turned purple.

Below them, sleeping bags came out. Zero-One piled wood on the fire. Laughter rambled up the rock formations.

"Gator. I'm not a particular fan of caves. I know this is a fancy-schmancy kariz. It's still a cave. Y'all, the last time I was in a damned cave was when we ran into underground gases. Don't mean to jinx us nor nothin'. I'm bringing it up because if we're putting together a pack to go in there, I think having gas masks with our gear might be good. We don't know if one area is safe and another not."

"Striker. We can do that. It won't add much weight. All right, we need a plan. Let's not get cocky. Remember, Zero-One didn't go through Hell Week and BUD/S, but DZ trained them for black ops. And they outnumber us, which is one risk. The other is we don't know what their operating orders are. We follow the laws and customs, and we can meet force with like force. But looking down there, they have long rifles with bullets, and ours have wires. They have range on us. If we're going to fight, which I'm not ruling out, we need to be in tight."

"Blaze for Ash. You double-checked that your grandma's face was on the back of the truck?"

"Ash. She's down there smiling at us. By the way, Hoover pissed on their tires."

"Jack. What are we looking for, quickest plan or easiest? Easiest, we leave someone on rotating overwatch and wait for them to move on. Walk in, find Saadiq. And that was what I was going to suggest, minimizing harm. But Striker's right. That scenario would have worked for Rupert. Saadiq is going to try to get out. And after what Gator said about how the black plays and what Deep said about the depth of the fall. I think we need to be aggressive."

"Blaze. Well, we aren't walking into their camp and asking pretty please with sugar and cream on it."

"Randy. Since Ash mentioned Hoover watering the tires, we did something like this when I was a Ranger, but I'm reworking the scenario with stun rifles. We wait for someone to take a leak. My guess is they're going to use the spot right below where you're at Striker, so they're not pissing into the wind. One of us leans over the boulder, covered in the ghillie rag. We wait until they've got their dick in their hands. We reach down, stun the guy on bare skin, count three, and then pull our finger off the trigger.

"Gator. He'd scream, and that would cover the sizzle."

"Blaze. And someone, if not all of them, are going to go over and see why their friend's on the ground."

"Jack. You were joking, Randy. But it's not half bad. The rest of the team goes into the kariz while they're not looking. The guy at the top needs to yank the prongs out of his skin and disappear."

"Striker. Let's run that through as if it's us sitting around our campfire."

"Randy. We feel safe and warm. A friend is screaming and then not able to move. What would I think? I'd think they were playing a joke on me. But we don't come from the same culture. I have no idea how *they* would react."

"Striker. What needs to happen is for two men to get into the kariz as fast as possible and for the rest of the team to protect the entry."

"Ash. When Hoover was baptizing their truck, I think I forgot to mention that I accidentally stabbed their tires, and they lost air. Those trucks aren't going to be able to chase us down."

"Striker for Ash, you brought the scent sources."

"Ash. Affirmative."

"Striker. You and Hoover are going in. Randy, you're our best navigator. You're going in."

"Gator. Striker, I have experience in there."

"Striker. You're wave two if it's needed. We're going to leave Blaze up here on watch. Everyone else, let's head down. And I'll explain my plan."

Once they were on the ground, the men huddled up. "Those men trained. Anything we do, they have a plan and a counterplan. What we need is something from out in left field," Striker said with a grin. "I think it can work. It might be a little painful for our sleepy brethren out there, but they took Saadiq from us, so it's on them. One thing I learned in New York City was that Hoover will sing on command."

"Sonny loved it." Ash reached over and scrubbed a hand into Hoover's fur.

"We first get Hoover to scent on the second-unconfirmed blanket and see if that interests him. If it doesn't, we need to rethink. If Hoover likes it. Ash walks him into the cave a bit and commands him to sing."

"To what end? Make Zero-One think that they have a goblin?"

"My hope is they'll have a nervous reaction of some kind but still feel compelled to go and check on Saadiq. They move up, unsure what's making that noise. We have our stun guns and stun rifles at the ready. When they mass up to decide who is going in and who is standing watch, we lift out from under our ghillie cloths and shoot the wires into them. Each of our team is going to have to get two people. Count three and pull your finger off the trigger."

"To make sure that happens," Jack said, "maybe shoot one person, and see who jerks and screams, to get your next target. You don't have to wait to say three. Just find a warm body that's confused."

"They'll run," Randy said.

Striker shrugged. "I'm good with that."

"If they run for their trucks, they're stuck." Ash crouched down next to Hoover and got a tongue bath reward. "They might be afraid to shoot their guns if they're in a tight ball. If they run back toward their camp, could they see to shoot? Depends on their scopes, right? If they're night vision scopes, we can't hide. And those guns have bullets. Right now, we have the upper hand with our night vision goggles. I'm for this plan."

The men moved forward.

"Blaze. Does that mean I'm not going to be able to stun gun a man while he's taking a piss?"

"Striker. We'll try to use that on a future mission. All right, gentlemen, we are in silent mode. Ash, you're up."

With their night vision goggles, they owned the night. The men moved into places around the entrance of the kariz. Kicking at the area to ensure no loose rocks would trip them up, they pulled their ghillie cloths around their shoulders.

Ash held the bag with the blanket under Hoover's nose, and Hoover's snout went into the air, snuffing and chuffing. He leaped forward, dragging on his lead. "Ash. That's a positive hit. We're a go. I'm positioning Hoover at the entrance. I need a signal that Zero-One is approaching, then Hoover and I will proceed on the scent trail."

After a ten count, Striker turned toward the kariz entrance. "Striker. Ash, are you in place?"

"Ash. Affirmative."

"Striker for Ash. Sing!"

Whatever song Ash had chosen for Hoover to sing along with was haunting. The unholy yowls echoed off the rock walls and rode the wind into the men's camp.

The men wrestled themselves out of their bags.

"Blaze. You'd think their sleeping bags were filled with hornets or scorpions. They're fighting themselves out of their sacks like it's a cage match. All right, they have their weapons. They're searching for the sound source. They realize it's coming from the cave. Conferring. Conferring. They're walking in a huddle. If this is Zero-One, they've lost their V formation. They're right up on you, slowing with each step. Keep that singing coming, Ash."

The leader seemed to decide he'd be watch as the other men went in. One of them raced back to the camp and grabbed chemlights that he handed out. Gator had said that the white light from the flashlight made it harder to see inside instead of easier. The men took their time snapping the lights.

"Striker. Okay, Ash, that's enough. Let Hoover get on that scent trail."

When quiet descended, the Zero-One men's nerves grew worse. Now, they wouldn't be able to locate the source of the sound; it could be anything or anywhere.

They huddled again.

"Striker. Pick your closest two targets and call them out. I have my twelve o'clock with the bare chest and one o'clock the guy with the striped pants."

Quickly, the operators chose their targets.

"Striker. Execute. Execute. Execute."

The probes flew out, stabbing the men's skin with a barb to hold them in place. Zapping sizzles filled the air, along with the men's shrieks as they jerked and twerked.

Three seconds, and it was over.

The electricity shot in that amount of time was enough to squeeze the glucose out of the muscles and leave the person unable to move.

One man still stood. He jumped back, lifting his rifle with a guttural cry. Out of the cave flew the team fur missile, launching right at the man as his finger slid into the trigger guard. Hoover's powerful jaws clamped down hard as Ash ran from the cave to call off Hoover and praise him for a job well done.

The team rose from under their ghillie rags to zip-tie the men on the ground and pull out the probes.

With Randy's knee on the rifleman's back, Striker called Blaze down from overwatch, then turned to Ash. "How'd

Hoover stop the shooter when he was supposed to be tracking Saadiq?"

Ash called, "All clear, Saadiq, come on out." He turned to Striker. "Because Saadiq was right around the corner. The hunt was over in thirty seconds."

Blaze rounded the boulder. "I missed out on all the fun. Hey! There you are, Saadiq. Man, we've been hunting you for days."

Saadiq wrapped his arms around Blaze for a big hug.

"Men," Striker commanded, "let's take this reunion on the road. Load up. We need to hightail it to base and see if we can't get there to meet Lynx and Margot."

"What are we going to do about them?" Randy asked, gesturing toward the pile of zip-tied assets.

"They're black ops. They'll figure this out," Striker said. "Let's go."

38

Striker

Iʀᴀǫ
Monday

Tʜᴇ ᴍᴇɴ ʜᴀᴅ ᴘɪʟᴇᴅ ɪɴᴛᴏ ᴛʜᴇɪʀ ʙᴏʀʀᴏᴡᴇᴅ ᴠᴇʜɪᴄʟᴇs. Rᴀɴᴅʏ was up ahead. Both drivers used night vision goggles.

"Your family is waiting for you at the American base," Striker said. "We're taking you there now."

"No headlights?" Saadiq asked, his voice wary.

"Yeah, we keep running into folks we'd rather not chat with," Gator said. "We're not a hundred percent that they're not watching us in their satellite feed, but if they're just trying to run us down, no point in making it easy for them."

Saadiq's body was stiff with tension. "What day is it?"

"We crossed over into Monday," Striker said. "Now, I have a question for you. How did you get to the cave, and how did you get back out?"

"I drank a bottle with a date rape drug and woke up to

what smelled and felt like a cave, which was very perplexing, especially in my dazed state. Whoever took me there, they left me with a glow stick. It wasn't much light in an atmosphere that seemed to absorb light. There was an odd flatness to that black. Wanting to see better, I dropped the chemlight into a bottle of water to make a lantern. With the water amplifying the illumination, I could see much better."

"They left you with water. Anything else?" Jack asked.

"There were boxes. But nothing very helpful beyond survival. The boxes were old MREs and cases of water. Not many. Enough for maybe a week. A bucket for waste. A bucket, I suppose, for washing." The road sounds rumbled into the cab as Saadiq shared his story. "I was looking around when I accidentally knocked over my lantern water bottle. It rolled to hit the wall. I went out of the room and tossed my bottle, and it, too, rolled back down to me. In my time in the States, I had a friend who was a spelunker. I went with him sometimes to check it out. I remembered that each time we descended into caves, right?"

"Right," Striker affirmed.

"I reasoned that you don't go into a cave and climb up into the dome of the hill or mountain. But then the Nile flows south to north, so never say never. To me, the back of the cave should be down, and the front of the cave should be up. That would make sense in the formation of a cave, but feeling along the walls, this seemed to be ancient and carved by man. Still, I thought that out must be up. So that's what I did. I tried to navigate up the incline."

"Smart move, Saadiq," Striker said. "And that brought you all the way out of the hole?"

"At one point along the way, it was flat. I couldn't tell which way the ground inclined. That happened several times, and I'd roll my water bottle lantern to find out. This last time, as I bent to pick up the bottle where it hit the wall, I saw that my bottle stopped on top of an old chemlight covered in powdered dirt. I lifted it, wondering if that was a chemlight that Chris had used."

"Rupert," Striker said. "The man you helped is Rupert Shaw, a British reporter."

"Rupert Shaw?" Saadiq tried on the name. "Have you spoken to him?"

"We were supposed to have picked you up in your last location, but we missed you. They gave us Rupert. He's on his way home to England. He was reporting out a story here in Iraq a year and a half ago when he was drugged and removed from his hotel room."

Saadiq's labored breathing huffed air past the rigid lungs, squeezed tight by adrenaline. "He was in there for a year and a half?" Saadiq's body went limp from the shock, and Gator had to brace him.

"You're out of there," Striker said. "We have you. Iniquus knows we have you. The State Department knows. The Pentagon knows. The CIA knows. The more people who know, the safer this trip is."

"The CIA knows?" There was desperation in his voice.

"My commander apprised Langley that Iniquus is tracing our vehicles on satellite. JASOC hired Iniquus to find you and take you to the American base to meet your family. The Pentagon will pound on Langley's door if you're not on that cargo plane with your wife."

"Zahra?" Saadiq's voice was a whisper of disbelief.

"Along with your mom, sister, and daughter. Your whole family is waiting for you at the base."

Saadiq took some time to process that information. Then he asked, "But what will we do from there? We can't live forever on that base."

"We're trying to get there in time to meet the next flight out. It'll be an uncomfortable flight to Washington, D.C. There, someone from the State Department will meet the plane on the runway. They have your documents. They'll walk you to a different plane that will take you to St. Kitts. Iniquus has a southern campus there, and we will house you while you get your feet under you. You can obtain citizenship in St. Kitts with an investment in a home. We'll help you with that. You may decide that you would like to live there. Or not. If you decide you'd rather be in the United States, it will give you a safe place to live as a family while Iniquus helps you to move through the paperwork. Coming from St. Kitts instead of Iraq might ease that path. Either way, we have you on our radar now. We'll make sure you get where you want to be."

Saadiq put his hand on his heart. "Thank you, my friends."

"So, finish your story," Jack said, reaching up to adjust the goggles over his eyes as he steered around the curve of the road. "You said that you thought the old chemlight might have been something Rupert left behind?"

"Yes, in the end, it wasn't hard at all. As I said, the first secret was to keep my body moving on an upward slope. It was subtle but perceptible. And the second thing was finding that old glow stick. As I lifted it, I realized there was a cord attached. It was difficult to see, but I could feel that even though covered with dirt, it still had a grip. I dribbled some water on it to test, and I was right. This was the military cordage, the kind treated with tar to keep it from getting wet and rotting. I also saw that sticky cordage went forward of me and back. I figured out which way was uphill and followed the line. Very soon, I was out in the night air, and I see you all taking control of the men who captured me."

"Gator!" the calls went up.

"You are Gator?" Saadiq asked. "Why is it that your men cheer you?"

"Back in his days as a Marine Raider," Striker said, "Gator laid that line to help his fellow jarheads out of the kariz. You found his line."

Saadiq stared at Gator for a long moment. "That seems miraculous."

"It's how we found your cave," Striker said. "Gator recognized the shawarma shack in the village. Lucky for you, Gator never forgets a good meal."

DEEP HAD COMMUNICATED THE TEAM'S POSITION TO LEXI AND Margot. When their vehicles pulled into the base, Margot stood with Saadiq's family at the entrance.

Jack stopped to let Saadiq out to run and embrace his loved ones.

The emotions of a reunion were complicated, joy and relief mixed with ebbing anxiety and pain.

Striker and Gator got out, unloading the gear from the back.

As Jack drove the truck away, Striker pulled Margot aside. "Where's Lynx?"

"She's flying back to Amman and heading back down to the Dead Sea. She said her mission is ongoing down there. My orders are to hand over the family to Strike Force control. Check." She smiled. "I'm going to the airport in the morning to fly west and meet up with Panther Force."

Margot and Striker watched the family, embracing and talking all at once.

"It's nice to have a happy ending. Rupert was heading

home. Saadiq's family reunited with a path forward. What could be better?" Margot asked.

What could be better? Striker thought. Angel could have signed the divorce papers already, and Lexi could be here flying home to their new lives with Cammy.

39

Lexi

JORDAN

When Lynx, Margot, and Grey drove onto the American base Sunday evening with Saadiq's family in the back seats, it hadn't felt like the victory that Lynx had anticipated. None of her stress fell away.

She felt the brewing storm, and in her mind was the children's tune, *Three Blind Mice*.

Her hugs and congratulations to the family were robotic, her head on a swivel.

"He's not here," Grey told her. "We have an asset that we were meeting. She was late getting in, and we must ensure everything's okay. It's not personal."

"Not personal?" Lynx pressed her lips together. "Okay, are you heading down to the Dead Sea now?"

"First thing in the morning. There's a six o'clock flight to Amman."

"I'm coming with you. I still have 'Mission Divorce Papers' to fulfill. How about we share the cab?"

MONDAY

LYNX AND GREY STEPPED OUT OF THE CAB AND THROUGH THE doors to see Angel sitting in the lobby next to a blonde-haired woman.

Angel raised his hand toward Grey with a smile, then leaned to whisper something to the woman as he slid a key card toward her. He stood to leave.

"Hey!" Lynx called out, finger in the air.

"I'll meet you upstairs. She has the key. I need to make a call." And off he strode toward the elevator bank.

The woman moved to greet Grey. "Hey there. I'm sorry for my delay."

"May I introduce a traveling buddy?" Grey asked. "This is Lynx"

Grey had a tenseness about his face that fell off when the woman nodded politely. "I'm Nicole Street." She held up the key card. "We're supposed to meet him in his room."

Grey stretched an arm toward the elevator banks. "Shall we head up, then?"

Lynx led the way to Angel's room and stopped at the door. "I'll just need a minute or two if you wouldn't mind waiting in the hall?"

"I can accommodate that." Grey glanced Nicole's way. It wasn't to see if she agreed but to assess her body language.

As they rode up on the elevator, Lynx, of course, had put it together.

318

Gator wouldn't have told his wife or sister about the mission to Syria to save Angel's life. But he would have shared the timeline at the country name. The person who had sent the message via Auralia Rochambeau could easily put together the familial connection between Gator and Auralia. Lynx would lay good money that her benefactor—the one who wanted to pay a debt—connected to Kaylie Street, the woman the team had saved on that same mission. This woman, Nicole Street, had the same familial face structure. Luckily for all involved, this woman seemed oblivious.

Lynx had trained to do intelligence work by the best of the best. There would be no tells about her face or body.

The knock at Angel's door got no response.

Lynx checked for a string but found none. Reaching into her bag, she pulled out her magical magic marker, pushed the tip into the hole in the bottom of the locking mechanism, and opened the door.

Grey trapped her hand with the marker and looked at the electronic tip. "I want one of these."

Lynx handed it to him and then walked into the room. "A gift."

The suitcase was gone.

The room was empty.

Lynx spun in place, throwing her hands over her head in frustration.

Grey turned to Nicole. "Would you mind waiting in the hall for just a moment?"

When Nicole shut the door behind her, Lynx hissed, "You all suck." She stabbed a finger at Grey. "And I'm done with this. Warn them at Langley."

"That's not going to help you, I'm afraid."

Lynx narrowed her eyes at him. "Care to expand on that?"

"I cannot."

Lynx plunked down on the corner of the bed, wrapping her hands around a knee. "Not CIA?"

"I cannot comment."

Lynx was hyper-focused, scanning his body for any tell that might help her puzzle through this conversation. "He told me you recruited him."

"That's correct."

"It's correct that he told me that, or it's correct that you recruited him?"

Grey's face broke into a bright smile. He pointed his finger at her. "You are as clever as he said you are. The answer is both."

"Just not for the CIA."

"I cannot comment. Classified."

"But my making a stink about Langley won't get me what I want, which is his signature on the documents."

Grey said nothing.

"He's working with you, Color Code. While you all are covert, you aren't black ops."

"We are not black ops. That would be the Numbers."

"Numbers have complete deniability. But if Angel were with Numbers, he wouldn't be working alongside you. And he could have easily solved the whole debacle with DZ and Zero-One." Lynx paused.

Grey tipped his head. "What was that thought?"

"I'm here because someone called me to tell me you were here. I'm telling you that so you know that this story is known."

"Do you think the person who called you has an ulterior motive?" Grey asked.

"I do. They want me to be happy. And in a world of crap, that someone cares about happiness is a miracle. But it also means that as black ops as you think that The Angel is, he's not. Too many people know. And when you see him again. Tell him that I'm bringing my relationship with him to an end as soon as I get back to the States." She stood. "A pleasure to see you, Grey."

"And you." Grey bowed.

And now she knew more secrets about Angel Sobado, namely, he does not work for the CIA. Her anger toward them had been misplaced.

It was JASOC that was going to get a visit.

As Lynx rode the elevator down to the front desk, where she left her roller bag with the concierge, she dialed Deep for him to arrange a flight home.

From there, things moved easily forward. She took the car to the airport and boarded the plane. She was on her way home.

Her bag was stowed in the overhead compartment of her redeye direct flight; Lexi accepted a cocktail from the flight attendant, then opened her phone to check the time, three in the morning, Tuesday. It would be around eight in the evening in D.C.

Striker, even in his military cargo plane, would beat her home.

After they had rested from their missions, Striker and she needed to get down to Miami and have a talk with Lynda.

When Lexi met four-year-old Cammy, everyone told Cammy that Lexi was Uncle Gavin's good friend. It was so odd to be down with Striker's family and hear them use his given name. It was funnier to hear Cammy call her 'Auntie Chica'—a name she'd invented on her own after Striker called Lexi 'Chica' as an endearment.

Auntie Chica—Aunt Cutie—which Lynx loved so much.

And as she thought that, everything shifted and warbled

as Lexi was hit with the full sixth sense experience of a *knowing*—Danger! Danger!

Three Blind Mice, see how they run! Danger!

Lexi searched frantically through the ether to attach the warning to something solid. Strike Force was safe in Germany. Saadiq and his family safe.

Cammy sprang into her mind. Help!

Lexi called Striker's father's number. It went right to voice mail. She dialed Mimi's number. It rang and rang until voice mail. Lexi called it back three times, growing frantic with each ring. Lexi planned to have Deep call the police to do a well check when a breathless Cammy answered the phone. "I knew you would help me!" Then the call dropped.

The next call went to voice mail.

The flight attendant leaned over her. "Please put your phone on airplane mode for take off."

Lexi didn't know what that phone call had done. But she felt that what she'd done was all that was needed of her.

The *knowing* faded. Her heart reseated. And Lexi felt peace.

Maybe that peace was knowing that when she got off the plane, she'd be back in Striker's arms.

40

Lexi

When Lexi walked off the gangway into the terminal, there were Striker and Cammy with flowers and balloons. Her heart sank. She didn't have the papers signed. She couldn't marry Striker. Not yet, anyway.

Pushing those thoughts aside, Lexi grinned at Striker's niece as she knelt with her arms wide.

Cammy threw her arms around Lexi's neck. "I've come to live with you."

Lexi lifted Cammy along with her as she stood to kiss Striker on the mouth. "Hey, you. You're a sight for sore eyes."

She set Cammy down as Striker took her luggage handle in one hand and reached for Lexi with the other. "No joy with Angel?"

"We'll figure it out. Let's talk about that later." She tipped her head to touch Striker's shoulder, then brought it back up. "Cammy's living with us now? Lynda agreed?"

"Funny story there that I think you'll appreciate."

"Funny as in ha ha or funny as in strange?" Lexi asked.

"Strange. Ready?"

"Yeah, I'm not sure." As they stepped onto the escalator, Lexi called out, "Hey, hold up there, young lady," to keep Cammy from dashing down the moving steps.

"I'm going to tell you anyway." Striker lowered his voice. "This is how my dad told me the story. The four of them were in the house—Dad, Mimi, Lynda, and Cammy. There was a huge thunderstorm, and the lights had been out for hours. Lynda had gone into the kitchen and passed out. Cammy found her. When Cammy started screaming, Dad said—now get this— 'they were like three blind mice all scurrying around trying to figure out what to do.'"

Lexi looked up to catch his eye before stepping back onto the floor. "No Butcher's wife with a kitchen knife, right?"

"That's not what you were humming."

"What's that?"

"When you were humming *Three Blind Mice* before I left for Iraq," Striker explained, "you only hummed the bars for 'three blind mice, see how they run.' You never sang past that, so I assumed it was a bunch of people running around trying to figure out a problem but that nothing would get amputated in the process."

"Lucky thing." Lynx grinned. "So what happened? Is Lynda okay?"

"Luckily, Mimi anticipated a need and had Narcan, but Dad couldn't get up and over to her. He had to talk Cammy through how to revive her mother."

"How is Lynda now?"

"Fine. She's in rehab, terrified she'll permanently lose custody of Cammy."

"The whole story is tragic." She reached for Cammy's hand as they passed through the automatic doors into the humidity of Washington, D.C. "I like the desert heat better," she said.

"Mimi and Dad told Lynda they weren't physically capable of caring for Cammy. And that they'd get social services involved if she didn't agree to give me temporary custody until she was clean, sober, and standing on her own two feet."

"Where are you parked?" Lexi shielded her eyes from the glare of the sun. Striker pointed, and they moved forward. "All this all happened when we were in Iraq?"

"Kate and Reaper flew down to Florida to bring her up."

"They are so wonderful. We are so lucky that we have them for family."

On the drive home, Lexi let the music on the radio and the relief of tension that had banded her muscles release.

She dozed until Striker squeezed her thigh. "Hey, Chica, we're home."

They piled out and headed up to the door.

Cammy came up, jumping from stair to stair, singing, "Three blind mice, three blind mice. See how they run. See how they run!"

"Cammy," Striker asked as he tapped in the code on the front door, "what are you thinking about right now?"

She followed Lexi and Striker over to the sofa, where she wiggled in between the two.

"I was remembering how I found my mom on the floor."

Lexi wrapped her arms around the child's slender frame. "That was a very scary time."

Cammy leaned back into Lexi's arms. "I've been scared like that before."

"Yes, you have." Lexi leaned to look Cammy in the eyes. "When you saw your mom, and you felt scared, what happened next?"

"Sometimes people do crazy things when they don't know what to do. I knew what to do. Call 9-1-1. But we couldn't see anything."

"You couldn't see? Why was that?"

"There was a big thunderstorm, and the lights went out. We were in the dark except for the light on my tablet."

"And that's how you found your mom?"

"I went to ask her where the flashlight was."

"Do you remember what happened next?"

"I was screaming for Mimi, and she came. Poppy couldn't get out of the chair because of his back. I was yelling 9-1-1, but Mimi didn't know where she put her cell phone. Poppy said his phone had run out of power. My tablet was our light. Mimi said she was going to take the tablet and run to the neighbors for help. I didn't want her to go. Poppy was stuck in his chair, and Mama was on the floor. I didn't want to be alone in the dark. But Mimi ran out anyway. Then Mimi's phone was ringing. I couldn't find it, but it rang again until I did." She looked up at Striker. "It was Auntie Chica. She said she'd always try to be there when I needed her because she's my fairy godmother. And I really, really needed her. And she helped."

"You were very brave." Lexi wrapped Cammy in her arms. "It sounds like you handled that emergency like a champ. So with Mimi's phone, you were able to call 911?"

"They told Poppy to use the nose squirter. And he couldn't get on the floor, so I squirted Mama's nose."

"Narcan," Striker whispered.

Lexi took the little girl's hand between her own. "You did a great job."

"Mama was sick," Cammy said. "That's why she was on the ground. She goes to a lot of doctors' appointments. Now, she's living in a place where the doctors come take care of her, and it's easier."

"That's right," Striker said.

Cammy twisted her body to lean into Striker. "Poppy said I can be with you until Mommy's feeling better. But that it might take a while." She jumped up from the couch and ran toward the kitchen, calling, "I need a cookie!"

Striker slid his hand into Lexi's. "Fairy Godmother." He kissed her. "Now, your turn. How'd things go with Angel?"

"Yeah, well, good news and bad news."

Striker canted his head. "How's that?"

"No signed divorce papers." She frowned.

"Why? What was his reason?"

"He didn't give me one. He just disappeared. But I did have a chat with Grey. Of course, everything is top secret—ultra hush-hush, so what he could tell me wasn't much. But I think I have a new insight and another way to get myself free. And the CIA isn't my golden ticket."

"How is that?"

"If it's okay with you, I'm going to keep this piece to myself until I see if it pans out."

Striker smiled. "Afraid to jinx it?"

"Exactly." She leaned up for a kiss. "Thank you for understanding that—understanding me. I promise, Striker, one way or another, we're going to get our *happily ever after*."

Cookie in mouth, Cammy ran into the room full throttle, jumped onto the sofa with Lexi and Striker, and squeezed them tight.

Striker reached his arms around both Lexi and Cammy. "Chica, I already have mine."

The END

Readers, are you ready for Lexi and Striker's Wedding?
Marriage Lynx coming this summer!

If you haven't read the story of how Striker and Lynx met, turn two pages for the first chapter or WEAKEST LYNX

The next book in the Strike Force Series will be **Blaze Ahead.**

If you haven't read Striker and Lexi's backstory, read the **LYNX SERIES**.
To learn more about Iniquus' Southern Campus, read **Rescue Instinct.**

If you'd like to know more about the Wombats, read **Danger Zone** and **Warrior's Instinct**.

If you'd like to know more about Sophia and space archaeology, read **Relic**.

If you want to know more about John Grey, read **InstiGATOR** and **Gulf Lynx**.

To learn more about Kaylie Street, read **Gulf Lynx**.

A LOOK INSIDE

WEAKEST LYNX (BOOK ONE LYNX SERIES)

1

THE BLACK BMW POWERED STRAIGHT TOWARD ME. HEART pounding, I stomped my brake pedal flush to the floorboard. My chest slammed into the seat belt, snapping my head forward. There wasn't time to blast the horn, but the scream from my tires was deafening.

I gasped in a breath as the BMW idiot threw me a nonchalant wave—his right hand off the wheel—with his left hand pressed to his ear, still chatting on his cell phone. Diplomatic license plates. *Figures.*

Yeah, I didn't really need an extra shot of adrenaline— like a caffeine IV running straight to my artery—I was already amped.

"Focus, Lexi," I whispered under my breath, pressing down on the gas. "Follow the plan. Give the letter to Dave. Let him figure this out." I sent a quick glance down to my purse where a corner of the cream-colored envelope jutted out, then veered my Camry back into the noonday DC gridlock, weaving past the graffitied storefronts. I recognized that the near-miss with the BMW guy probably wasn't his fault. I couldn't remember the last ten minutes of drive time.

I watched my review mirror as a bike messenger laced between the moving cars on his mission to get the parcel in his bag to the right guy at the right time. Once he handed over his package, he'd be done—lucky him. Even though I was handing my letter off to Dave, the truth was that wouldn't be my endpoint. I wasn't clear about what an endpoint would even look like. Safe. It might look like I was safe, that I had my feet back under me. But that thought seemed like it was far out on the horizon, and right now, I was just looking for something to grab on to, to keep me afloat.

When I finally parked in front of Dave Murphy's mid-century brick row house, I sat for a minute, trying to regain my composure. I'd pushed this whole mess to the back burner for as long as I could but after last night's nightmare… Well, better to get a detective's opinion. Dave had handled enough crackpots over his time with the DCPD that he'd have a better grasp of the threat level. Right now, even with all my training, I was scared out of my mind.

I glanced down at my hands. The tremor in them sent the afternoon sunlight dancing off my brand-new engagement and wedding rings. I felt like an imposter wearing them—like a little girl dressed up in her mother's clothes. *I'm too young to be dealing with all this crap,* I thought as I shoved my keys into my purse. I pulled my hair into a quick ponytail and stepped out into the February cold. Casting anxious glances up and down the street, I jogged up the stairs to bang on Dave's front door.

The screen squeaked open almost immediately as if he'd been standing there waiting for my knock. "Hey, Baby Girl," he said, stepping out of the way to let me in. Dave had been calling me Baby Girl since I was born because my parents couldn't decide on my name, and that was how I was listed on my hospital ankle tag.

"Glad I found you at home." I walked in and plopped down on the blue gingham couch. It had been here since I could remember. The fabric was threadbare, and juice stained by his five-year-old twins. On a cop's salary, fine furnishings ranked low in priority. Right now—edgy and confused—I appreciated the comfort of familiarity.

Dave shifted into detective mode—hands on hips, eyes scanning me. "Long time, no see."

"Where are Cathy and the kids?" I asked.

"They've got dentist appointments. Did you come to tell us your news?" He lifted his chin to indicate my left hand and settled at the other end of the couch, swiveling until we were face to face.

"Uhm, no." I twisted my rings, suddenly feeling drained and bereft. What wouldn't I give to have my husband Angel here? The corners of my mouth tugged down. I willed myself to stay focused on the reason for the visit. My immediate safety had to take priority over my grief.

Dave raised a questioning brow, waiting for me to continue.

"Angel and I got married Wednesday. I'm Lexi Sobado now." My voice hitched, and tears pressed against my lids. I lowered my lashes, so Dave wouldn't see. But his eyes had locked onto mine, and he never missed much.

"Married? At your age? No introduction? No wedding invitation? Why isn't he here with you now?" Dave angled his head to the side and crossed his arms over his middle-aged paunch. "I'd like to meet the guy," he all but snarled.

Dave probably thought I'd come here because my husband screwed things up already. I pulled the pillow from behind my back and hugged it to me like a shield. "I'm sorry. I should have let you and Cathy know what was going on—I was caught up, and I just..." I stopped to clear my throat.

"Angel and I got married at the courthouse, and no one came with us. Not even Abuela Rosa."

"Angel Sobado. He's kin to Rosa, then?"

I gave the slightest tip of a nod. "Angel is her great-nephew. I couldn't bring him with me today because he deployed with the Rangers to the Middle East Thursday. That's why everything happened so fast. He was leaving." The last word stuck in my throat and choked me.

Dave leaned forward to rest his elbows on his knees. Lacing his fingers, he tapped his thumbs together. "Huh. That's a helluva short honeymoon. Married Wednesday. Gone Thursday." Dave's tone had dropped an octave and gained a fringe of fatherly concern.

His compassion gave me permission to break down. But those Angel-emotions were mine. Private. Right now, I needed to hold myself in check long enough to get through my mission of handing off the letter. I shifted my feet back and forth over the rug as I glared at my purse.

"Might even explain the expression on your face," Dave said, narrowing his eyes. He slouched against the arm of the overstuffed couch.

Stalling wasn't going to make this any easier. I reached a hesitant hand into my bag, pulled out a plastic Zip-loc holding the envelope, and held it up for Dave. "The expression is because of this," I said.

Dave took the bag. After a brief glance, he hefted himself to his feet. Over at his desk, he pulled on a pair of Nitrile gloves, then carefully removed the letter.

DEAREST INDIA ALEXIS,
O my Luve's like the melodie
That's sweetly play'd in tune!

As fair thou art, my bonnie lass,
So deep in love, am I:
And I will love thee still, my dear,
Till a' your bones are white and dry:
Till a' your veins gang dry, my dear,
And your skin melt with the sun;
I will luve thee until your heart is still my dear
When the sands of your life shall no more run.
And fare thee weel, my only Luve,
And fare thee weel a while!
And I will come again, my Luve, so I can watch you die.

DAVE READ THE WORDS ALOUD THEN STARED AT ME HARD; HIS brows pulled in tight enough that the skin on his forehead accordioned. "What the—"

"Someone shoved the poem under the door to my room, and it's scaring the bejeezus out of me." I gripped the pillow tighter.

Dave peered over the top of his reading glasses. "Last night? This morning?"

"Wednesday morning." I braced when I said it, knowing it would tick Dave off that I didn't bring this to him immediately. Ever since my dad died, his buddies had stepped in and tried to take over the fathering job, even though I'd be turning twenty in a few days.

True to my expectations, Dave was red-faced and bellowing. "*Wednesday?* You waited two whole days to tell me you've gotten a friggin death threat?"

Yup, this was exactly the response Dad would have given me.

Dave jumped up, pacing across the room. Obviously, he didn't think this was someone's idea of a joke. Fear tightened my chest at his confirmation. I had hoped he'd say, "No worries—someone is having fun pranking you," and then I could go on about my life without the major case of heebie-jeebies that tingled my skin and made me want to run and hide.

"It was our wedding day." I worked to modulate my voice to sound soft and reasonable. "I only had a few short hours before Angel had to take off. So yeah, I decided to focus on us instead of this." I motioned toward the paper in his hand.

Dave took in a deep breath, making his nostrils flare. "Okay." I could almost see his brain shifting gears. "When you first picked up the letter, did you get any vibes?"

"You mean, ESP-wise?"

He nodded stiffly; his eyes hard on me.

Vibes. That wasn't the word I would have chosen to explain my sensations. "I didn't hear anything. It was more like an oily substance oozing over me." I tucked my nose into the soft cloth of the pillow and breathed in the scent of cinnamon fabric freshener. "I vomited." My voice dropped to a whisper. "It felt like evil and craziness, and I can still smell that stench." A shiver raced down my spine.

Dave's lips sealed tightly; he was probably trying to hold back a litany of expletives. Finally, he asked, "That's all?"

"Yes."

"Did any of your neighbors notice anyone unusual lurking around? Did you check with management and run through the security tapes?"

"Dave, didn't you hear? My apartment building burned to the ground three weeks ago. I assumed you knew. It was on the news."

Dave's eyebrows shot straight up.

"I've been living in a motel the Red Cross rented out for all the families displaced by the fire. But to answer your question, no, nobody saw anything, and there were no cameras trained on my motel corridor." I curled my lips in to keep them from trembling. I was used to holding my emotions in check. I trained myself to present a sweet exterior, a costume of sorts, but right now, I was filled to overflowing, and my mask kept slipping out of place.

"Shit." Dave ran a hand over his face. "I had no idea. I'm letting your parents down. Apartment burned, married, husband gone, and now a death threat." His eyes narrowed on me. "Do you think that about covers all of your surprises for me today?"

I paused for a beat. "Yeah, Dave, I think that's it for today." Okay, even if he was like family, the way Dave was talking pissed me off. I was frightened. I wanted a hug and his reassurance. What I was getting was... Dave's brand of love. He wouldn't be this red-faced and agitated if he wasn't worried about me. Tears prickled behind my eyelids, blurring my vision.

"Hey, now. Stop. We'll get to the bottom of this. Did you already let Spyder McGraw know what's going on?"

I wiped my nose with the back of my wrist. "Spyder's still off-grid. I have no idea when he'll get home."

"Were you assigned a different partner while he's gone?"

"No, sir. I only ever worked for Spyder—he sort of wanted to keep me a secret." I still couldn't believe Mom had sat Dave down and told him all about my apprenticeship with Spyder McGraw. Under Spyder's tutelage, I was following my dream of becoming an Intelligence Officer, learning to out-think and out-maneuver the bad guys trying to hurt American interests. And like anyone heading toward a life in the intelligence community, my skills needed to go under the radar. Now that my mom had died, only four people—Spyder, the Millers, and Dave—knew that side of my life. I would prefer Dave didn't know.

"Still, did you consider bringing this to Spyder's commander? Iniquus would probably give him a heads up. Get a message to him."

"Iniquus is my last resort. Sure, Spyder told me to talk to them if I ever found myself in trouble." I sucked in a deep breath of air. "Bottom line? He never wanted them to know I worked for him, well, for them. Safety in anonymity and all that." My fingers kneaded the stuffing in the pillow. "Besides, I guess I was hoping this would all just go away."

Dave's eyes were hard on me. "You know better. Once some psycho's caught you on his radar, you're stuck there until someone wins."

"Okay, so I make sure it's me who wins."

"Exactly right." He considered me for a minute before he asked, "You've kept up with your martial arts training?"

"I have a sparring partner who's pretty good. We rent time at a Do Jang twice a week."

Dave lowered his head to read over the poem again. He put the letter and envelope back in the Zip-loc and placed it on his mantle. Pulling off his gloves with a snap, he looked down at them. "I hate these things. They give me a rash. Look, I'm going to take this down to the station and open a file. If you get anything else, I want you to bring it to me right away. Understood?"

"Yes, sir."

"This is the only poem, letter, communication of any kind you've gotten?"

I nodded. For the first time since I walked into Dave's house, I became aware of sounds other than our conversation and the thrumming blood behind my eardrums. A football game played on TV. I glanced over as the announcer yelled some gibberish about a first down, then moved my gaze back to Dave. "You must have taken graveyard shift last night," I said.

He picked up a remote, zapped off the TV, and sent me a raised eyebrow.

"It doesn't take a psychic. You look like an unmade bed."

Dave ran a hand over his dark hair, thick on the sides, sparse on top. He hadn't used a comb today or bothered to shave. He was hanging-out-at-home comfy in jeans and beat-to-hell tennis shoes. It looked like the only thing I was interrupting was the game re-run.

"Double homicide. Turned into a long night up to my ankles in sewage."

"Yum." I tried on a smile, but it was plastic and contrived.

Dave narrowed his eyes. "We need to move you. Pronto. It's priority one. You need to be someplace secure where I can keep better tabs on you."

"I've been looking since the fire, but I haven't found anything."

"Would you consider buying?" he asked.

"Yes, actually—I'm looking for a low-cost fixer-upper I can work on to help me get through this year without Angel." I followed Dave into the hallway. "Diversion, and all that."

"How about here, in my neighborhood? I could keep a better eye on you—and you won't be showing up at my door with a suitcase full of surprises." He grabbed his coat from the

closet and shrugged it on. "I'm taking you over to meet my neighbor. She has the other half of her duplex on the market." He looked over his shoulder at me. "You shouldn't be running around without a jacket." He handed me an over-sized wool parka that smelled like raking leaves. He kicked a Tonka truck out of the way, and we moved out the front door.

On the front porch, I slid into the shadows and took in the length of the road—no cars, no barking dogs, everything quiet.

Dave glanced back. "Coast is clear."

I tucked the coat hood up over my ponytail. Screened by Dave's broad back, I started across the street. Down the road, a car motor revved. I reached under my shirt and pulled out my gun.

Enjoying the read?

FIND WEAKEST LYNX IN eBOOK, PAPERBACK AND NOW HARDCOVER.

THE WORLD of INIQUUS

Chronological Order

Ubicumque, Quoties. Quidquid

Weakest Lynx (Lynx Series)

Missing Lynx (Lynx Series)

Chain Lynx (Lynx Series)

Cuff Lynx (Lynx Series)

WASP (Uncommon Enemies)

In Too DEEP (Strike Force)

Relic (Uncommon Enemies)

Mine (Kate Hamilton Mystery)

Jack Be Quick (Strike Force)

Deadlock (Uncommon Enemies)

Instigator (Strike Force)

Yours (Kate Hamilton Mystery)

Gulf Lynx (Lynx Series)

Open Secret (FBI Joint Task Force)

Thorn (Uncommon Enemies)

Ours (Kate Hamilton Mysteries)

Cold Red (FBI Joint Task Force)

Even Odds (FBI Joint Task Force)

Survival Instinct (Cerberus Tactical K9 Team Alpha)

Protective Instinct (Cerberus Tactical K9 Team Alpha)

Defender's Instinct (Cerberus Tactical K9 Team Alpha)

Danger Signs (Delta Force Echo)

Hyper Lynx (Lynx Series)

Danger Zone (Delta Force Echo)

Danger Close (Delta Force Echo)

Fear the REAPER (Strike Force)

Warrior's Instinct (Cerberus Tactical K9 Team Bravo)

Rescue Instinct (Cerberus Tactical K9 Team Bravo)

Heroes Instinct (Cerberus Tactical K9 Team Bravo)

Striker (Strike Force)

Marriage Lynx (Lynx Series) 2023

Blaze Ahead (Strike Force) 2023

Coming soon, more great stories from the ex-special forces security team members who live, work, and love in a tightly knit family.

WWW.FIONAQUINNBOOKS.COM

Fiona Quinn's Amazon Page Link

(https://www.amazon.com/Fiona-Quinn/e/B00OTQE926)

READERS

Readers, I hope you enjoyed the journey with Lexi and Striker. If you had fun reading **STRIKER**, I'd appreciate it if you'd help others enjoy it too.

Recommend it: A few words to your friends, book groups, and social networks would be wonderful.

Review it: Please tell your fellow readers what you liked about my book by reviewing **STRIKER** on Amazon and Goodreads. If you do write a review, please send me a note at FionaQuinnBooks@outlook.com so I can thank you with a personal e-mail. Or stop by my website www.FionaQuinn Books.com, to keep up with my news and chat through my contact form.

My great appreciation ~

To publicist, Margaret Daly

To my editor Kathleen Payne

To my cover artist, Melody Simmons

Beta Force, who are always honest and kind at the same time.

To my Street Force, who enthusiastically supports me and my writing.

To M. Carlon

Thank you to the real-world military who serve to protect us, our interpreters, and our allies.

Thank you to all of the wonderful professionals whom I called on to get the details right. Please note: this is a work of fiction, and while I always try my best to get all of the details correct, there are times when it serves the story to go slightly to the left or right of perfection. Please understand that any mistakes or discrepancies are my authorial decision-making alone and sit squarely on my shoulders.

Thank you to my family.
I send my love to my husband and my great appreciation. T, I've known you longer than I have not, and my world is all the richer because of our shared lives.

And, of course, thank YOU for reading my stories. I'm smiling joyfully as I type this. I so appreciate you!

ABOUT THE AUTHOR

Fiona Quinn is a USA Today bestselling author, a Kindle Scout winner, and an Amazon Top 40 author.

Quinn writes smart, sexy suspense with a psychic twist in her Iniquus World of action-adventure stories, including Lynx, Strike Force, Uncommon Enemies, Kate Hamilton Mysteries, FBI Joint Taskforce, Cerberus Tactical K9, and Delta Force Echo Series.

She writes urban fantasy as Fiona Angelica Quinn for her Elemental Witches Series.

And, just for fun, she writes the Badge Bunny Booze Mystery Collection with her dear friend, Tina Glasneck, under the name Quinn Glasneck.

Quinn is rooted in the Old Dominion, where she lives with her husband and children. There, she pops chocolates, devours books, and taps continuously on her laptop.

Visit www.FionaQuinnBooks.com

COPYRIGHT

CPSIA information can be obtained
at www.ICGtesting.com
Printed in the USA
LVHW100549240723
752986LV00001B/94

9 781946 661753